Mistress Mackintosh & the Shaw Wretch

Mistress Mackintosh & the Shaw Wretch

BRIDES OF CHATTAN

Rose Prendeville

ERIDANI PRESS

First published by Eridani Press.

Cover by Poshie

Names: Prendeville, Rose, author.

Title: Mistress Mackintosh and the Shaw Wretch / Rose Prendeville.

Description: First edition. | Nashville, Tennessee : Eridani Press, 2022.

Identifiers: ISBN 978-1-955643-06-1 (trade paperback) | ISBN 978-1-955643-07-8 (ebook)

Subjects: LCSH: Highlands (Scotland)—Fiction. | Man-woman relationships—Fiction. | Romance fiction. | Historical fiction. | BISAC: FICTION / Romance / Historical / Scottish | GSAFD: Love stories.

Classification: LCC PS3616.R452 | DDC 813/.6—dc23

LC record available upon request.

For all the girls with scoliosis
and all the ones who were told "You can't."

Chapter One

MOY, INVERNESS-SHIRE, 1725

Jory hoisted her skirts and clambered onto the slick stone embrasure, looking out across Loch Moy. The autumn air was brisk, scented with forest musk: hints of pine and moss and *freedom*. If she jumped from this height, she could probably clear the island, but how far would she plunge before thrusting back to the surface? How deep was the loch? And, fettered by the trappings of feminine fashion, could she really make it to dry land on the other side? Would even a stronger swimmer make it, weighted down by skirts and stays?

The stays, at least, she could do something about. And the skirts, for that matter. If she was going to break with her family and leave propriety behind, she might as well do it in her shift. Better that than being bartered or sold off to whatever horrid clansman her uncle would find to take her off his hands.

She huffed at that. She could take herself off his hands, no man required. Hadn't she proven so, earning the better part of her dowry by herself? But still, he thought it his sworn duty to find someone to *take her off his hands*, and he'd been telling her as much since the day she stabbed a Gordon at the age of thirteen.

At least if she left now, whilst everyone was distracted in the Hall, she could make her way home to Inverness and collect her dowry before he had a chance to promise it away. How much might her uncle offer, above and beyond what was hers, with two daughters of his own still to wed?

Jory took a deep breath to settle her nerves and then was startled by a flash of movement as a rider galloped towards Castle Moy.

They took the guards by surprise, the Clydesdale's hooves thundering across the bridge like rumbling war drums. The soldiers raised their swords defensively, and the rider slowed enough to flash his clan badge, so they stepped back and allowed him into the bailey yard unimpeded. In one, fluid leap he dismounted, tossed the reins to a stable lad, and then charged into the keep without a backward glance.

Only once he disappeared inside did Jory dare to breathe.

Moments later his boots slapped the bastion stairs, and then he stepped out onto the parapet and stopped, as though Jory were a doe he didn't want to frighten away.

"Feasgar math," he gasped.

She blinked and burst out laughing.

"Is it? A good afternoon?" Jory asked him. "One would think not, and you riding up like the hounds of hell were at your heels."

He must have known she'd observed his arrival, but her reminder brought a pleasing flush to the tips of his ears even as a shadow fell across his moss-colored eyes.

"Come down from there at once," he ordered.

Jory turned back to face the forest across the loch.

She'd recognized him immediately—not when he startled her nearly into slipping as he barreled across the bridge, but the moment she saw him on the battlements—Finlay Shaw, the younger brother of the Tordarroch. For half a moment she thought, disgraced in battle or not, if he was the Highlander her uncle expected her to marry, then her sentence might not be *all* bad. At least he was handsome.

But no. She didn't need a husband commanding her hither and thither, and she had no notion of accepting one. *Marriage means war*, she reminded herself. Dowry in hand, her life would be her own to do with as she pleased. The second money was exchanged, though, her every moment—asleep or awake—would be at the mercy and pleasure of her husband. *No thank you*. No, she would not get down.

"Please," he said more softly, turning his demand into a request.

"Afraid they'll think you rushed up here to push me?" she teased.

When he didn't respond, she turned to look at him again. His face had lost the fullness of youth, but it was still the same square jaw and hungry eyes she'd watched scrabble in the bailey years ago.

He didn't recognize *her* of course. They never did. And why should they? She looked fine enough—until they noticed one shoulder was too high and a little bit hunched, and then all they could see was a disfigured, burdensome shrew. They never had the imagination to see how helpful she was, how she might ease their burdens instead of adding to them.

"I'm not ready to come down."

He sighed, stepped closer, and Jory braced herself to be manhandled. It was what men did best, wasn't it? If he grabbed for her and she struggled, she might slip and hit her head, or perhaps worse, go over the wall and be dashed on the rocks instead of making it safely into the water. Instead, he climbed up alongside her, so close his blue and green plaid brushed her skirts, impossibly making her thigh tingle as if the soft wool had actually touched her skin.

There was an earthy tang about him, the mingled scents of

3

horse and clover and road dust. It shouldn't be appealing, and yet it made a refreshing change to the stale sweat and sour ale of her Mackintosh cousins down in the Hall.

"If you jump," he reasoned, "then I shall be forced to follow. I'm an outcast as it is. I cannae simply let you drown."

"You're an outcast as it is, so you might as well look the other way."

"One may be fallen, but one can always sink lower," he said soberly.

"Is that what you believe?" she asked, for, though she didn't know the details of his disgrace, it seemed as though Finlay Shaw had fallen about as far as a man could go.

"The Church says—" he began, but she cut him off with a forced laugh.

Did he presume she was some kind of whore driven by guilt to suicide?

His fist clenched as she laughed at him, right in the folds of her skirts, though he still didn't lay a hand on her, and for some reason his restraint made her sorry for laughing.

"This isn't some desperate cry for help," she said. "I can make it across."

Now it was his turn to laugh, and Jory didn't loathe the sound. It discomposed her stomach like she hadn't eaten for weeks, but she didn't despise the feeling, however much she wanted to. Well, she had laughed at him first, hadn't she?

"In those clothes? Nae, mistress, I think not," he scoffed, and she couldn't disagree with his assessment.

It was a stark reminder that she'd been trying to convince herself to leave the heavy garments behind, and she huffed once more. He'd ruined her escape even before joining her on the castle wall, from the moment of his frenzied ride into the bailey.

"I won't be deterred."

He looked down at her, an appraising sort of look which made it hard for her to breathe, but Jory lifted her chin and glared right

4

back at him, refusing to wither, challenging him to recognize the girl she'd once been.

"No, I dare say you willnae." Then he smiled softly and stood up impossibly straight, smoothing the wrinkles from his sark and plaid. "Verra well," he said. "Shall we go on the count of three?"

"We?"

"I told you, mistress. If you jump, I shall follow. So we may as well go over together."

She pursed her lips, scowling at him. Was he serious or testing her resolve?

Jory took in his broad shoulders and muscled biceps straining against the fabric of his shirt, his taut forearms exposed by rolled-up sleeves. Even if he abandoned the heavy plaid and jumped in stark naked, would so much muscle sink straight to the bottom of the loch?

Either way, she'd be wiser to abandon the plan for now. She might abide until nightfall, right after moonrise, and sneak out through the postern. There would be less noise without the splash, less chance of injury or discovery.

"You don't look like much of a swimmer," she lied because she couldn't let him know he'd bested her.

"Och. I may not have spent every day of my youth on this water like the Borlum's brood, but I can hold my own with the beasties beneath. On three?"

"I should never forgive myself if I kept you from your evening meal, Mr. Shaw," she tried again.

He cocked his head, realizing she knew him, but of course everyone did. Even before the fighting in 1715. She only hoped the reminder of his dinner would be enough to deter him from forcing her to jump.

And then his stomach grumbled, and he stepped back down onto the walkway, reaching out—to grab hold of her if she went ahead and jumped as much as to help her down.

She gave the opposite shore one last, longing look before

smirking at his proffered hand and hopping down unaided, just to prove she could.

Retracting the hand, Shaw combed it through his tangled hair, still damp with the sweat of his ride. "I'm afraid you have me at a disadvantage, mistress."

"Marjorie Mackintosh. They call me Jory."

"Pleasure." He offered a courtly bow despite her curt reply.

She rolled her eyes at him to keep from smiling, then thought better of it and added, "I thank you. For your... concern. Please don't... If you don't mind, I... That is..." .

"I willnae mention it."

Relief washed over her, and this time she did let him see her smile before she turned and continued on her way.

"May I ask the reason, mistress?" he called after her. "For such a grand flight? Are ye here against your will?"

"Here?" Jory looked around the castle walls and shook her head with a sigh. "No. No, I like it *here* just fine. But I will not be the property of any man. And they'll learn that soon enough."

———

FINN STARED OUT THE WINDOW OF OLD MACKINTOSH OF Borlum's private chamber, his back to the desk where the Borlum and Angus stood, heads bent together in discussion. They weren't best pleased with his manner of arrival. He'd been dragging his feet, letting Sparradh forage along the banks of the loch to delay the inevitable, when he'd spotted the lass on the battlements. At first, he'd thought her a threat. Then he'd assumed her to be in some sort of distress.

The whole Chattan Confederation had been at table when Finn strode in, ignoring Old Borlum's surprise and Angus's angry bellow in his haste to reach her before she could jump. Then she'd smiled at him up there on the battlements, a real smile, rare and light as a butterfly. It made him want to safeguard all her secrets, and so he'd given her his word and now wasn't at liberty to explain or defend himself. Still, he didn't know why he'd been summoned at all—either to the castle or to this palaver.

Years ago, he was included as a silent witness to the plans between the Borlum and Finn's eldest brother Robert, back before the '15. But since the fated battle at Preston—where his callow blunder cost many men's lives including that of the girl's blue-eyed father—no one, and most especially not Angus, had invited him to discuss such matters, not as a soldier or as the younger brother of the Tordarroch. And that was fine by Finn. So why now?

When the door opened and the Borlum offered a welcome, Finn turned from his post in time to see the lass, Marjorie Mackintosh, enter with her uncle. Though she wasn't as fair as her cousins, surprise crept up her sun-browned neck in a lovely shade of crimson as she registered Finn's presence. Their glances met for a moment before she quickly dropped her gaze to the floor, revealing a tiny crease between her brows which he found himself wanting to smooth, if only to see once more those surprising brown eyes, so different from the rest of the blue-eyed Mackintosh line.

She glanced back and caught him staring, then turned her head away to face her uncle, but not before the same tightness in his chest jerked all the way down to his groin. With her head turned, the curve of her neck gave Finn the impression of a demure whooper swan at sundown. He took a breath and brought his hands, which had been clasped behind his back, to rest folded in front lest his body betray him any further.

At least now he knew they had no intention of asking his opinion on strategy, not with a lady present, but what the devil was going on? Had someone spied them on the embrasure and reported their behavior as untoward? If they were now to be taken to task, could he defend her propriety without giving her intentions away?

Finn cast a glance at Angus, but his brother remained as inscrutable as ever.

"I've had a visit from Father Burnett," the Borlum began without preamble, and Finn remembered the lass's adamant assertion she would not marry. He hadn't realized it was to be quite so soon.

For a fleeting moment, the space of an untaken breath, he wondered if he could possibly be her intended, the one who'd be asked to shelter her, small and fragile as a bird—though he suspected she'd have pushed him off the embrasure if she heard him call her fragile. But of course, the notion was ridiculous. She'd no wish to marry, and lovely as she was, her kin would have no trouble finding someone far more suitable than he.

"A wealthy benefactor desires, as do we all, for a return to the old ways—for papal churches and religious orders, for lives of prayer and beatification. He offers his grounds on the coast near Aberdeen to be used as a secret convent and invites each of the clans of Chattan to select a few cherished young women to take the holy vows."

Finn may not be a strategist, but he was canny enough to realize the benefactor would be from some rival clan, and the maidens sent to him, merely the currency of a new alliance. It was no different than the strategic marriages of decades past and decades yet to come. But it didn't sit well. Would these lasses be safe? After the systematic dismantling of the Catholic Church in Scotland, it was no wonder convents had gone underground, but what was to stop this one from being discovered and destroyed by Protestants? And what had any of it to do with him?

He stole a glance at Mistress Mackintosh who was watching the laird, head tilted, as if peering across a foggy sea.

"Because of your devout and pious disposition, you've been chosen as the first from Clan Mackintosh to be so honored."

Finn's stomach sank, though he couldn't say why. Of course she'd be a nun, this alluring young woman, so opposed to a man's touch she preferred the risk of drowning in Loch Moy. How could he have ever allowed himself to suppose otherwise?

The men all turned to her, watching for some reaction, though she still seemed far away, as if hearing them from the bottom of the loch.

Her kinsman nudged her, and she blinked at the laird.

"A secret convent?" she asked, allowing something like a smile to tug at her soft, full lips. "In Aberdeenshire?"

"Aye," the Borlum nodded benevolently. "You leave tomorrow. Tordarroch has offered up his heir to escort you safely."

"He's not my heir," Angus muttered, and Finn's face burned as he glanced over to see if the lass heard.

She was studying him, and despite his shame, Finn's cock jerked to attention beneath his kilt once more.

"Escort her? Me?" he choked out.

"Aye," Angus said with an almost bored tone. "It's not particularly dangerous, and we've real work to do here. You're good enough and the only one can be spared."

Finn's cheeks flamed anew, and, as if catching himself, Angus turned to the girl's uncle for reassurance.

"You've no need to worry. She'll be delivered safe and intact, or he'll have me to answer to."

Bloody hell.

FINN'S APPETITE ALL BUT ABANDONED HIM WITH ANGUS watching his every bite, and he picked at the cold mutton and cheese without tasting any of it.

"I remember a time when the Tordarroch would call for ye, and you'd come running so hard and fast you'd trip over your own wee shadow."

"I came as quick as I could, brother."

"Brother," Angus spat. "Aye, and there's the difference, isn't it?

Though I wonder if you'd be half so slow to turn up if it was Robert summoned you."

Sighing, Finn tore a bannock in two and studied the pieces, one half a little larger than the other, but two opposite ends of the same loaf. "Tell me, for I cannae decide which makes you despise me more: that ye wouldnae have become chief if Rob was still living, or that it's me you blame for putting ye there?" His gaze flicked up to meet his brother's scornful one, but Angus didn't acknowledge the barb. He would only fight back when he picked the time and place.

"I expect you to undertake this journey to the coast wi' all due haste. The priest, Father Burnett, requested the lass by name. Her reputation precedes her, it seems. And Finn, she's to be a nun. She must retain that reputation."

Heat scorched down the back of Finn's neck, his brother's words echoing off the walls as though the empty Hall itself was privy to his most secret desires and mocked him for it. He shoved his plate away and stood to face Angus. "What do you take me for?"

His brother shrugged. "I ken soldiers."

"That's right, I *am* a soldier, Angus. Not a bloody nursemaid. Why does her kinsman not take her?"

"Her uncle is needed in town. So I offered you as a favor to the Borlum."

"Yet you dinnae even trust me to behave with honor. So explain to me why you've tasked me with such a... menial..." He struggled to find the right word for such an insulting assignment, but before he could spit it out, Angus cut him off.

"It's a job for the lowest of the low, and you, Finlay Shaw, are the lowest I've got."

"I'm your heir, whatever you tell them."

"I have no heir."

At his full height, Finn had almost an inch on the chieftain, and he drew himself up straight and tall. "I'm still your brother," Finn said, daring Angus to deny that too.

"And I am your chief. So act like it and follow my order."

"I have proven myself time and again. What do I have to do—"

"Deliver the lass to Bearradh Dearg," Angus said, withdrawing a letter from his breast pocket, sealed with crimson wax. "And don't come back without a signature swearing the Watch will look the other way when we start blowing up bridges."

"The Black Watch? What have they to do wi' a Catholic convent? The Campbells, the Grants—they're all Protestants."

Angus offered him a smug grin. "Aye, but the Gordons and the Grants have decided a centuries-old alliance is more important than the Pope, so we get to the Watch through the Grants, and we get to the Grants through the Gordons."

"Gordons?" Finn nearly choked on the half-chewed bannock, which turned to sand in his mouth, and he could swear he caught a malevolent twinkle in his brother's eye.

"Get this right, for the clan and the cause, and then *maybe* you'll have proven your worth as my heir."

Finn sighed. It always came back to the bloody Jacobites. And worse—Clan Gordon.

"I willnae let you down," he mumbled, tossing the bread back on his plate and turning towards the south staircase and the sanctuary of his quarters.

"I'm told the girl is frail," Angus called after him. "You were always so adept at nursing..."

Finn waved his acknowledgment but didn't stop or turn back. He couldn't stand to see whether his brother's face was filled with compassion or resentment.

For years Angus had hired him out as a stable hand to a pig farmer near Tordarroch Castle, and, eager for absolution, Finn had gone without complaint. Then it was cleaning chamber pots, and at first he'd assumed this was just one more in a long line of punishments for his failure ten years ago at Preston. But perhaps this time it was also penance for an even deeper wound. As the middle son, Angus was always jealous of Finn's relationship with their ailing mother—a closeness Angus could have enjoyed himself if he'd but tried. Like everything else, it was somehow Finn's fault he never tried.

And now he was to be saddled with an invalid and a prosaic quest. And a Gordon.

On their own, he and Sparradh could reach the coast in a few days. With a delicate woman riding aside, would even a full sennight be enough?

In his quarters, Finn tore off his shirt and flung it away, picturing the lass standing resolutely upon the embrasure, the wind whipping her skirts and hair. She'd never appeared frail to him. She seemed...

He plunged his whole head into a cool, clean wash basin left behind by the chambermaid. Water sloshed over the sides, but he held his breath and forced the image of the lass's penetrating eyes to recede from his memory.

Chapter Two

After slamming the door of the chamber she was sharing with her younger cousins, Jory leaned against the wall, trying to catch her breath. She'd been so close to escaping, she could scream.

And what would she have done if she'd made it across the loch? It would take hours to reach Inverness on foot, and then? Sneak into her home to liberate her dowry before boarding a coach bound for Edinburgh? There was talk of starting a medical school at the university. In breeches and a hat she could pass for a man, sit the course, become a real doctor.

The plan had sounded so reasonable when she'd hatched it in the carriage on the way to Moy: disguised in trousers she would take whatever job they'd offer at the university, prove to them how competent she was so they'd have to admit her. Then along came Finlay Shaw with his ginger beard and those arms. She'd have gotten away with it and made do, half-dressed or otherwise, if only he hadn't found her out.

"Jory, where have you been?"

Her youngest cousin, Maggie, burst in with Wee Ellen right behind, looking for all the world as though someone had died.

"We've been looking everywhere. Da said he was going to speak with you." Wide-eyed she added in a whisper, "Along with Himself."

"Yes," Jory said, sitting down on the edge of the bed, suddenly too weak to stand.

Wee Ellen, only a year younger than Jory, sat next to her, so light the down mattress hardly dipped. She clutched Jory's sleeve and opened her mouth as if to speak, but what was there to say?

Jory patted Ellen's hand. "I'm two and twenty, a spinster, really. Given the choice between this and marriage, I suppose this is the lesser of two evils." At least she wouldn't be walking on eggshells, learning what would and wouldn't set a man off, for there was always something, wasn't there?

"Is it true the Shaw Wretch is to be your guide?" Maggie asked gleefully. "You should've seen him, striding into the Hall with the devil on his back and not a word to Himself or his brother!"

"Don't call him that, it's unkind," Jory chided.

"But everyone does! His own clan despises him, though I dinnae ken why when he's so awfully handsome."

Ellen shot her sister a censuring look.

"What? He's not so pale and freckled as most of the Shaws, and his nose is almost straight."

Ellen shook her head, looking up to the heavens for patience.

The younger girl sighed and flounced onto the bed. "You're so old fashioned."

"She's also right," Jory said, though she'd be hard pressed to admit which of her cousins she was referring to.

There were too many contradictory emotions jostling around inside her brain, bumping into each other—elation and fury, relief and disappointment. She wouldn't be forced to marry. That in itself was a cause for celebration. But holy vows? Was it all some perverse joke?

She'd never expected to marry *well*, of course not, with a back twisted like the branches of a curly oak tree. During the odd burst of optimism, when she wasn't plotting her departure, she'd imagined proving herself reliable and worth the trouble to someone of her choosing. Clearly her uncle thought such an outcome unlikely, and his assessment stung more than it probably ought.

At least a journey to Aberdeenshire would afford her the opportunity to disappear.

"Not my good handkerchief!" Maggie squealed. "Just tilt your head back."

Turning towards her cousins once more, Jory saw Wee Ellen's nose dripping blood. "Again?" she asked and dug through her trunk for a small medicine bag. She'd need to pack it later, but she'd leave the yarrow behind for them. Crushing some of the leaves, she mashed them into a small lozenge and then cupped the back of Ellen's head as she pushed the compound up into the sanguineous nostril.

Ellen smiled gratefully, and Jory patted her cheek before dropping the small jar into her cousin's hands and telling Maggie, "Not too large or she'll have trouble removing it."

Maggie nodded, but Ellen tried to return the jar as Jory began to sort through her things.

"Perhaps there's an herb garden at the convent. If not, I suppose I'll start one of my own."

Would that be allowed? Were the nuns taught a skill? Allowed to study healing and midwifery, to work among the people with a little plot of earth for growing medicines? Or would the convent's inhabitants be bound to silence, speaking only hymns and prayers of matins, vespers, and compline, keeping their own counsel all the hours in between?

It didn't matter, really, because Jory didn't plan to find out.

Her good handkerchief safe, Maggie flopped down upon the bed again and gazed dreamily up at the ceiling.

"Da's determined Wee Ellen shall wed a MacKenzie, but he says there won't be enough dowry for me to entice a man of worth. I'll likely follow you to the convent in a few years." She sighed dramatically, as only a fourteen-year-old could. "And there I shall perish of a broken heart."

Jory rolled her eyes, but Ellen chuckled at her sister and squeezed her hand.

"Unless..." Maggie bolted upright. "We could switch places! You could convince Da to let *me* have the MacKenzie. You'd love a nice quiet convent by the sea. You'd thrive there."

Ellen laughed at her sister's dramatics and sponged the dried blood from her cheek and mouth.

Turning back to her trunk, Jory asked, "Did you borrow my sewing kit again?"

"Yes," the girl replied cautiously. "I'll run and fetch it now." She scampered out, leaving Jory and Ellen alone.

Ellen peered curiously at Jory's pile of belongings.

"I don't imagine a nun needs so very much," Jory said, ignoring a twinge of guilt for leaving out the part where packing light would make it easier to abscond with her dowry. If anyone would keep her secret, it was Wee Ellen.

She ran a finger over the seams of one of her skirts, some of her finest stitching. But she couldn't take it all, and anyway a saddlebag would hold more than she'd been planning to carry only a few hours earlier. "Besides, we're riding."

Ellen frowned, most likely fretting about the impropriety of Jory being escorted by a rough and tumble soldier without any kind of chaperone. Jory's stomach did a little somersault at the same notion.

"I'll be perfectly safe," she said. "Finlay Shaw would no more look at me than his own sister." If he had one. Her stomach did another flip. "Besides, I'll have my sgian dubh."

Her trusty little knife lay comfortably nestled deep within her pocket. She hadn't needed to use it in years, but she'd be ready. She was always ready. And perhaps this arrangement, this banishment to the coast, was her atonement, long overdue.

She didn't consider herself particularly pious. If she believed the sermons, her own soul was already damned to the fires of hell, for hadn't she committed the gravest sin of all when she stabbed that boy nine years ago? Did her uncle think dedicating her life to God would somehow wipe her past clean along with his part in hiding it? Or was this simply a way to unburden himself of an unmarriageable niece with a crooked spine?

FINN PUNCHED HIS PILLOW AND FLIPPED OVER ONTO HIS stomach. He couldn't decide which part of the conversation ate at him most. It wasn't unusual for Angus to assign him a lowly task for which he refused to spare a *reliable* soldier. Nor was it particularly shocking for him to insinuate that Finn, or more accurately Finn's cock, couldn't be trusted. But underneath it all there was a niggling suspicion his brother might be eager to see him fail.

He had no particular objection to the journey. Indeed, it was beautiful country and it had been some years since Finn had seen the sea. Neither was it an objection to the lass. She too was beautiful, but he could keep his cock in check. Hadn't he done as much for twenty-five years? Not that he would need to. Mistress Mackintosh was to be a nun, and even if she wasn't, she'd said herself she had no use for men, and if she didn't despise him already, she surely would the moment she heard the story of his disgrace in '15. Nae, that certainly wasn't his worry. Nor was it the opportunity to prove himself worthy of his chieftain's trust. At its root, Finn was angry because he still needed to prove anything at all after a decade spent trying.

Perform this one final task and all might be forgiven. But would it ever, really, when it never had before? Or would he continue to live this half-life, bowing and scraping to appease an anger which had no desire to be extinguished? Had Angus ever even liked him? As boys they'd argued and scrabbled endlessly.

His brothers took it in turns to torture him when they weren't ganging up on him together. But with Rob there was always a glimmer of brotherly affection. Finn never doubted that if things went too far his eldest brother, heir to the clan chief, would put a stop to it. Rob was teasing, most of the time, to toughen Finn up, whereas Angus had a wolf-like hunger to prove the second son more worthy than the third.

He punched his pillow again, secured the plaid around his waist, and went for a walk.

How could this simple assignment be the one thing to finally allow Finn back into the Tordarroch's inner circle? He couldn't work it out. Either his brother was simply dangling a carrot to ensure his obedience, or Finn was too dim to understand why the Borlum and Angus thought an alliance with the Black Watch could be trusted, too stupid to understand why anyone, but especially a Shaw or Mackintosh, would ever trust a Gordon. Then again, he'd never been much good at strategy.

Finn couldn't say what drew him back to the battlements in the dead of night, but there he walked, and there he found her. Not atop the embrasure this time, thank heaven, but leaning against the parapet wall staring out across the loch just as before.

"Are you going to stand there all night or are you here to push me in?" she asked by way of a greeting.

He couldn't help smiling. Something about her flippant banter —instead of the forced politeness or outright disdain he normally met—eased the tension in his jaw and across his shoulders. "Glad ye decided not to jump?"

She tilted an ear towards him like the petals of a flower turning towards the sun, but she didn't quite look his way. "I haven't decided yet."

"Haven't ye?" Did she mean she was undecided about jumping or about being glad? He took a step closer and was hit by a waft of lilac and liniment. It reminded him of home, the way you don't quite realize what your home smells like until you return after a time, and wasn't that odd, when Finn wasn't even sure where home was anymore?

He shook his head to clear it. "Ye've escaped marriage. It seems the perfect solution, if you don't mind me saying."

She snorted. "Does it? Spared the marriage bed, but still, my life is not my own."

Well, and whose life was their own when it came down to it? Finn drew even with her and leaned onto the next embrasure, a wall of solid stone between their faces. The smooth rock, icy against his bare chest, helped slow his beating heart. Why did it beat so fast, like he'd been running instead of merely speaking to her? "I suppose that's so, mistress. And how would ye spend it, if your time were your own?"

"You first."

He laughed but quieted when she began to speak once more.

"I... What does it matter, Mr. Shaw? When such a thing can never be?"

The way she said his name made him shiver—or maybe it was the hopelessness in her voice, or merely the frigid breeze whipping his torso. He wanted to press her for an answer, but with his luck she would change her mind and throw herself into the loch.

"Are ye warm enough?" he asked instead. "Perhaps you should come inside."

"I'm just fine." She drew her plaid earasaid more tightly around her arms. "You're the one who's half naked."

A little thrill shot through him at the word.

Had some sort of wizardry conjured her out of the darkness? One moment he'd been alone, climbing the narrow, twisted stairs, holding his breath as though the bastion had no space for both him and air. He was thinking of how she'd stood on the wall, defenseless, but somehow strong. The lass had consumed his thoughts, and in the next moment, he emerged from the staircase and she was there, staring out across the water and speaking bold as you please of nakedness.

"Does it offend ye, mistress? My nakedness?" he asked, wanting to see her reaction to his saying it out loud too.

"No. If you wish to catch your death, go right ahead," she taunted. But she frowned when he pulled the plaid up to cover his top half as well. Was she actually disappointed by his hasty concession to social graces?

"If I do catch my death, I hope you'll pray for my soul."

"Of course. When I become a nun, I'll pray for you."

"Thank you, mistress." An awkward silence followed, and then Finn said, "Ye'd do well to get some rest. It'll take at least five long days of riding to reach the coast."

"Five days?" she demanded, stepping away from the parapet to stare him down.

"Aye." He straightened up and met her glare. "For a lass not accustomed to long days in the saddle, five at least."

She sneered at him. "Let's do it in three."

He laughed out loud, but she whirled on her heel and stalked away.

Chapter Three

The next morning, Jory secured her satchel to a borrowed saddle and stroked her bay mare's flank. Nell was a solid, gentle creature, and she found herself almost looking forward to the ride.

Ellen traced the stirrups with one hesitant finger.

"I'll be fine," Jory assured her.

"Oh, Jor. Promise you'll write the moment you arrive and tell us everything," Maggie begged, clutching Jory's cloak.

She took one cousin's hand in each of hers and squeezed. "Promise," she told them both, because wherever she landed, she would find a way to let them know.

Across the bailey yard, Finlay Shaw watched her as he tightened his own bags, heavy with what must be Jory's dowry, not enough for a decent husband but plenty for the Church to take her in. What a sneak her uncle was, to have brought it with them to Moy and never let on about his plans.

The flutter in her stomach burst apart like a chattering flock of starlings scattered to the wind, but she netted them all back down and made up her mind to speak.

Marching across the courtyard, she rehearsed exactly what

she'd say. But when he squinted down at her, hands on his kilted hips, and asked, "Nearly ready, mistress?" her practiced speech eluded her.

Freshly shaven, he looked a good deal younger than his twenty-five years, though his eyes were still as ancient as the elm tree near her home in Inverness.

"Mistress?" he asked again, calling her back to herself.

"My dowry." She nodded toward the nearest bag. "I should be the one to carry it."

His squint deepened, and he ran a hand over his russet tangles. "Aye, maybe so, but it'd be too dangerous. And it's done now," he added with a shrug.

"Dangerous?" Had he guessed her intention to flee? Or did he presume she couldn't hold her own against bandits?

Scowling, Jory considered reaching out and liberating the bag herself. But if her escort already didn't trust her, such action wouldn't help her cause, nor her impending flight. Besides, he was indisputably quick with a sword and could probably catch up her slender wrist the moment she reached out. His strong grip would fully encircle her arm and hold it fast.

"Well... then... wouldn't thieves expect it to be in your saddle-bags, instead of mine?"

He blinked and laughed a little. "I suppose so."

"Then will you not reconsider?" she demanded.

Shaw shrugged and shook his head. "I'm sorry, mistress. There's nothing to reconsider. But you needn't worry. It'll be perfectly safe. Best say your goodbyes now." He nodded back to where her aunt and uncle had joined her cousins' farewell party.

She huffed before stalking back to her horse, resolving not to speak to him again until he relented. She'd thought Shaw might be different, but he was just like the rest of them, certain he knew best.

Even if he was merely a puppet doing the Borlum's bidding, she wouldn't speak to him no matter how much he laughed that surprising laugh of his—surprising, because it was so unexpectedly pleasant, so free of irritation at her demands—surprising, because she couldn't remember hearing him laugh as a child.

Everything about him was unexpected: from his breathless arrival on the battlements yesterday, to his joining her upon the embrasure, to his seeming amusement every time she was—well if she was being truthful with herself, every time she was rude.

She wasn't generally ill-mannered. She didn't consider herself an impolite person. She treated her uncle and the Mackintosh of Borlum with deference, the shopkeepers of Inverness with respect. But something about Finlay Shaw made her want to straddle the line of impropriety. And instead of reacting with violence or anger, he simply laughed.

It almost felt like approval, and it was as startling as the gentle timbre of his voice and the teasing glimmer in his grey-green eyes. But it was also unsettling to not know where the line lay between what would amuse and what would anger.

Then again, perhaps her rudeness was nothing next to his own kin. The *Shaw Wretch* had likely grown a thick skin years ago because it was either that or spend every moment stung by insults.

Like young Maggie, she didn't know the details of his fall from grace. When the others came back from the Rising, he returned in name only, referred to as the Shaw Wretch, spat with venomous whispers by any speaker who dared mention him at all. And when he finally did visit, he kept to himself, lurking on the fringes, leaving Jory to burn with curiosity.

He was a puzzle, Finlay Shaw, and Jory had exactly three days to figure him out and then steal away, off to a new life disguised as a gentleman in Edinburgh, before he could turn her over to the convent by the sea.

"Is he simply awful?" Maggie whispered with delight, shattering Jory's reverie.

"Keep an eye on her. She's bound for trouble," Jory told Ellen, who nodded her agreement.

Stepping between his daughters, her uncle grasped both of Jory's shoulders firmly—the closest he'd ever come to an embrace. "You do this family a great honor, Marjorie. Your father would be verra proud."

Tears pricked, and she blinked them back because if this would be the thing to make her father proud—being bartered to the god of an underground faith in order to have any worth to Clan Mackintosh—then she'd be right to run.

"Thank you," she managed to rasp. "For arranging this next chapter of my life."

He squeezed her shoulders once more and stepped away. Then her aunt rubbed Jory's arms and followed him, allowing her cousins to surge forward and enfold her from both sides.

"Don't forget us," Maggie wept, though her cheeks were flushed with the romance of tragedy.

Wee Ellen stood on tiptoe to kiss Jory's cheek.

"Mo cho-ogha, mo chridhe," Jory whispered.

They clung to each other, Jory and Ellen, just for a moment, and as she tried to pass to her younger cousin all of her own strength and determination, Jory felt a peacefulness settle over her like she was taking some part of Ellen with her as well.

And then he was there, offering a hand to help her into the saddle.

It was time to part. But not forever. Jory would make certain of that.

Determined not to allow Shaw the satisfaction of her gratitude, she gave his proffered hand a withering look. Then she hefted herself indecorously onto the sidesaddle unassisted and lifted her chin, daring him to laugh or comment.

When he didn't, she expertly turned Nell and rode out of the bailey yard and across the bridge, not a backwards glance at him or those she left behind.

It was better that way. She didn't want him to see her grief, and she couldn't bear the thought of Maggie chasing after her dramatically, waving her best handkerchief, eager to burst into wailing at a glance from Jory.

Each time he tried to catch her up and ride two abreast, she would urge the bay mare faster. Let him think she would gallop poor old Nell to death before she'd give in. Eventually he fell back and allowed her to take the lead.

When they came to a fork in the road, he still hung back, waiting.

They'd been traveling south most of the morning, so the left-hand path peeled off to the east. Would the right-hand lead her to Edinburgh? With little hope of fleeing in broad daylight, she chose the left. After a moment, Shaw let out a shrill whistle bringing Nell up short.

Jory glared over her shoulder to see a smug face grinning back at her.

He nodded towards the right-hand path.

She glanced at the eastern sun and then back at him.

"Aye, that'll take you east for a bit, and then due north. We'll go down through the Cairngorms before we head east."

She rolled her eyes, but urged her mount down the correct path, trying not to smell his fresh clover scent as she passed.

Jory contrived to ask him again for her dowry the first time they stopped to water the horses, but then she realized no one, not even the Shaw chief, had been there to see him off.

It was normal, she supposed, for men to come and go. After all, he'd be back soon enough, but she found herself angry all over again: at her uncle for handing over the dowry to her escort, at the Tordarroch for not deigning to bid his brother a safe journey, and most of all at herself for caring whether Shaw was upset by the slight. No, most of all at Finlay Shaw for making her care. And so, before she'd had a chance to break it, her vow of silence was renewed.

. . .

EXHAUSTED BEYOND COMPREHENSION BY THE TIME THEY MADE camp on the edge of a forest, every muscle ached, but Jory was determined to build a fire.

It galled her to admit, but she knew without asking, they hadn't made it even a quarter of the way to Aberdeenshire.

Let's do it in three. She'd been so boastful, and now the day had put her in her place.

As she gathered up twigs for kindling, she tried to picture their location on a map, to assess her opportunities to disappear. If she waited until the last possible moment and vanished into Aberdeen, she might have more men than simply Finlay Shaw scouring the city for her. The priest might search too, along with the convent's benefactor and perhaps the full power of the Catholic Church, whatever that might mean these days. But if she took off from here, wherever *here* was, could she survive on her own long enough to reach Edinburgh? Could she trick Shaw into revealing how far away that city might be?

Either way, first she must reclaim the dowry he so staunchly refused to hand over.

He'd withdrawn into the woods to hunt, and perhaps this was the best opportunity she might ever have to leave, but she was bone weary and famished. Even if she managed to mount Nell again, one more minute sat upon the horse would see her crumple off the saddle to be trodden by the old mare. No, tonight she must sleep. She could find a way to flee tomorrow.

Night fell all at once, like a blanket, and though she'd done it many times, Jory couldn't spark the flint to save her life. She tried again and again, as the disconcerting sounds of darkness crept closer.

"This is ridiculous," she muttered, her hands, trembling with fatigue and cramping from having gripped the reins all day.

Suddenly there was a hulking shadow at her side, and she

flipped her sgian dubh outward before realizing it was only Shaw. He swayed out of reach just in time, hands up in surrender.

"May I?" he asked, gesturing towards the flint still clutched tightly in her other fist.

Jory shifted away from him, unwilling to concede defeat. She'd started fires before, for heaven's sake.

"I ken ye can do it yourself, but let me help. Please?" He wrested the stone gently from her fingers with his left hand, the right still held up in deference to her knife.

Once the fire was roaring, he set to work cleaning a rabbit he'd trapped while she was gathering sticks. Jory had expected to dine on nothing more than the dried fruit and cheese from their provisions, and the aroma of sizzling meat made her stomach rumble with anticipation.

"I'm sorry it isnae more lavish," he said, trying to break the silence she'd imposed between them.

She glanced from him to the rabbit. What did he think she was accustomed to in Inverness? Roasted pheasant with a soup and fish course every evening?

"There aren't a great many inns along this road," he tried again. "Though perhaps tomorrow."

Imagining a warm inn with a cozy peat fire perked her up, until she remembered she intended to slip away before the next dusk fell.

Likely she'd be sleeping rough again tomorrow, with no one to spark the flint but herself, and only the memory of her cousins' gentle snoring for company. Their breathing and stirring were the sounds of night for her as sure as the distant cries of owls and foxes, as sure as the soft hum of a far-away lullaby. How would she sleep without them nestled close beside her?

The screech of some distant creature echoed through the darkness, and Jory's head spun automatically to seek out its source. She was loath to seem frightened in front of Finlay Shaw, but he appeared not to notice, rising to stoke the flames. Then he said, "Dinna fash. The foxes and wolves and the like willnae dare draw too near the fire."

"I wasn't worried."

"So ye *can* speak! I thought perhaps the Borlum had cut out your tongue before leaving."

She rolled her eyes out of habit.

"Careful they dinnae stick that way."

So much for the privacy of darkness. Chuckling despite herself, Jory tried to think of a cutting retort. In truth, she wanted to pepper him with questions—about the convent, about Aberdeenshire, about why he'd been chosen to accompany her. Instead, she heaved a weary sigh and looked up at the emerging stars.

"Are ye cold?" he asked, offering her a horn cup she assumed contained whisky.

"Not in the slightest," she lied, but she caught a whiff of the proffered cup and turned her face to him. "Willow bark tea?"

He shrugged, and she accepted the warm drink gratefully. He really was full of surprises, this *Shaw Wretch*.

It didn't change anything though. He could be as gallant as he pleased with his tea and his offering to help her mount and dismount, but it wouldn't matter. She may have appreciated his straight, strong nose from afar when they were children, no longer quite so straight but no less fine—and back then, as now, she may have admired his tender way with his horse and tenacious handling of the sword—but until he relinquished her dowry, he was nothing to her.

THE ICY DEMEANOR THE LASS HAD ADOPTED THAT MORNING was finally nearing a thaw, but what had caused it? Was she simply afraid to speak to him—nae, to even look upon him—with no chaperone to ensure his behavior remained pure?

Only, her cold shoulder didn't strike him as fearful, nor did she seem the sort of lass to care very much what other people thought. Perhaps the pain of parting from her family had turned her surly.

She was close with her cousins, clearly. As Finn had turned to mount Sparradh, a touch so feather-light he almost thought he'd imagined it had brushed his forearm before being snatched quickly away. The elder cousin, the quiet one, had handed him a folded note with crisp, clean writing. It said simply, *Take care of her*.

To leave such comfort, she must feel quite anxious facing down an unknown and unexpected future far from her family and friends. For all her bravado, a convent in Aberdeenshire was a long way from the life she'd known in the Highlands. And being sent away so suddenly, with only the likes of him as an escort— aye, it would make anyone sour and grasp at control whichever way they could get it, even if it was only by riding ahead of him.

Well fine, the rear had provided a better vantage point from which to study her. She was clearly a trained rider, handling Nell with ease, and exhibiting none of the fear lesser horsemen tried in vain to hide.

He'd gone out of his way to select the right horse for her: patient yet energetic, surefooted and able to keep pace with Sparradh, but steady enough to control while riding sidesaddle. Perhaps his abundance of caution had been unnecessary. Her seat, though slightly strange and unbalanced at first glance, was prac- ticed, and she was responsive and secure even as she navigated the rocky Highland terrain. What surprised him was her ease in a sidesaddle, for he half expected her to don breeks and insist on riding astride like a man.

After continued observation—for what else had there been to look at?—he determined that she held herself a bit askew to remain balanced in the saddle. She adapted her stance to account for some slight curvature, one shoulder was higher than the other, and her hips undoubtedly the same, like the horizontal branches of a beautiful old yew tree he'd climbed as a boy. The branches were always stronger than they looked, the perfect place to hide and clear a cluttered mind.

Riding for so many hours must be excruciating for the lass, though she uttered not a single complaint within his hearing. So he had taken the time to gather some willow bark when he was hunting. Because he worried it wasn't just being stripped from the bosom of her kin that left her hating him.

Had someone imparted the events of the '15? They'd have painted a picture for her of his brothers, wounds festering in a squalid prison even as he escaped unharmed.

Perhaps a well-intentioned friend of her youngest cousin had shared the woeful tale. The girl was only a few years older than his nieces. Even a loose-lipped servant might have let slip, for who among the Shaws didn't know the infamous story of Preston?

Surely none would be so cruel as to dredge up her own father's death under the auspices of care and concern. Or Finn's responsibility for the whole bloody disaster? Her father's lifeless face still haunted him. Did it haunt her too? Was that why she despised him?

When he'd offered her the rabbit there was such a look in her eye. It said she'd rather starve than accept a thing from him, but then her stomach bellowed like a hind in heat and gave her away.

And what did it matter if she did hate him, when he'd soon deposit her on the steps of a convent never to be seen again?

Still, at least she was drinking the tea. Hopefully the tincture would help to ease any pain from the day's ride. She was shivering less now she'd drunk it, at least.

Finn moved the horses nearer for a little added windbreak, and then sat close enough to see her features in the firelight—to provide further warmth, was all. She glanced at him but didn't outwardly object before turning her attention back to the sky.

"Polaris," he said, pointing up at the North Star.

She looked where he was pointing, and he took the opportunity to lean a little closer.

"The big yellow one." He pointed again. "And Ursa Major's just there."

"My father knew all the names of the stars," she said. "He taught me a few before he died in the Rising."

Finn's tongue turned to ash in his throat, threatening to choke him. "At Preston?" His voice came out a guilt-stained whisper, but she simply nodded—oblivious to his discomfort, unbothered by his mention of the battle, intent only on the stars.

"I like the one that looks like a pigeon flying over."

"Cassiopeia? The M shape?" he asked, swallowing hard, happy for the astral distraction. She was quite clever to see that constellation as a bird. "Aye. It's a good story. She's followed, over there, by Perseus," he said, pointing further to the northeast.

Silence fell between them again as they looked up into the vast night sky. But Finn had gotten a taste of her voice, and he needed more.

"D'ye know the myth of Cassiopeia?"

She didn't answer but shook her head slightly, still looking up.

"She was a queen."

"Of Scotland?"

"Och no. Of a kingdom far away known as Aethiopia, where the king was called Cephus."

"Aethiopia," she tried the word out, like she was tasting it, and Finn shivered though he was anything but cold.

"Aye. Together they had a beautiful daughter named Andromeda. See those stars that make a square?"

She leaned closer to him for a better look, so close they were almost touching, and a familiar yearning jerked beneath his plaid and made his lungs constrict.

"I think so."

He cleared his throat. "That's Pegasus. And in between," he

pointed from the square back to the M, "is Andromeda. The chained maiden."

"The chained maiden," the lass repeated softly once more.

The bitter tang of willow bark tickled Finn's nose with each frosty puff of her breath.

"Aye. Ye see, Cassiopeia was a vain woman, bragging to any who'd listen about her daughter's beauty. She went so far as to claim Andromeda was even more lovely than the nymphs of the sea."

"Scandalous," she scoffed.

" 'Twas indeed. The nymphs, mind, were vainglorious in their own right. They petitioned the great god Poseidon to punish Cassiopeia. To appease them, he sent a sea monster to attack the kingdom."

"A sea monster? Like the one Saint Columba saw in Ness?"

"Aye, but meaner. In his *infinite wisdom*, Cephus believed the only way to save his kingdom was to sacrifice Andromeda to the monster." He glanced at her. Did she see parallels to her own life, feel she was being sacrificed to the Jacobite cause because of the cowardice or ineptitude of her clan?

She sniffed and murmured, "Sounds about right."

"So they chained Andromeda to a rock in the middle of the sea."

"What happened to her?"

Finn hesitated. "Perseus rescued her."

She huffed her disappointment, and for the first time in his life, Finn was disappointed in Perseus too.

"He ran the monster through wi' his sword, liberated Andromeda. They wed, and begat nine children."

She huffed again, but this time it sounded more like a laugh. "I like my version better."

"About the pigeon?"

"Yes."

"Will ye tell it to me?"

32

She turned her face away from Andromeda, back towards the M shape of Cassiopeia.

"There was a girl who befriended a pigeon," she began, and Finn's gaze was drawn to her face rather than to the stars. "The kind of pigeon that carries messages back and forth. Only she didn't use it for messages. She kept it locked in a cage all the time."

Was Mistress Mackintosh the girl in the story or the pigeon in the cage? He needed to know but was too afraid to interrupt her and ask, as though she'd dissipate and join the stars.

"You see, she'd lost her mother, and she was desperately lonely. She couldn't bear to lose the pigeon too. But the pigeon was a bird. It yearned to fly free. It broke her heart to see her friend look so sad, so she brought it fresh boughs and berries from the forest—anything she could think of to make it content.

"But it wasn't content, not really. Even so, it loved the girl, and at night it would sing for her. One day, it sang a haunting lullaby which had been her mother's favorite. Except she'd lost her mother long before she ever found the pigeon and kept it in a cage.

" 'Where did you learn that song?' she implored, for it was in a language she didn't remember.

" 'I heard it upon the wind,' the pigeon told her.

" 'It was my mother's song,' the girl said.

" 'If you let me out, I'll follow the song to the ends of the earth and carry a message to your mother upon the wind,' the pigeon promised.

"The girl was torn. She didn't want to part with her friend, but she missed her mother terribly, so finally she agreed and gave the pigeon a message for her mother."

"What did she say?" Finn whispered, longing to pass a message to his own mother, gone these thirteen years.

She looked down at the cup in her hands.

"All the things she didn't know how to put into words. All the notes in the lullaby, all the pain in her heart. All the questions she'd been too afraid to wonder.

"Finally free, the pigeon flew out her window. She watched it all the day, swooping and twirling through the trees, and she began to despair. She thought perhaps it had tricked her. But the pigeon simply needed to wait until nightfall, and when the stars crept out, it followed them all the way to her mother. In the morning, it returned as promised.

"'Your mother says to tell you you're brave,' the bird reported. 'And you're mighty. And even so, she'll always be here with you.'

"And from that day on, the pigeon was allowed to fly free. And whenever the girl needed her mother, it would carry a message to her through the stars."

The lass looked up at the constellations again, a small sad smile tugging at her lips, and how could Finn possibly leave her behind in a cage in Aberdeen?

H E RESTED FITFULLY ALL NIGHT, TOO WELL WRAPPED IN HIS plaid to toss and turn about as much as he was wont, until the wind picked up. Then he could hear the girl's teeth knock together from three feet away as she shivered under her earasaid, though she lay closer to the fire. He watched her for a moment in the flickering light and then made the decision, knowing full well it might earn him a blade buried to the hilt between his fourth and fifth ribs. Still, he couldn't let the lass freeze to death, now could he?

He sidled over a few inches. Then, when she didn't stir, he crept closer still, until finally there was only a handbreadth between them and he could spread the end of his tartan over her. She nestled into the wool, warm from Finn's body heat, and immediately curled onto her side, dragging more of his plaid away with her.

Finn tugged it back and finally settled down to sleep, no

longer bothered by her teeth rattling themselves half out of her head. No, now he was kept awake by the scent of lilac and peppermint balm, by her back up against his, and by trying not to feel her bony shoulders or the soft shape of her arse as she unconsciously burrowed into him, or the hardness of his cock begging to respond in kind.

The moment dawn began to trace its gold-drenched fingers across the twilit landscape, Finn rolled away from her, taking his plaid with him, and slipped into the trees to relieve his bladder. He was dead tired and facing down a second long day in the saddle. Yet, standing in the forest breathing in the damp, musky earth tinged with wood sage as the brisk autumn air nipped his skin, the knowledge that he'd spend the day sparring with Mistress Mackintosh invigorated him.

His stomach grumbled and he carefully studied the trees. Last night he'd heard the coo of some nearby pigeons. How surprised she'd be, waking to a breakfast of fresh eggs after a cold night sleeping rough. He scanned the base of each tree for tell-tale white droppings and finally spotted a nest just out of reach. Securing his kilt and glancing around for adult birds, he shimmied up the trunk until he could reach the delicate limb, then stretched out to carefully extract two ivory eggs. Maybe he wouldn't tell her they came from pigeons.

She was gazing blearily into the glowing embers of last night's fire when Finn returned with breakfast. He watched her from the safety of the clearing, her tangled mop of dark brown curls framing her cheeks, legs tucked up to her chin like a child, ensconced within her own plaid, and suddenly his low back felt cold with the loss of her.

She turned towards him as though reading his thoughts, and he cleared his throat before emerging from the shadows of the woods.

"Madainn mhath. And did ye sleep well, mistress?"

She smiled faintly. "I dreamt I was a bird."

"Oh, aye? Carrying messages and the like?"

"Just flying," she said, noticing the hands he kept behind his back. "What do you have there?"

"Och, it's nothing. Only eggs and chanterelles to break our fast."

The way her face lit up, she reminded him of a tiny hedgehog —pretending to be all prickly on the outside but quick enough to smile at one who's gentle and brings tasty treats.

"Where did you find eggs at this time of year?"

He shrugged, trying not to look too pleased with himself for being able to make her face do that.

Setting the bounty of delicate, pale eggs and orange, funnel-shaped mushrooms gently in her folded lap, he said, "Faeries left them, maybe."

"Faeries?"

"Aye. Everyone knows the woods are full of magic the closer you get to Samhain."

And was it wee folk he could blame for making him feel so strange, so eager to please a maid who could never be his?

Chapter Four

Her skin had pricked like hen flesh before Jory noticed him lurking in the shadows. Then he came out speaking of faerie eggs and chanterelles and magic, and she half wondered if he were some rogue druid sent to tempt her away from the sisterhood. It wouldn't prove much of a challenge, and not only because she had no intention of taking vows.

It felt almost improper to accept such decadence from a man without a chaperone. But she was hungry and there was no one to question her propriety out here, the faeries notwithstanding, so she nestled the food amongst the dying embers, and soon they had a hot and delicious breakfast.

"How are ye?" he asked timidly as they ate. "Are ye sore at all, I mean, from the ride?"

She was, in fact, very sore from the ride and from passing the night on the cold, hard ground, but what good was complaining? It wasn't his fault she was being sent away, and the last thing she needed was to be treated like some sort of fragile butterfly, constantly under observation.

"I can still travel, if that's what you mean. You needn't fuss on my account, Mr. Shaw."

"Well, good then. Eat up and we'll make ready."

She'd felt momentarily sorry for her sharp tone. But then he took charge, in his gruff, irritating way, and she was glad she'd been short with him.

Standing, she brushed the dust from her skirts. "If you're concerned about bandits, would it not be wise to divide my dowry between the two of us? Carry some on each horse?"

He stared at her stupidly, tilting his head to the side as though she spoke the riddled language of a Sphinx.

"No, of course not," she answered herself sullenly, turning her back on him to mount unaided. "Do you think we'll make it to an inn tonight?"

"Maybe. I suppose it depends on you."

Everything always depends on me, Jory thought. She certainly didn't expect to rely on anyone else—ever.

"Good," she said, with all the confidence she could feign. "I'll be relieved to sleep in a real bed. And eat a proper meal."

Then she turned Nell to the east, leaving the braw Highlander to scramble with the fire before following along behind.

In truth, both meals had been perfectly delicious and after the long hard day, she'd slept solidly. She couldn't help goading him though, feeling him out, testing his limits. Because vague memories as wispy as the reflections of sunlight bouncing off a stream reminded her of feeling cold, and then extremely warm and cozy. Startled awake at some point, she'd found herself pressed close against his solid form, breathing in the scents of clover and horse dander that clung to his plaid.

Jory's skin tingled to think of it. Had they each rolled closer to the other in their sleep, huddling together at last, back to back, for warmth? What would her family say? Ellen would go white with horror, and Maggie would be beside herself, gleefully begging for details. Her aunt would pray to Mary, and her uncle... well... It was his fault she was there to begin with, so his opinion didn't signify.

It was her uncle's fault, too, that she must become a nun—*her* a *nun*! It was laughable and infuriating all at the same time. She preferred the Latin names of plants to solemn Latin prayers, preferred quiet solitude for making up stories rather than for penance and reflection. Her—a nun. She, who had sinned and was not sorry. No, after years of attempting to summon one iota of regret, she could at least admit the truth.

She wasn't sorry, and God could smite her down if he chose to.

"Is something funny to ye?" Her companion nudged his Clydesdale almost even with her old mare, and this time Jory didn't pull away.

"Life is funny is it not, Mr. Shaw?"

"Call me Finn, if ye like. Tell me, what's so humorous about life, then?"

"Two days ago, I thought I was to wed, against my will, a man I didn't know. Instead, I find myself promised as a bride of Christ, whom one can never truly know, can they? I'll be a bride in name only, given over to a bridegroom from whom I cannot even seek the comforts of a married woman, few though they may be."

Some part of her expected to be struck down dead on the spot for blasphemy, and it made her hot all over to speak so plainly.

Since when had she ever yearned for the touch of a man? Never. But the fact she was denied it without any voice in the matter, like a gelding put to pasture, made her burn with a smoldering rage.

"Ye really dinnae want to be a sister?"

"I do not."

"Did ye... did ye dream of your wedding day then? When you were a wee lassie?"

It shouldn't sting that he didn't remember her. She was no one, only a lesser Mackintosh waif, a half-orphan whose uncle had taken pity on her and brought her along as a companion to his daughters. Her uncle wasn't the chief nor anywhere near the line of succession as a second cousin to the Borlum. It shouldn't sting, but it did.

"No," she answered honestly. "I suppose I was too practical for such girlish daydreams."

He snorted appreciatively, but he wasn't laughing *at* her, so she let it pass.

"I came by it honestly. My father had to ask five times before my mother agreed to wed. She always said that marriage was Church-sanctioned war. I don't know if she truly meant it, but the notion that marriage was war amused my father very much. He repeated it often."

"Was she unhappy, d'ye think?"

No one had ever asked her that before. Not even Maggie, who was nothing but a whirlwind of questions day and night.

"No. Merely strong-willed. And what of you, Mr. Shaw?" she asked, changing the subject. "What was your childhood like?"

"Och," he said, letting out the rein again to draw up fully even. "About what you'd expect, I reckon, being the third son of the laird. And it's Finn."

Jory remembered exactly what it meant, *being the third son of the laird*.

"I was trained from the time I could stand, to do my duty."

Was he insinuating her desire for freedom was the abandonment of her own familial duty? But if there was reproach in his voice, she couldn't hear it no matter how hard she tried.

"And I'll do mine. What can you tell me about this priest? And the man who builds a convent for him?"

Finn shook his head. "Only that he didnae build the convent. It's housed in an old family castle. And if the alliance they seek holds, it'll be a big help to the Jacobite cause. I'm sorry, I wish I knew more."

She flicked her gaze at him sideways. He was his laird's younger brother. Surely he knew more than he was letting on. Surely he was lying. But why?

"Though," he added brightly, "I think you'll like Aberdeenshire. Ye can taste the salt in the air, and—"

"I won't," Jory said, much more emphatically than she meant to. Not because there was anything to dislike about the coast, and not because she was determined to hate it, but because she had no intention of sticking around long enough to form an opinion.

IT HAD BEEN PLEASANT WHILE IT LASTED, RIDING TWO ABREAST, sneaking sidelong glances at the lass instead of staring at the arse-end of a flatulent horse. But then Finn managed to say exactly the wrong thing, as he always inevitably did, and now he was right back where he began.

When it was time to water the horses at midday, he whistled to get her attention, since she insisted on riding so far ahead. He'd learned well enough yesterday that Mistress Mackintosh didn't approve of being whistled at, and for some reason the knowledge he could vex her from afar delighted him.

She was feisty and confounding, and when he spied her in the shadows of the parapet for the second time two nights ago, his heart had stopped for a moment, presuming she was there to jump once more. Knowing her exile to the coast was not quite the welcome reprieve he'd assumed would make his duty somewhat less pleasant, but he'd given his word to Angus, and if she didn't wish to marry, what was the alternative? She'd grow accustomed to her new life in time, but they had to be realistic. Didn't they?

"You needn't whistle. I'm not a dog," she grumbled as she slid from her saddle, tossing him the reins so she could wash her face and hands in the stream.

"So that's what your voice sounds like. I'd nearly forgotten," he sassed.

After hobbling the horses where they could drink their fill, they each dipped into their separate provisions of cheese and bannocks, but Finn was determined to get her attention again. He situated himself comfortably against the trunk of a shady pine tree, removed a handful of dried strawberries from his sporran, and sighed blissfully—and loudly—as he closed his eyes and dropped one of the ruby morsels onto his tongue.

"Are those *strawberries*?" she asked, right on cue.

He opened one eye, pretending to notice her for the very first time, looked around, and pointed at himself feigning surprise.

She eyed him for a moment before allowing a small laugh, and Finn relaxed. He almost thought he'd overplayed it.

"Aye, they're strawberries, and I'll share them with you if ye're nice to me."

A shadow flitted across her face, and he regretted saying it, but there it was.

"Perhaps a trade? Some hazelnuts?" she offered, producing the prize from one of the pockets deep within her skirts.

Finn nodded his agreement, though he had hazelnuts of his own, and slid over to make space for her to lean against his tree. She hesitated before hitching up her skirts to join him, and then held out a dainty handful of nuts.

Hazelnuts had always been his favorite treat as a lad. He took one, and filled her cupped hand with sweet, dried berries.

"I'm not accustomed to riding side by side," she confessed stiffly, not quite an apology, but it was progress.

"I can see that. Well, you know, it's a lot like walking side by side. Except the beast does the walking."

She blinked and burst out laughing as she had when he arrived breathless on the battlements wishing her a good afternoon. He might've felt a bit foolish, but her laughter was somehow a salve along the rough edges of his feelings. He liked hearing it, knowing he'd been the one to cause it, almost more than he liked vexing her. It had a musical quality, like the tinkling of glass in a spring-time breeze.

"So easy, is it?" she asked, like someone who'd learned from experience the difficulty of making new friends.

"Gets easier the more you practice."

"The more you grow accustomed to being down wind, I imagine." She turned a mischievous eye on him.

Was she suggesting he smelled?

"Ha?" he asked.

She nodded towards the nearby stream and said, "Either you or your horse could do with a swim. Though it's certainly eau de barnyard, I'm willing to give the benefit of the doubt to the horse."

She was! She sat there, prim as you please, accusing him of needing a bath. And after he'd given her strawberries.

He felt flushed all over, but he tried to keep his face impassive. Had she lain awake half the night, smelling his foul stench, wishing he were not so near? Was it an unpleasant chore for her to sit beside him even now?

"Aye, well, I'll warrant it isnae Sparradh," he agreed. "There never was such a well-groomed laddie as he."

She laughed again, and he risked a glance at her only to find an unexpected warmth dancing on her pursed lips. Perhaps she was only teasing him to obscure her reasons for preferring to ride alone. Well. He'd teach her to tease—two could play at that. Besides, for reasons further south than his oxters, a cold splash might do him good.

He frowned and nodded. "My apologies, mistress. I'm not accustomed to the company or sensibilities of fine ladies such as yourself."

She laughed a third time, choking it off short when he rose and strode towards the stream, stripping off his plaid as he went.

How desperately he wanted to sneak a look back as he discarded his sark as well, to drink in her shocked expression, to know if she was watching or primly averting her gaze. His cock jerked freely with the notion she might be appraising his every curve and sinew even now. She'd likely never seen a grown man's backside before.

He waded into the stream until the brisk water reached his hips, so cold it made him gasp and immediately rectified any problems of propriety as his arousal shrank back down to size. Then he splashed his face to ease the burning in his cheeks and neck, hoping the flush would diminish before he had to turn back and face the shore.

Slapping at the water, he cursed the cold as if swearing would warm it, and then there was a shift in the current, followed by a tiny gasp. Finn spun around, the frigid water lapping at the hairs below his navel.

The lass had followed him in, submerged up to her neck, the silly fool, and from the look of her, naked as the day she was born.

He opened his mouth and closed it, gawping like a salmon.

"Well, if you're going in, it's only fair I ought to," she stammered. "Be a shame to find out it was myself I was smelling all along."

His lips twitched, but he managed not to laugh. "Downright embarrassing," he agreed, sinking lower into the water so half his chest was covered like hers.

"Don't you try anything, Mr. Shaw," she said, slapping the water in his direction, so it splashed him in the face.

He turned his head so it didn't catch him full in the eye, but he didn't even wipe it away, just let it drip down his cheek and back from whence it came. "I would never," he said calmly, though he felt anything but calm. He kept his gaze firmly on her face, not allowing it to wander, or for his imagination to fill in the gaps. It was struggle enough to keep his arousal in check despite the icy bath.

"I mean it." She splashed him again. "Stay on your side."

"I was here first," he said splashing her back.

"Surely a gentleman such as yourself can share a whole river."

"A gentleman, am I now?"

He sloshed more water her way, and because she was smiling with her lips open, the cold water caught her in the mouth and his own teeth ached as she grimaced.

"A gentleman—and here I thought I was nothing more than the Shaw Wretch."

He meant to say it in a light, teasing tone, but there was an edge he hadn't been able to hide.

"I never called you that," she confessed softly.

"Why not?" he asked, and he desperately wanted to know the answer. "Surely you've heard the stories."

"We're apt to catch some virulent fever if we stay here much longer. Turn your back."

He watched her for a moment. What could she possibly do if he refused to turn around? What had she even been thinking, following him into the river? But only a wretch would shirk basic courtesy, and she alone had never called him one. So he turned and strained his ears for the sounds of her retreat.

"Don't turn back until I tell you," she called.

"Nae, mistress."

"Swear it."

"On my holy iron and the soul of my dear departed mother."

The faint sounds of swishing fabric and light footsteps wafted back down from the shore. Mercy, but the lass took an eternity to dress. How had she removed it all so quickly, the skirts and the stays and whatever all a lady wore? It was like the difference between cracking an egg and trying to piece the shell back together.

"Not to rush ye, mistress, but that chill you mentioned is starting to seep into my bones."

She didn't answer, but Finn could still hear her moving about under the trees and Sparradh chuffing and stamping in a way which made him shake off any lingering arousal and grow instantly alert. Was something out there, some predator his horse was sensing?

"Mistress?"

He counted to ten and then turned around.

She wasn't standing there, naked or otherwise. In fact there was no sign of her at all, or his Clydesdale, just the dingy white sark he'd stripped off his back and Nell grazing beneath the pines.

"Sparradh?"

Finn exploded from the river, yanking his shirt over his head and onto each wet arm, and turning a complete circle in search of his plaid. It should have been there—right there, feet from where his top had lain, halfway back to the blasted tree.

He rolled his neck in frustration and then he saw it, her own reddish plaid, fluttering on a limb of the tree.

She'd taken his kilt. He was going to strangle her.

Finn swiveled his head for any sign of the lass, but she was well and truly gone, and on the back of *his* steed, no less. Confounded, damned, headstrong woman.

He tied the shirt tail between his legs and gingerly shimmied up the tree trunk, much as he had in pursuit of eggs for *her* breakfast, if slightly more skin was exposed this time.

Finally he caught hold of her heavy plaid and untangled it from the limb. Then he folded it upon the ground and enveloped himself in the scent of her, smoky lilac and birch, a scent he felt certain he may never clear from his brain after this. Once properly attired, he examined the mare. Cursing under his breath, he eased himself gingerly into the sidesaddle, slinging his right leg around the pommel far more awkwardly than he'd observed the lady do. He nearly lost his balance when he kicked but eventually turned Nell about and began to follow the heavy tracks Sparradh left in his wake.

Bloody sleekit vixen from hell.

Chapter Five

Jory couldn't believe what had just transpired. She didn't know why she so enjoyed deviling poor Shaw, but when he first stood up, she feared she'd angered him. And then he'd dropped his plaid to the ground and she saw his strong, muscular legs, and then he tore the shirt off over his head and she saw everything else.

His backside was taut and sculpted like marble, and she found herself staring at it for far too long before it occurred to her to look away. Jesus, Mary, Joseph, and the wee donkey, but the air had grown hot and thick all of a sudden.

When he'd walked into the river stark naked without a care, it had occurred to her if she didn't abandon him—if she allowed herself to be locked away in some horrible tower in Aberdeenshire—she might never be so near a young man again, and for once in her life, that seemed like a very great shame.

And so she got the devil in her, and if that hadn't been brazen enough, she saw her opportunity to escape and took it.

She hadn't meant to steal the horse. Well, she *had* meant to, but she hadn't planned to take Finlay Shaw's beloved giant of a horse. She thought he might let her go if she slipped quietly away with Nell, especially if she was difficult to find or he didn't notice the missing dowry right away.

She'd only planned to remove the money from his saddlebag, but the sack was closed tight with a complicated knot, so then she thought to take the whole thing and be on her way. When her effort was foiled by another secure knot, she swung herself up and made her escape. *Stupid, stupid, stupid.* It was all she could do to remain astride the massive beast, barely steering, though she cared not which direction they careened, as long as it was *away*.

At first she attempted to ride aside in the saddle, but quickly realized if she was going to keep her seat she must straddle the Clydesdale with her petticoats bunched up to her waist and her outer skirt stretched wide exposing her stockings. Her legs weren't quite long enough for her to even reach the stirrups, indeed she felt like a rag doll atop a dragon, digging her heels into Sparradh's billowing sides and clinging to the horse for dear life.

She had no idea how much of a head start she'd managed, for of course he would attempt to follow. How many minutes or precious seconds did he wait before emerging from the river? Did he teasingly chide her for taking so long to dress, oblivious of her departure? How much time was wasted in retrieving her plaid from the tree? She was rather bitterly proud of that little afterthought.

Straining to catch any sign of her pursuer, all she could hear was the wind howling in her damp ears and the rumble of the Clydesdale's massive hooves. Her only hope was that Shaw would be slowed down enough to lose their erratic trail as they careened across the countryside.

She needed time and space to think. Perhaps she could make it to a village, slice the leather thong attaching the bag to the saddle, and disappear with the money, leaving just enough behind to cover the damage, as well as a warm bed and a hot meal for Shaw and some oats for the horses.

Yes. That was exactly what she'd do, what she should have

done back at the river, but it had gotten the better of her—their naked, virile splashing and the cheeky grin, tugging at the corners of his mouth like it did when he was a boy and didn't want to give too much away.

It had all made her too flustered to think straight, the splashing and the grinning and the dropped kilt, and those arms, right there in front of her, as though they'd finally kept their promise to burst the seams of his shirt. And now she was wrapped in his plaid, and it smelled of campfire and pine needles and clover and none of the reek she'd accused him of, and she'd stolen his horse and nothing was going according to plan.

Would he be in very much trouble back at Moy for losing her? Or would they expect as much from the *Shaw Wretch*?

One may be fallen, but one can always sink lower, he had said. Surely they wouldn't blame him for her selfish ways.

After what felt like hours clinging to the back of a storm cloud, Sparradh slowed a little, allowing Jory to hoist herself upright and take proper hold of the reins. At this pace, she even began to enjoy the ride—the crisp wind nipping her nose and cheeks offset by the warm sun smiling down on her.

Once she tracked the sun and turned the Clydesdale southward, it became exhilarating trotting towards her future. She could disappear in Edinburgh. With enough money in her purse to rent a little room, she might even apprentice while she earned her medical degree. And then, after proving herself as capable as any man, she would let down her hair and show the world who she truly was. She would finally, finally live her life on her own terms.

Perhaps it was her dream, such tempting of fate, the single moment of hubris which put a peat bog in her path. For no sooner had she pictured it than the Clydesdale ground to a halt and refused to move. After a futile attempt to encourage the horse to walk on a little further, Jory slid from the saddle, sinking up to her ankles in the marshy bog.

Fool, she chided herself, turning a full circle to survey her predicament, each step making a sucking squelch. *Prideful, ridiculous, cotton-headed fool.*

She ran a hand down each of Sparradh's legs, murmuring gently, and coaxing him to lift the hoof so she could examine his feet. Poor thing had lost a shoe. *Now what?*

Jory guided him out of the marsh and looked around, but there was no sign of the missing shoe.

Shaw would catch up to his Clydesdale soon, and when he did, she didn't want to be within striking distance. So she took her sgian dubh and sliced the ties on the first saddlebag like she should have done if she'd been thinking clearly back at the river. But when she reached inside, there was no coin, no ruby ring which had once been her father's. The bag held merely a leather-bound journal, a few apples, and some cheese.

Biting back the rising panic, she cut the other bag's tie, then let out a furious bellow when she reached inside to find nothing but more provisions. Where was her dowry? Where was her whole future?

Bile started up her throat, and with it, the unfamiliar taste of despair. Could the whole lot be safe in Finlay Shaw's sporran? Or had her uncle kept it? Had she been given over to the Church without a penny for her keeping?

Jory sank to the ground next to the Clydesdale and, feeling faint, lowered her head between her knees.

AT FIRST, IT WAS EASY TO TRACK SPARRADH AND THE LASS—FAR easier than deciding what to do with her once he found her. Where she thought she was headed, Finn couldn't begin to guess. In truth, he was surprised and a little impressed she'd managed to hang on.

Sparradh was gentle enough when he wanted to be, but he

could get frisky when the air was crisp and the midges weren't biting. And he was certainly not used to such a light load, why he probably felt as though he were carrying a wood sprite, and from the depths of his prints, they were fairly flying. Finn half expected to come upon her sprawled across the ground, broken into a dozen pieces, each piece another thorn embedded in his conscience.

She both intrigued and infuriated him, this fledgling of a woman who spoke of pigeons and was destined to take holy orders, but who would toy with an unclad man in the river and then for some confounding reason up and steal his damn horse.

After a while, his leg cramped something fierce in the petite and unfamiliar saddle, and even Nell's spirits seemed to flag. No sooner than he would find the trail, he'd lose it again, the Clydesdale and the lass nowhere in sight.

If he didn't find her... what then? Angus would have his bollocks for tea. He hardly even needed an excuse. Would his brother banish him from Shaw territory? From the whole of the Highlands? Nae, from Scotland herself if Angus had his choice. Would he become a mercenary then? A hired sword for the English? That would stick it to Angus and the lot of them good and proper. Or he could try his luck in America, though it sounded like unrest was building there by the day.

No, he was better off continuing to wage his own private battle to make amends with Angus, to restore himself and his name. He had to see this mission through, which meant finding the lass and delivering her to the convent trussed hand and foot if he had to. And if he didn't find her, perhaps he could persuade some other maiden to take up orders in her place, though Angus had said the convent asked for her explicitly.

FINN THOUGHT HE MUST BE IMAGINING A SPECTER WHEN HE finally glimpsed the figure in the distance, shoulders slumped in defeat, trudging alongside a horse. *His* horse, who appeared to have lost a shoe judging by the way he favored one foot.

It pleased Finn to know the lass got down and walked. It was the sensible thing to do, of course, the humane thing, though light as she was Sparradh might not have even noticed the difference. But he'd known plenty of horsemen who insisted on riding their partially shod mounts, and it seldom ended well for the horses.

Though she'd stolen from him and ridden headlong into a bog, Finn felt a warmth and kinship to Mistress Mackintosh because no matter how exhausted, she was willing to get down and walk. Still, despite his own enthusiasm to dismount, he was willing to let her walk a little bit longer, at least until he felt satisfied she wouldn't try such a foolhardy thing in future.

When the sun dipped low on the western horizon, and her plodding steps looked more and more labored, Finn took pity on her and rode around in front, bringing her to a stop. She didn't even look surprised or disappointed to see him, merely resigned and defeated and lost.

Without a word, he untangled himself from the blasted sidesaddle and unbuckled the thing to stow it with Sparradh. Then he mounted Nell once more, seating himself atop the saddle blanket, and reached a hand down to the lass. She stared through him, but allowed him to hoist her up onto the mare and settle her between his legs. He pried Sparradh's reins from her clenched fingers and chirruped for the horses to continue on their way.

The lass was asleep against his chest in minutes.

He probably ought to be angry. She'd nearly cost him everything—not only the hope of regaining a place at his brother's right hand, but if anything had happened to Sparradh... He shuddered to think about it. Pathetic though it was, the Clydesdale was just about his dearest friend, and Sparradh aside, what if something had happened to the lass herself? Finn didn't need yet another soul on his conscience. Not her. He'd never be able to forgive himself.

It was dark when they finally reached an inn on the outskirts of Tomintoul, and the longer the evening wore on without a word of apology or regret, the more irritated Finn became.

She stood silently, watching him curry the horses and inspect Sparradh's foot, her plaid about his waist while she was wrapped cozily in his own kilt. She didn't pretend to be of any help, simply stared at him with deep, anxious eyes, and so Finn coddled the horses more than necessary to delay going inside. Only when he couldn't put it off any longer, he led the way back to the inn without a second glance at her, though he listened to know she followed wordlessly behind.

He requested one room for them to share, and her glance flew to his in alarm, though she had sense enough to hold her tongue. He shot her a warning look anyway, and she turned her gaze stony, staring straight ahead.

She was dead on her feet, and when she didn't move to follow him, he laid a heavy hand on her shoulder and turned her towards the stairs leading up to their single room.

As soon as he closed the door, though, she whirled on him. "Will you be sleeping in the barn then?" she asked, but the fire was gone, and that scared him more than a temper would have.

"And leave you here untethered to take off for God knows where? I think not, mistress, however much ye insist I smell like a stable. I shall pass the night here wi' you."

Now it was her turn to look ashamed, a tinge of red creeping into her cheeks betraying her as Finn's ears were wont to do. She tried to stare him down, but he was a master of such games, and when he refused to blink, she broke away and surveyed the room instead.

"There's only one bed."

"Aye, I can see that."

"There are two of us."

"How clever ye are."

She reached up to slap him, and he caught hold of her wrist, fully encircling it with his fingers. She swallowed.

"Why'd ye run?" It wasn't a question, but a demand, and for some reason it made her purse her lips and set her jaw. Then there was a knock at the door and a young girl on the other side called, "Dinner for ye."

Finn opened the door without letting Mistress Mackintosh out of his sight, lest she bolt again, and the young maid entered, placing the savory-smelling tray upon a small table in the corner near the hearth. She glanced nervously from Finn to the lass, and he tossed her a coin from his sporran, so she curtsied clumsily and closed the door on her way out.

Mistress Mackintosh made to follow the girl, but Finn slid to the side to block her way. She tried to go around him on the other side, and again he stepped in front, tilting his head and squinting down at her in a way he'd been told by more than one cousin made him look haughty.

"Why did ye run?" he repeated.

She threw up her hands and retreated across the room. "Why do you care?"

"You stole my horse, my plaid. Made me chase ye half the day. I've a right to know."

"It doesn't matter. You want to take me to Aberdeenshire, and I've no desire to go. It's as simple as that."

"Ye're lying," he said, taking a few exasperated steps forward.

Last night, looking up at the stars, there'd been a sort of honesty between them. But now it was all anger and hurt cloaked in half-truths and bitter words. "My honor is on the line, mistress—my future. I've a right to know why ye're so determined to destroy it."

"Your future," she scoffed, because of course she knew his honor was already lost to him. "You're a man. You can have any future you desire. The food's getting cold."

"The food can rot," he said, taking another step closer. It did smell like the best meal he'd ever been offered, but they had squared off like two wildcats, and things must be resolved between them before they supped or they would fester like a dirty wound.

The lass, however, was disinclined to make amends, and she reached for a bannock. He caught her wrist once more, perhaps delighting a little too much in the touch and the power surging through him. She moved to strike him again, with the other hand, and he caught that one too, trapping her. But the flash of fear in her face right before she lifted her chin defiantly turned his stomach and took the fight right out of him.

"Why?" he asked once more, squeezing her wrists before relaxing his grip.

Sensing the change, she yanked her arms away.

"Because I don't want to be a nun." She scurried to the opposite corner, almost as far away from him as she could get, and crossed her arms defensively over her chest.

"But why take Sparradh?"

"Obviously he wasn't my first choice." She sighed heavily and slid down the wall a little. "I needed my dowry from your saddlebag, and your knots were too good."

He tried to ignore the surge of pleasure at her complimenting his knots.

"But I dinnae have it."

"I know that. *Now.*"

Finn stepped forward to sit on the edge of the bed, and she flinched a little. He'd scared her before—well, he'd meant to, at least in the moment—but now? He felt filthy and cruel, and so he stepped back again to give her space. "I told you two days ago I didnae have it. The first time ye asked."

"No." She shook her head. "You said you couldn't give it to me."

"Because I didnae have it. Your uncle had it sent direct from Inverness before we even left the castle."

She slid the rest of the way down the wall in utter defeat, and Finn did the only thing he could think of. He fixed her a plate of food.

Chapter Six

Eating, but not tasting the lamb stew or bannocks, Jory merely chewed and swallowed in rhythm with Shaw's own chewing and swallowing, slowly—as though it might be possible to prolong the meal forever.

Her dowry was sent ahead without her. It was probably there already, so if she wanted it back, she'd have to take it. Was she bound straight to hell for plotting to steal from a priest?

A head-pounding ache began to settle into every muscle, the last two days catching up to her. Shaw, at least, seemed somewhat chastened, either by the conversation or the breaking of his fast, and he moved the empty dishes outside the door for the mousy little maid to retrieve—or for Jory to forget about and trip over, waking him up with a god-awful clatter if she attempted to flee. But there was no leaving, not now. Not without the funds to transform herself and begin her life anew.

He loomed over her, offering a hand up from the floor where she'd eaten her dinner alone.

"Come." He nodded toward the bed. "Strip down to your shift and lie prone."

"Don't be ridiculous."

She glanced at his waist where he still wore his belt. Did he mean to punish her after all for stealing Sparradh and all the other trouble? When he didn't strike out earlier, despite her repeated efforts to goad him into it, she rather thought he'd forgiven her. She wasn't even very afraid now, only bitterly disappointed.

Would he hit her? Force himself on her? Brand her, as she'd heard some evil men liked to do? What did she really even know of him, beyond the boy he once was? Except that he could make her laugh, make her shiver just by looking at her, and that only a few hours ago she'd felt safe within his braw arms.

"Come now," he said gently. "I willnae hurt ye."

Jerking her chin to hide a nervous swallow, she huffed, "Won't you?"

He held out his hand, but Jory didn't accept it, instead pushing herself up the wall to stand defiantly before him. It had been years since she'd been whipped, and she didn't relish the thought of it coming from Finn's powerful arms, no matter if he was within his right, which she would argue he was not until the day he cut out her tongue.

Except she didn't have any fight left in her, and anyway, she knew well enough when she was outmatched. If she pulled her knife on him now, she'd have to be prepared to use it.

With trembling fingers she reached back to unlace her stays, making a tangle of them until he stepped closer.

"Let me help." Then he took her shoulder and gently turned her so he could reach the laces.

His fingers were long and thin, perfectly suited to managing muddled knots.

Once free from her stays, he helped her step out of the skirts as well, her hand on his shoulder for balance. And then she stood before him, wiping her sweaty palms on her shift, trying not to chew her bottom lip. More covered than she'd been in the river, but far more nervous than she had been then too, she folded her arms protectively across her chest.

"Face down," he said softly, gesturing toward the bed.

She glared at him, stomach threatening a reprisal of sour stew, and reminded herself to breathe.

He nodded towards the bed once more, and when she complied, he spread his plaid over her. She knew it was his, because the earthy scent of him still clung to the soft wool all these hours later, and it surprised her how soothing she found the aroma. But why order her to undress only to cover her right back up?

"I willnae force ye, but it'll be better if ye take off yer shift—"

"Better—?" Jory scowled back at him, but his face was soft, even shy.

"I promise not to look."

Puzzled and hardly breathing, Jory watched as he turned away. His belt remained safely fastened around her own plaid at his waist, and so she slipped the shift over her head and settled back beneath her covering.

She jumped when he tucked the wool close around her. Then he took her left foot, slid off the knit stocking, and began to rub: the heel, the arch, the toes—every bit that ached from her long walk through the woods. He circled her ankle and took his time with long, sure strokes, pressing into all the places that hurt but not deep enough to cause pain.

"Is this all right?" he whispered.

When her surprised, "Yes," came out inaudibly, he paused until she said it again.

After her feet, he worked his way up each leg, so sore from the way she'd gripped Sparradh. When he reached her thigh, he adjusted the plaid to expose more skin than was proper, but less than what might have been, and then he gently worked the ropey, jumping muscles around her hip, kneading them until she thought she couldn't stand another second, and then moving on, along her low back, chasing the sharp lines of pain as though forcing them down and out of her body in puffs of smoke.

Jory melted into the bed as he worked first one side and then the other, finding by touch alone all of the most tender muscles across her back, her neck, her shoulders. He worked as though he could read her mind or her skin or the very marrow of her bones, as though each inflammation was actually a flame, drawing his hands like moths from one to the next.

The room was silent except for the crackling fire and a distant churr of crickets, interrupted only by Finn's soft murmured questions from time to time. "Still all right? Is that too much? Dinnae forget to breathe."

Breathe?

She could hardly string two thoughts together, let alone inhale and exhale, but when she did manage to, it was only in questions: *What is this? What's happening?* and *How?*

Her father had taken her to Edinburgh once when she was very young, and the physicians there stretched and prodded her painfully before putting her into an iron corset meant to force her to grow straight and tall. She managed not to cry during the visit, focusing on her father's ruby ring and the way it danced in the light. But during the long, jostling carriage ride home she buried her face behind a book and silently wept.

When they finally arrived back in Inverness, Jory could hardly move without wincing, and not only because she felt like a turtle on its back. But, despite her undergarments and padding, the awful contraption had chafed her bloody. As soon as her father saw the ugly sores, he ordered the thing taken away, reasoning that a softer, normal corset should do just as well.

She'd always wondered—if she'd been stronger or her father's heart made of stone—might it have been a success? Would her spine be straight today?

Her uncle, too, had brought in healers over the years, and some had even tried to alleviate the pain of her curvature with pressure and stimulation of the musculature, not unlike Finn was doing, and yet completely unlike what Finn was doing.

No one in her life had ever touched her like this. And when they would ask where it hurt or she was bold enough to offer direction, her words fell on deaf ears and she found little relief where she needed it most. Finn barely needed to ask, but still, he listened and responded, spending more time on her low back and neck despite the obvious deformity of her shoulders. It was... was it a terrible sin to describe it as divine? Well, she was already bound for hell anyway, and this was the most religious experience she'd ever had.

He had learned the technique at the knee of his mother's physician. Arthritic and inflamed for most of Finn's young life, she tried her best to hide it, but he could see the silent pain behind her eyes even on good days. And there were more bad days than good ones towards the end. It was the same pain he saw reflected in Mistress Mackintosh's determined gaze, made all the worse by his forcing her to walk so far.

Knowing of her curvature, he'd still coddled his wounded pride and punished her for causing it. He was petty and wrong, and all he wanted now was to take her pain away, the pain which he'd caused along with all he had not.

He lowered the plaid to expose her full back, and beneath her soft, glowing skin, it told a story. Bending in the shape of an S, her left shoulder was higher than her right, pulling and straining, and hunched slightly forward as though it was in such a hurry to get on with life that it was dragging the rest of her along with it.

As a boy, he'd rubbed his mother's feet and hands, the base of her skull and around her temples. She always said he had a knack for it, which made him feel special, like they shared a bond, just the two of them and not his older brothers. Not the heir, not the spare, but still Finn mattered.

This time was different. With the lass, he felt such stirrings as threatened to get in the way of his healing touch.

At least she no longer seemed afraid of him. But oh, bloody hell, she was going to be trouble.

Finn lay awake most of the night on the floor between the bed and the window he'd cracked open to let the peat smoke out. He tried to lie still and not fidget, but each exhale and murmur left him on high alert. All night his mind raced, calculating how much of a delay this detour would cause.

Angus was expecting him back with the agreement about the Watch. How long would he wait before sending a trusted rider out in search of them?

How much longer would it take to reach the coast? And would it be morally right for him to force a young woman into holy orders if she didn't wish to go?

All night he kept his mind busy with any thought it wanted to think, so long as it didn't drift back to the lass, alone in bed, a bed he could easily have joined her in, were he man enough. A bed he didn't want to be anywhere near.

That was the real reason he hadn't rented two rooms. He needed to prove to God, to Angus, and to the lass herself that he was the master of his own will and could resist his baser impulses, no matter how sweet the reward. He was the architect of his own particular torture and the vow of chastity he'd taken after the '15.

As dawn slipped its way into the corners of the room, highlighting Jory's cheek with liquid amber, he had no answers to his questions, only a headache and a list as long as his arm of things he needed to do. Traveling with the lass was a bit like juggling bees—no sooner than you thought you had things under control, you were stung without warning. But the thing about bees was they only stung when they felt threatened. Henceforth, he would have to be more careful not to get stung.

Chapter Seven

It was late when Jory woke on the third morning of their journey, and she found herself unable to look Finn in the eye, as though he might read her most secret thoughts and know the depth of longing his peace offering had wrought. They danced around each other with a shy awkwardness she'd only observed in newlyweds, eating their bannocks in silence before he ushered her out to the stables.

"Have you found a blacksmith to mend the shoe?" she asked, and though ragged, her voice sounded almost normal.

"I've been to the smithy for a shoe, aye. But I've no need for a *farrier,*" he corrected her gently. "I'll place the shoe myself. And you'll help."

"Me?" she exclaimed, stepping back into a great steaming pile of dung. She wrinkled her nose but refused to give him the satisfaction of making too much fuss.

"Aye." He grinned, trying not to laugh at her predicament. "You'll do fine. I've been shoeing horses since I was knee-high to a Clydesdale."

Picking up the back right foot, Finn removed a brand-new

shoe from his sporran and aligned it with Sparradh's hoof before selecting a large nail.

Jory winced. At one point yesterday, it had felt like she was walking on a carpet of upturned nails. "Won't it hurt?" she whispered.

"Nah. Hole's already there." He slipped the nail through the shoe into the existing hole and began to hammer it in.

"What exactly am I to do?"

"Pet his nose and tell him what a pretty laddie he is."

So Jory caught Sparradh's velvet-soft nose and murmured comforting words.

She pretended not to notice when Finn glanced up at her with a delighted, smug little grin.

When the hammering was complete, he broke off the tips that had poked through the other side of the hoof and then held Sparradh steady so Jory could file down the nubs. Then he smacked the Clydesdale's flank and said, "All right, now it's your turn."

"Mine?" she squeaked.

"Turn around," he said, and for some reason Jory complied without argument, one hand still on Sparradh's silky neck.

When Finn grasped her ankle, she let him lift her foot up like he'd done with his steed, but instead of hammering, he brushed off the muck she'd stepped in when they first entered the stall.

"I could have done that myself."

"Aye."

"Shall we gather some provisions before we ride?"

Gently, he released her foot. "We've a stop to make first."

"Where?" she asked, turning to face him. He was quiet and intense this morning, but not out of sorts.

Last night, after... everything, she'd slept better than she could recall sleeping in years, maybe ever, deep and restful. She awoke feeling refreshed and ready for whatever the next leg of the journey had in store.

He took a step closer, and a flash of last night's dream feathered her memory—a dream of him in bed beside her.

"I'll show ye," he said, and strode past her, motioning towards the front of the stall and the exit beyond. "Mind where ye step."

Once outside the stable, Finn rested his hand on the small of her back to guide her down the dusty road, and this touch, too, did things to her that a lady ought not to have done. Even through her stays, her back felt warm and fairly tingled beneath his hand, and again she was transported back to last night and the gentle way his fingers kneaded deep into the tender spots along the base of her spine.

They stopped outside a cobbler shop, where the CLOSED sign was just being flipped around, and she looked to Finn quizzically, but he opened the door and gestured her inside.

"Madainn mhath, madainn mhath," said the squat little proprietor, running a hand over his downy white hair as they entered. "What can I do for you both?"

Jory looked to Finn, unsure exactly why they were visiting a cobbler when her boots were in perfectly fine condition, and as near as she could tell, so were his.

"I was hoping you might see fit to lengthen the heel on the lady's right boot," Finn said, to Jory's surprise. "One leg's shorter than the other," he explained to the old cobbler, who came around to see.

"No." Jory shook her head, heat burning in her cheeks. "No, I have a curvature, that's all," she admitted.

"Aye," Finn agreed. Then to the cobbler he added, "The right leg."

The old man looked from one to the other, then took a stack of thin sheets of wood meant for making low-heeled slippers. He peered at her through shiny round spectacles and offered an intrigued nod.

"Lift your skirt an inch or two if you please, madam."

"I don't... my legs aren't..." Then she gave in to curiosity and did as she was bidden.

Finn put one hand on each hip and she sucked in her breath in surprise, but it did seem as though his hands weren't level.

"Lift your leg," he whispered, tapping her right hip. "A bit higher. Stop."

The old cobbler stooped down to slide first one, then another tiny wedge under her heel until she could actually rest her weight on them.

Instantly the ache, which had been her constant companion, shooting up and down her leg, eased. The pain had been with her so long Jory almost didn't notice it until it was gone, and then she felt like she could properly inhale—for the first time in how many years?

She looked back over her shoulder at Finn, amazed. "Incredible," she gasped.

His schooled features burst into a broad grin, and he winked at her like a rake, but Jory forgave him and faced forward once more, grinning herself.

THE COBBLER FINISHED HIS WORK IN THE EARLY AFTERNOON, and Finn surprised Jory by insisting they should rest another night at the inn. So much for making the journey in three days, but she wasn't about to disagree.

"Why did ye not tell me you wanted to take your money and go?" he asked, as they walked slowly back to their lodging, giving her a chance to grow accustomed to her new gait.

"Would you have given it to me if I had?"

"I didnae have it to give."

"But would you have? After your brother and the Borlum entrusted you to see us both delivered safely to Aberdeenshire?"

He took a breath and frowned, and his non-answer told her all she needed to hear. He was simply a man and too afraid of the consequences to take such a risk.

"Of course you wouldn't," she said, reaching up to pat his cheek without thinking, as she would a child she adored but was disappointed in, letting him off the hook because a creature cannot change its very nature. "You're a good little soldier."

He caught her hand against his ginger stubble, and his eyes flashed for the briefest moment.

"There it is," she said, slipping free from his grasp.

"What?"

"A look that shifts like a shadow on the shore. One minute so tender, like you could—" She cut herself off before she could reveal too much of what she read in his face. "Well. And then in an instant you look as though you want to snap me in two."

"Well and maybe I do."

His voice was low and gravelly, almost a growl. Was she such a blastie that she liked being growled at?

"A man can want two things at once."

They stared at each other for a moment, the muscles in his jaw twitching like he had so much more to say, but then he sent her back to the room to rest, so he could make preparations for tomorrow's departure.

Rest, however, was not forthcoming. Jory couldn't still her mind enough for that.

Every time she tried to read, she saw his twitching jaw and flashing eyes. When she laid down, she felt his hands on her, not to satisfy his own lustful needs, but in service only to her.

She'd heard women in Inverness speak of intimate moments with their husbands—what they did and didn't do—and she couldn't help wondering. If he was so attentive last night, took direction like a soldier even from a hapless female, even when he was annoyed with her, what would he be like in his marital bed?

Both her cheeks and her loins burned with the lustful thought, but what could she do? Unthink it? She could sooner make the River Ness flow backwards.

She tossed and turned for what felt like hours, trying to forget about Finlay Shaw, to focus instead on her plan. How hard could it be? Wait a week, watch the comings and goings at the convent, find her money, and slip away in the dead of night. Would she be forced to hide in Aberdeen for a time, or could she make haste to Edinburgh then and there?

The bed linens were a twisted jumble by the time a knock sounded at the door.

"Are ye decent?" Finn called, and she rather wished she wasn't, but she rose and let him in.

"Would ye be wanting to eat down in the tavern tonight?" he asked. "I heard a balladeer warming up his voice as I passed through."

It was all so perfectly normal, like the world wasn't supposed to be ripped away from her with the stroke of a pen in a few days' time. Once her dowry was recovered, Jory would have to watch every penny, to forgo every frivolity at the risk of being discovered.

She wasn't one for pretending things that could never be, but the earnest apology pouring from every quirk and furrow of his stupid, handsome face made her desperate to imagine a future where she could have everything she wanted and more. "How lovely," she agreed. "It's been some time since I've heard proper musicians."

"I'd have thought opportunities were abundant, living in town," Finn said, but she could swear his ears turned pink with pleasure at her enthusiasm.

"Only when my uncle invited them to dine."

So he held out his arm in welcome, and she nearly skipped down the stairs to get away from Finlay Shaw and his gentle blushing.

The innkeeper brought them ale and roasted chicken dressed

with apples and rosemary, neeps, and all the bannocks they could possibly want, and Jory wished they could remain at the inn and grow old there. In short order they were both stuffed to the gills, waiting patiently for the entertainment to begin.

His ale empty, Finn went to the bar for another, though Jory was content to drink the watered-down table wine, the better to keep her wits. She sat comfortably, watching the balladeer tune his lute, until a shadow fell across the table.

"All alone are ye, lass?" a rough looking young fellow with close-cropped blond hair asked.

"No," she said.

"You're a pretty thing, aren't you—isn't she pretty Iain?"

Iain nodded far too long, like his head was a wobbling toy. "Like a pretty sable kitten," he said.

"Nah, this one's all grown up, eejit. Aren't ye, lassie? Not a kitten at all. This one here's a wildcat."

Jory glanced towards Finn, oblivious and penned in at the bar. Slowly she reached in her pocket for her trusty sgian dubh, staring straight ahead, waiting for them to draw closer.

"Wot's'a matter? You think you're too good for us, kitten? Too high and mighty to give us a smile then?"

Her right fingers twitched around the familiar handle, and then the blackguard grabbed her upper arm, wrenching it towards himself as she tried to yank it away, not wanting her knife exposed until she was ready to use it.

"I'll teach you how a kitten should behave. You'll be licking my bollocks and purring in no time."

She needed him to step a little closer, but then Finn crossed the tavern in two long strides and grabbed the lout by the shoulder, nearly lifting him off the ground, looking for all the world like he might punch him right in his pimply, red nose. Through gritted teeth he said, "That's no way to speak to a lady. You'll be wanting to apologize."

The other man laughed at Finn, clearly too deep in his cups to know what was good for him. "We were just making friends, weren't we kitten? Go on now, I saw her first. I'm going to take her upstairs and teach her how to respect a man."

Her arm now free, Jory withdrew the knife but kept her hand ensconced in the folds of her skirt.

"I dinnae think you will," Finn said, hauling off and socking the sot right below the ribs, as the murmurations around them went silent, not a sound but the scraping of chairs and stacking of cups at the bar.

The smaller man doubled over, wheezing for breath and his two friends shrank back against their own table.

Finn looked from one to the other. "Which of you's next? The eejit, perhaps?"

They shook their heads in unison.

"Get him out of here then," Finn said, nodding towards the door, and the two scrambled to drag their friend outside between them.

Finn sat close beside Jory, sliding her down the bench towards the wall and away from prying eyes, and she let him, still staring straight ahead, the sgian dubh clenched tightly at her side.

The innkeeper set a fresh tankard before Finn and nodded in thanks. "All right?" he asked, pulling at his frizzy beard and eyeing Jory.

"Ah. Mead, perhaps?" Finn asked, and the taverner nodded and went to pour the drink. "Ye're safe," he whispered to Jory, hesitantly rubbing her back with his left hand, placing the other upon the knife in her lap.

"I was safe the whole time," she said fiercely, though, now it was over, her body had begun to shiver.

"Aye, sure." He stroked her hair and down her back, much the way he would soothe Sparradh, and moved the knife gently back to her pocket. "D'ye want to go upstairs?" he offered, but Jory didn't want to move or be treated like a bairn.

"No." She pressed her left hand flat into the table to still its quaking. "We came to hear music."

The taverner returned once more with the requested honey wine, along with a dram for each of them.

"Slàinte," Finn told him in thanks, and he nodded before returning to his post at the bar. "You're cold. This'll warm ye."

She wasn't cold, but she took the cup in her trembling hand and tossed it back with ease, breathing through the burn to belie her inexperience with whisky.

Finn smiled at her. "Slàinte mhath," he said before drinking his own.

"Slàinte mhath," she murmured.

Once the shock had worn off and the alcohol had soothed her, Jory began to feel quite cozy nestled in between Finn and the smooth stone wall, warmed by the smoky haze from the crackling fire.

An ethereal, ancient voice entertained them with soft Gaelic ballads. The tune was a familiar one. It took her right back to dancing with Ellen in her auntie's kitchen while the adults listened to a concert in the next room.

Gradually, everything came back into focus: the sounds of boots scraping and drinks being poured, the smell of freshly baked bannocks, and Finn—all horse and hay and clover.

But her mind kept straying back to the two buffoons who wanted a kitten. Would she have stabbed them? Or was that merely a story she told herself when she froze?

"You don't believe I can handle myself, but I can," she blurted out during a break in the singing, when a young local harpist played an interlude so the balladeer could wet his tongue.

"Truly, you're the most capable lass I've ever met," he replied, and her cheeks burned at the compliment, even though she could hear an unspoken *but* behind his words. *But you're still just a lass.*

"I had to once," she confessed. "Handle myself."

"Did ye?"

"Only once." Her head felt floaty instead of the horrible sick feeling which would usually accompany the memory. "You can't trust any of them," she said.

"Who's that?" he asked with a half-amused expression on his face.

"Men. Especially Gordons."

His brow furrowed for a split second, and she thought she must have said the wrong thing, rudely hurt his feelings once again, only this time without intending to.

He took a long drink and then said, "No, you cannae."

"You can't even trust the ones you're related to."

He tipped his head towards her in agreement.

"I never had prospects," she explained. "On account of the curvature. Scoliosis, they call it—the learned men of Edinburgh. From the time I was twelve I heard the same thing. 'Och, Marjorie, you'll need triple the dowry if any man's to take you on with shoulders like that.'

"They tried to make it straighten, but it didn't work. So when my father died and left me a modest amount, I knew it wouldn't be enough. I took on scrubbing, mending, helping deliver babies... earned what little I could any way I could find. Not because I really wanted a husband, but needs must. Then I got the idea I could buy my own hand off my uncle—show him that I could earn my own keep—so then I'd be free to live whatever life I wanted."

"What would that life look like?"

Instead of answering, she drained the rest of her mead. "Doesn't really seem like stealing to take money I earned myself—money meant for my keeping."

"No," Finn agreed, putting an arm around her. "No, it doesnae sound much like stealing at all."

Chapter Eight

The horses were saddled and eager to resume their journey bright and early the next morning, and Jory was surprised to find she was ready to greet the day as well. She didn't mind so much riding side by side with Finn, or the cautious way he glanced at her from the corner of his eye, as though making certain she was still there. When she caught him, he'd smile sheepishly and turn away, studying the ground or scanning their surroundings for danger. Each time it sent her stomach fluttering in a not-unpleasant sort of way.

Sitting at the inn, she'd missed the whip of fresh, brisk air on her cheeks as Nell cantered along, and the opportunity to observe the changing countryside—a stark contrast to the rugged Highlands of home. Her flight from the river two days ago had been so helter-skelter, clinging to the fearsome Clydesdale with all her might, she hadn't taken time to observe the changing landscape or vegetation.

"I really should stop and pluck some of this yarrow," she called to Finn, pointing out the white flowers growing on either side of the road.

"There isnae time, mistress, not if you'd like to make it to another inn tonight."

"A quarter of an hour, I promise. Whoa," she added to Nell, pulling the reins and not bothering to check whether Finn kept riding. He would wait. And if he didn't, she'd know where she stood.

"You are the most headstrong lass I've ever met," he grumbled, but he brought Sparradh to a halt alongside her.

"Shockingly *not* the first time I've been told as much. One of my finer qualities, I think." She stooped to pluck a handful of the trusty herb, drinking in the scent of pine resin and rich damp earth.

Finn harrumphed but didn't comment, instead sliding off his mount to look over her shoulder.

"What use has yarrow, then? Balancing out the humors, is it?" His breath tickled the back of her neck, and she pursed her lips to keep from giggling.

"You could say that. It's an excellent coagulant."

"Like witch hazel?"

She turned to look at him over her shoulder. "A little. You know quite a lot about medicinal herbs, Mr. Shaw."

"For a man, d'ye mean?"

"For a soldier."

He shrugged. "I could say the same of you."

"For a woman, you mean?"

"For one so young."

She turned back to the yarrow. "Books."

"Mmphm. Will ye be long? There's a willow grove just yonder. I could scrape off some more bark, if ye like."

"Oh, please!" Jory agreed, though she found herself strangely relieved when he didn't go far and stayed within her eyeline.

He was an unusual one. Two nights ago he had her wholly in his power, after she'd treated him terribly, stolen from him, and risked injuring his horse. He could have thrashed her that night, and her uncle would likely have supplied the strap for him to do it. But instead, he'd tended to her—saw her fed and then comforted, and then fitted with a brand-new boot heel to ease her weary bones.

She puzzled over his patience as she gathered the white flowers, taking perhaps more than she needed without Ellen's nosebleeds to tend, but it was plentiful, and the most useful of plants.

When she straightened up and stretched her sore back, she found Finn returning, his hands filled with chips of bark, along with some verdant leaves and a solitary sprig of white flowers.

"Find something else?" she asked.

"Aye." He stowed the willow bark in a saddlebag, then handed her the large wide leaves before placing the flowers in her hair, right behind her left ear.

"What?" she asked, her free hand reaching for the plant and catching his hand still there.

"White heather." He smiled. "It's meant to be magical. They say it marks—"

"A faerie grave!"

He tilted his head, curious, perhaps, to hear one so practical as she invoking his Samhain faeries. "A hallowed ground, where blood has ne'er been shed."

"Isn't it bad luck to pick it?" she asked.

"Not so long as you present it to a lovely lass."

A flush crept over her, tickling heat from her scalp to the backs of her knees. How did he keep making her so flustered? It wasn't a state she was accustomed to.

"And the leaves?" she asked, inspecting them thoroughly, so she wouldn't have to meet his penetrating gaze.

"Wild lettuce."

"For luncheon?"

"For a tincture—pain, sedation. Colic. Even dropsy."

"Dropsy?" she gasped, holding the lettuce up to the light. "Truly?"

"Aye. Are ye impressed?" he asked, rocking back on his heels, thumbs in his belt.

"A little. But I'll be more impressed when I see it in action," she said, handing the lettuce back.

He shook his head and helped her into the saddle. "You're a hard one to please, mistress."

"Not so hard as all that, I hope." She smiled, and now it was his turn to look away, the tips of his ears beginning to pink.

"How are you feeling today? D'ye need to chew some while we ride?" He held out a small piece of willow.

In truth, she'd much prefer another rub down later, but she accepted the offering before he might guess her thoughts. "Thank you. Shall we go?"

"As you wish."

This time, unlike days prior, she waited for him to mount before slapping the reins and clicking her tongue at Nell. And this time, unlike days prior, she was glad when he made conversation.

"So books, aye?"

"My uncle may not be the laird, but he has a fine library, and I had free run of it."

"Verra generous. Did you live wi' your uncle then?"

"Mostly. My father was away a great deal, and he didn't know what to do with a motherless child. My aunt and uncle were kind to take me in. As for the library, well... I was meant to be reading novels and poetry—works suitable for a young lady. And I did, of course. But there was much more of interest to me than poetry."

He smirked at her. "You were a sneak."

"I prefer to think of myself as an overly ambitious student. There was one time though..." She grinned with the memory of it. "Wee Ellen and I slipped into the library after bedtime because I was determined to get my hands on a volume of anatomy." She glanced at Finn, and his eyebrows were raised, attention fixed on her, waiting for the rest of the story. "There were guests for supper, so we expected no interruption. But then Ellen heard footsteps, and there was no time to hide, so I shoved the books I was holding down my nightdress."

"A dress? I'd have pictured you running amok in breeks day and night," he teased, and Jory rolled her eyes at him.

"It was Uncle, of course, coming to find some treatise or other to lend his dinner companion, not happy at all to find us out of bed. He lectured us quite sternly as he searched for the right book, and one of my mine slipped from my dress and fell.

"As he spun around, Wee Ellen stamped the floor, kicking the book under a chair, and proclaimed to have seen a spider." If he'd seen her selection, well, anatomy would have been a bridge too far for her uncle. Ellen had certainly saved her further tongue lashing, if not worse.

Finn smiled and shook his head.

"Of course, the best education was while earning my dowry— tending to the townsfolk alongside our healer or the midwife."

"First hand knowledge is always best, isn't it?"

"Invaluable," she agreed. "Do you speak from experience?"

"Aye. There was a family physician who visited Tordarroch quite often. He was always verra kind to me, allowing me to hover at his knees like an irritating wee midge. I thought he put up wi' me because I was brilliant, of course, but in hindsight, it was like as not only because my father was chief."

Jory laughed. The *Shaw Wretch* was full of surprises. "I'm sure he considered himself lucky to have such a magnificent apprentice."

Finn offered her a shy, sideways smile. "Is that what I was then? An apprentice? I suppose my brother might have been happier if I'd become a physician," he added, the smile disappearing as he turned contemplative, maybe even a bit sad.

Jory wished she could offer him a tincture to ease his rumpled spirit. His mother being too sickly to leave her bed, let alone make the journey from Tordarroch to Moy very often, Jory could only recall seeing Mrs. Shaw the once, but she well remembered her absolute warmth and tenderness, and as a little girl, she'd secretly wished Finn's mother was her own. Even when she passed, leaving behind three young sons—the youngest but a few years older than Jory—she'd felt the pain of their loss, but envied their chance to say goodbye.

"Perhaps," Finn said softly before clearing his throat and trying again. "Perhaps he tolerated me because he felt sorry for me. My mother... she wasnae well. Not for most of my childhood."

"So the physician visited often?"

His face turned rueful. "The physician took up residence. He taught me to palpate her musculature to ease the aching, and which herbs could safely relieve pain."

"Firsthand knowledge," Jory said.

"Aye."

"I'm sure you were a great help to them both."

He pulled himself back from some far-off reverie and cleared his throat once more, casting his gaze heavenward. "Dinnae ken. But I did spend hours at her bedside reading tales of Arabian Nights and King Arthur and Grecian heroes."

Ah. "The stories of the stars."

"Aye, the very same."

Again Jory felt a pang of jealousy mixed with sadness, for what wouldn't she have given to spend such time with either of her parents? Though her father survived her mother by more than a decade, he was seldom around.

It was why she hadn't begrudged him the trip to see the physicians in Edinburgh. As miserable as the steel corset had been, Jory cherished the carriage ride to the city, getting to know her father better and hear his stories.

Her one fear had been not returning in time to accompany her cousins to the gathering at Moy. But her worries were in vain. They had returned with time to spare, and that was the visit when she met Finn's mother.

78

Jory had, of course, seen Finn before—usually wrestling in the bailey with his brothers and cousins. She longed to fight like the boys did, to learn the art of the sword, to strike and parry against a living, breathing opponent. Instead, she was forever being chastised because she'd soiled her pinafore or because she wasn't allowing the maid to lace her stays tightly enough to straighten her spine, or for poking her nose where it didn't belong when all she'd dared to do was ask the questions how and why.

She was nine years old and meant to be confined to her quarters with Wee Ellen practicing needlework, but she had in fact changed into a shirt and breeches to clamber about the castle in a naughty game of hide-and-seek with a scullery maid. Whilst hiding in a wardrobe of richly-pungent cedar, she heard shouting from the bailey yard. Racing to the nearest window, she looked down on three young boys fighting three much larger boys with wooden swords. She recognized Finn amongst the smaller lads immediately.

As she had many times before, she pressed her nose against the glass and imitated his thrusts and jabs, the way the sword was like an extension of his arm, the way he blocked and pivoted, shifting his weight to absorb or deliver blows. She marveled at how well he and his companions held their larger aggressors at bay.

"He's coming along quite well, isn't he?" a breathless voice asked, and she jumped, noticing for the first time Finn's mother, dressed only in her shift, clutching a plaid about her shoulders as she leaned against the next window watching almost-twelve-year-old Finn demonstrate his warrior prowess.

"They're unfairly matched," Jory observed. "One on one, I believe he could best any lad out there, but I'm not so sure about the other two on his side."

"You could be right," his mother replied.

Jory had studied her from the corner of her eye, splitting her attention with the skirmish still happening below. She smelled of anise and orange blossom, and traces of camphor, and her skin was very pale, like delicate bone, but the smile she shared with Jory was warm as milk and honey, and the love in her face as she gazed down at Finn rivaled that of the Virgin herself observing baby Jesus.

It made Jory heartsick for the mother she'd never had the chance to know, and she turned back to see the smaller boys beginning to wear out. Then suddenly, the two on Finn's side turned on him, joining the others so it was five on one.

"Foul play!" Jory had yelped as they began to surround Finn, circling him like a pack of hungry wolves.

"I suppose it's to be expected, as the youngest son of the laird. He'll always have something to prove." His mother had sounded so sad when she said it.

"It isn't right. I wish I had a wee sword—I'd teach them a lesson about ganging up."

"I believe you would," his mother said, pointing to a trunk in the corner of the room, and when Jory opened it, she was instructed to remove a boy's cap from the top. Then Mrs. Shaw beckoned her back and, turning Jory towards the window, she deftly twisted up her thick braid, pinning it under the cap. After turning Jory back around, the frail woman nodded in satisfaction and handed her a small wooden sword which had stood propped in the corner. "Go and help my boy," she said.

Jory had nodded solemnly, and as she flew out of the room and down the corridor she heard his mother call, "Protect his left side!"

Fast as she could fly, Jory had raced into the fray, screeching what she hoped was a terrifying, blood-curdling howl. It startled the boys, pausing their onslaught long enough for her to leap to Finn's left side. She had no training to rely on, nor to stifle her. She hacked and swung, holding her own. Back to back they fought until the others were well and truly bested, nursing bruises and sprains and sore egos. It was glorious.

And when, at last, their opponents shrank back towards the shadows to lick their wounds, Finn had roared the Shaw battle cry, "Touch not the cat!" And though some of the older boys on the sidelines had laughed and called, "Here kitty, kitty," Finn ignored them, turned to her and offered his hand, her heart fairly bursting.

He threw his arm around her shoulders, unexpectedly knocking her off balance, and the cap slipped from her head, her hair falling to her waist. He froze in horrified realization that he'd been assisted by a girl.

"What have you done?" he whispered. Already the snickering of some remaining bystanders had begun.

"I came to help."

"I didn't need *your* help."

"You did!"

"I'd rather fall a thousand times than have help from a wee lass," he yelled, pushing her down in the mud and running away into the keep.

It was the first and last words they'd ever spoken to each other, though she'd seen him from time to time, until their recent reunion overlooking the very same bailey yard and thirteen years gone by.

Chapter Nine

It was strange, speaking casually of his mother after such a long time, but somehow sharing a memory of her with the lass eased an ache Finn hadn't even realized was there. Angus didn't forbid it exactly. It simply wasn't done. Perhaps because it was a reminder of others they'd lost, of their father and of course Rob, the chief who should still be with them, and Finn's culpability in his passing. Or perhaps it was because of Angus's own guilt over not spending more time with their ailing mother as a lad, and his anger at Finn for supplanting him as her youngest child by the sheer temerity of having been born.

Whatever the reason, to speak of her was to bring a dark, brooding gloom to Tordarroch, and so Finn kept her memory in his heart. Mistress Mackintosh reminded him of her in some ways, though not the ways he'd expected when they first set out.

She wasn't the weak damsel her kin had painted her to be. Her stamina thus far had proven ten times what his mother could have endured, particularly towards the end. But they shared a ferocity, a determination of spirit, even a sense of humor. The lass might oft pretend to be annoyed by his teasing, but when she laughed, he heard the same melodic tones of his mother's laughter. He sometimes felt as though he only lived in between the times when he could make her cackle.

"You miss her very much."

"Aye," Finn agreed. "She understood me." It was too insignificant a statement to encapsulate everything he missed about his mother.

"At least you have the memory of her."

A pang of guilt struck him in the belly, sure as an arrow. "D'ye not remember yours at all?"

"Only what my father told me."

She went quiet for a moment, her face dreamy and far away.

"She grew up an orphan. But that didn't make her special, did it? As she was passed from home to home, she learned many different ways of healing. She'd a talent for it. So when my father fell at Dunkeld, they brought him to her. She nursed him back."

Finn's stomach twisted. He hadn't realized her father had survived the first Jacobite rising only to fall at Preston.

"He always credited her with saving him, but she always said he was far too stubborn to die. She followed him after that, his good luck charm, he said. Saved many men's lives at Glencoe. Eventually he wore her down and she agreed to be wed. Lost three bairns, one after another, but she survived all of that, only to be felled delivering her fourth. Because who's there to heal the healer?"

It was a rhetorical question, but Finn wanted to hear the answer, and his own complaining made him feel wretched and small. He tried to think of something amusing or even ridiculous to say, but she looked lost in the deepest of dreams, until she gasped, "Oh, look, Finn!" Not *Mr. Shaw*, but his given name, warm and full and lilting, and his name had never sounded more *him*.

He tracked her gaze in time to see a red hind dart out before them, and two more after it. Drawing Sparradh up short, he reached across to catch up Nell's reins as well, and while the lass watched the deer, he strained his ears.

It was windy, but over the rustle of the heather and creaking trees, he could just make out the lowing.

"What is it?" she whispered, and he put a finger to his lips to shush her. He slid off Sparradh and offered her a hand down, and then hobbled both horses and motioned for the lass to follow him as he crept through the trees to a clearing up ahead.

He knew by her sharp breath the moment the lass spotted them, three massive harts, and a field full of hinds, in audience just as the two of them were. The largest bucks already had their racks tangled together on the ground as the third looked on like he was keeping score. They circled and circled each other, then stopped.

The smaller of the two was the aggressor, younger and ready to take on the world. He disentangled his antlers for a moment and reared back for a push at the larger, but the older deer merely tilted his head to one side to throw him off, then tilted it the other way, easily defending each attack.

"Will they hurt each other?" she asked, and her concern—ever the healer, like her mother—made Finn smile.

"Och, nae, not so very much," he assured her, then pointed as the younger buck, clearly annoyed, locked antlers once more with his elder, forcing him to turn more weary circles. He shoved the larger hart backwards and backwards, until the larger tired of it, dug in his heels, and pushed the young buck all the way back to where they began.

The clacks of their antlers echoed across the field like the sound of his brothers slapping wooden swords, until at last they ran, heads locked, sideways over a ridge and out of sight, leaving behind the heavy scent of musk among the heather. More clacking echoed from the far side of the ridge, and then the younger deer came bellowing back and proceeded to mount the first female that didn't run away.

It was a quick affair, and Finn's neck burned and his own cock stood in recognition as he glanced at Mistress Mackintosh, whose mouth opened wide with surprise.

"Oh," she exclaimed, then glanced at Finn, catching him watching her, before they both turned quickly away, clearing their throats.

"Birds and bees," Finn muttered, kicking himself for not having led her back to the horses, and hoping she couldn't read his filthy yearning so easily as she'd read his face the day before.

"Quite."

"Hart and hind."

"Yes, of course."

"It's only natural."

"Shall we ride, Mr. Shaw?" she squeaked.

Could Finn elicit such a delicious sound from those lips on purpose?

Climbing back atop Sparradh right then was rather the last thing Finn wanted to do, but with no excuse readily at hand, he swallowed hard and headed back the way they'd come. "Aye. We're burning daylight."

"Well, it was you who insisted we stop."

"Aye. I'm sorry, mistress."

She was quiet for a moment, accepting his help to mount Nell while looking deliberately away, her fingers searing embers against the flesh of his palm. "Don't be. It was... enlightening."

Finn's stomach gave a little twist of shock, and he felt hot all over, as though he'd been baking for hours in a forge. *Enlightening?*

Something about the whole affair had been enlightening but not the deer.

It wasn't as if Finn had never seen beasts perform the act before, of course he had. But not with a lass—nae, a lady—at his side, let alone one who stirred the beast within himself. What would it be like to take her in a similar fashion, from behind in a grassy meadow with the perspiration of triumph still dripping off him? It didn't help that his bollocks ached and his cock chaffed against the saddle as he rose and fell in time with Sparradh's hooves.

It was a sweet mercy to stop for their noon meal within the shaded protection of a pine grove, where she took an immediate interest in a ring of toadstools.

"They look poisonous," Finn snorted as she knelt and examined the fungus up close.

Glancing over her shoulder the lass replied, "Maybe I'm in need of poison," and when his eyebrows shot up, she smiled innocently.

"I think ye might go straight to hell if ye poison a priest."

"Who said anything about a priest?"

When his brows rose clear up to his hairline, she laughed with just enough wickedness that Finn decided he'd best be careful what he ate and drank henceforth. Perhaps the enlightened Mistress Mackintosh was a wolf in lace and stays.

Even so, it was pleasant, lazing beside her, each pretending to be unaware of the other, while lacewings and hoverflies flitted about them. He leaned back against a soft, moss-covered stone, telling himself it was time they were off again. Four days in, and they were barely halfway to the coast after the detour to Tomintoul. Still, it wouldn't hurt if he rested his eyes for a moment.

When he opened them, the sun had drifted far too many degrees. He could hear voices, at least half a dozen of them. And the lass had wandered out of sight.

At least Sparradh was right where he'd left him, nibbling on some clover, and Nell stood hobbled on the Clydesdale's other side. But the voices were getting closer, and a sick chill ran down his back.

Studying the ground for any sign of her, even light as she was, Finn could make out soft tracks away to the right. He coaxed Sparradh and Nell deeper into the pines and then followed her steps until he found her at the edge of the woods, rooting around in the dirt.

Careful to stay out of reach of her little knife, Finn knelt and whispered, "Back up quickly, mistress. We've got company."

She glanced towards him, clearly startled, and then turned back to her digging, determined to finish her work. But there was a foreboding deep in his bones he couldn't explain. He only knew they mustn't be seen, and so he risked a hand on her shoulder and bent close to her ear. "Leave it. Come wi' me. Now."

"Let me finish gathering these avens first."

"Mistress..." he implored before the rumble of hooves got her attention. Shouts of laughing riders drifted their way, and she shrank into the shadows, just as Finn gave up being a gentleman and pulled her back, before the party of men rode by.

"Am Freiceadan Dubh," he whispered when their dark green kilts and standard came into view.

"Why would the Black Watch be active here?"

"They travel the whole north country in small groups," Finn said. "Keeping the peace." He spat his disdain for that particular load of manure, missing her boot by inches.

"Please, Mr. Shaw!" she exclaimed. "There's no call to be crude."

He clapped a hand over her mouth and dragged her deeper into the woods, snarling, "Wheesht! Keep yer voice down, woman."

She shoved him off, folding her arms across her chest. "How dare you lay a hand on me, sir," she whisper-shouted.

"I apologize, mistress. Though I wouldnae have to, if ye'd just heed my words."

"Have they any real authority this far outside the Highlands?" she asked.

"The Watch have authority wherever they decide to exert it," Finn replied, and her confidence flagged at last.

"It's not as though we've done anything illegal," she said in a small voice.

"Tales I've heard, it's not as though it matters."

The Watch were given their authority because of the '15, and Finn would swear they could smell the stench of Jacobite on a man. He'd encountered them more than once in the past year, and once was more than enough.

"Mark me, mistress, those bastards are as slippery as eels."

"Are you so loyal to the Stuarts, then?" she asked as he helped her into the saddle.

He offered a non-answer in reply. "I'm Catholic, same as you."

In truth, Finn didn't much care who sat on the throne of England. Catholic or Protestant, it would still be an Englishman ruling the Scots and no mistake.

"Would you despise me then, if I said I weren't a Jacobite?" she asked.

"Dinnae let your uncle or the Borlum hear you utter those words."

"They're not here. I'll likely never see either one of them again," she trailed off as though only realizing it for the first time, and a pang of guilt nipped at him for his part in it. "But would you though?" she persisted. "Despise me for it?"

"Nae."

She grinned at him. "Don't let the Tordarroch hear you say that."

"He isnae here," he parroted her words in a teasing tone. "You're from Inverness, aye? Were ye there? When Lovat led the siege against MacKenzie?"

The lass shook her head. "Sir John sent my uncle to Moy requesting reinforcements, and he took us with him for safekeeping. Were you there?"

When he didn't answer, she looked over at him, and he very much regretted having mentioned it.

"Nae," he said because not answering didn't make her look away. "Nae, the Shaws were with William Mackintosh at Preston."

Her face clouded for a moment. "My father was at Preston. Was it terrible? Fighting? You'd have been awfully young..."

Finn glanced at her sweet, concerned face. And how old could she have been at the time? Twelve? A child.

"I was there," he hedged. "I wouldnae say I fought."

Compassion bloomed across her face like the heather of the moor, as she studied him. No doubt she was construing scenes straight from her imagination, trying to fill in the gaps he wasn't yet ready to share.

"Young enough to be enamored of the adventure, and too young to be of any use," he added to stop her from writing her own version of his story.

"Well, age makes fools of us all," she said sympathetically, and he was grateful when she let it go.

"Aye, that it does, mistress. That it does indeed."

FINN KEPT THE LASS IN THE SADDLE FAR LONGER THAN WAS good for her, but every time he thought to stop for the night, someone walked over his grave giving him a chilly unease, and he pressed on. She didn't complain, but she kept casting him sideways glances, and he knew her well enough by now to read the unasked, "Aren't we there yet?" in her weary posture.

Poor lass was practically asleep sitting up, and so, though Finn would've liked to put even more distance between them and the Watch, he led Sparradh off the road and into the woods.

Despite her exhaustion, the lass lit a fire while Finn went in search of dinner, but all he could find was bloody pine marten.

She jumped and then froze when he approached, once more reaching for her sgian dubh, as though that little knife could ward off all the evils of the world, but what protection could it truly offer?

"Only me," he said.

If she'd been a lad, she'd have learned to protect herself, and it suddenly struck Finn as backwards that the fairer sex were not taught as much or more.

He stepped closer to where she knelt beside the fire and set down the marten. When she reached for it, he caught her hands.

"Yer fingers are like ice," he said, clasping them between his for a moment before releasing her to skin the wee beast.

"Pine marten?" she asked, trying to hide her disappointment when she recognized the pelt.

"Bit late to catch much else," he said, not an apology exactly, though he was rather sorry.

"Of course."

"Maybe you could use the fur for mitts," he offered, holding the pelt up, and she nodded tiredly before rummaging through her satchel.

Locating whatever green bit she'd been after, she chopped it finely with her little sgian dubh, and then pushed herself up to sprinkle it over the spit he'd fashioned, tinging the gamey scent with a more aromatic smoke.

When she caught him watching her curiously, she explained, " Avens and wood garlic," the plants she'd collected that afternoon.

It still tasted like pine marten of course, there was only so much you could do with a few fresh roots, but the meat was more appealing than any other time Finn had eaten it, and he relished it all the more for her contribution.

Chapter Ten

A dream woke Jory with a start in the wee hours of the morning. Day five: it should have been the day they arrived at the convent, but she couldn't find it in herself to feel sorry that they still had so far to go.

As the cobwebs of sleep began to clear, she was already forgetting the details of her nightmare—something about being buried under spiders—but she couldn't shake the eerie feeling of eight thousand tiny feet skittering across her skin.

She rolled over to face Finn, situated much closer than she remembered him lying down the night before. Asleep he looked young and sweet, very much the boy she'd known all those years ago. His hand was curled up near his brow and he frowned a little as he slept.

Awake, he seldom looked serious. Always teasing, anything for a laugh, yet he was never cruel. His easy nature almost set him apart from other men of her acquaintance, the ones who were quick to anger and brooked no opposition. But in quiet, unguarded moments, she could see the weight of an entire generation on his broad shoulders and she knew that deep down, a man couldn't be anything but a man. Even one who jested and restrained himself from throwing her own haughty words back in her face. *Let's do it in three.* What a brat she must have seemed.

Usually nothing and no one could stir Jory to laughter. It had been one of her uncle's chief complaints besides her physical deficiencies—she was too stoic, too humorless and serious. She should smile more, laugh more, flirt more, and generally make more of an effort. Jory wasn't dour on purpose, but she didn't find things particularly funny most of the time.

She would try to humor him by smiling politely and excusing herself at the first opportunity, when really all she wanted to do was scream, "Why?"

It was exhausting having to be the one always *making an effort*. If she was to find love or even simply a tolerable match, shouldn't it be... not effortless exactly, she wasn't naive, but wouldn't it work out better for everyone if she didn't put on a show during the early days of courtship? Not that there had ever been a courtship. If there'd been even a hint of interest, would she have been sent away to rot in a convent?

The funny thing was, she wasn't really making an effort with Finn. It was just simple. Somehow it was easier to get along with a man she had no interest in, because then they could both just be themselves, warts and all. If he vexed her, she would vex him right back. It didn't matter. And somehow it also became easier to tolerate a person once you'd watched them sleep.

He stirred and began to snore lightly, and, unable to stand the crawling sensation on her skin any longer, Jory tiptoed away in the direction of the stream where she'd washed her hands and face the night before.

One by one she removed her layers of clothing and shook each piece fiercely to dislodge any hidden arachnids, until she stood in nothing but her shift. Then she stripped it off for the same treatment before wading into the stream.

"Jesus," she gasped as the water hit her, stealing her breath before she could invoke Mary, Joseph, or the wee blessed donkey.

Longing for a proper bath, she'd meant to linger over it, but on the bright side, first her legs and then her arms began to tingle and fall numb. At least she couldn't feel the tickle of invisible spider feet any longer.

Now she thought only of getting dry and warm again, of the heat radiating from Finn's arm when it brushed up against hers as they both reached for another bite of marten, or from his chest as she rode nestled against him after causing his Clydesdale to throw a shoe. Of how hot his fingers had felt, each one like a branding iron as he worked her aching muscles and tender sinews, bringing chills to her flesh even as he lit it on fire.

How did he manage that feat? And could he pull it off a second time?

But she shouldn't be thinking about such things—about him. She was leaving, going to Edinburgh, and he was going home.

Jory danced around in the freezing water, trying her best to scrub every inch of herself as quickly as possible.

When movement on the shore caught her eye, she spun around and then froze, gasping at the sight of Finn stooping down alongside her clothes where the sun reflected off her sgian dubh. He turned his head away, trying not to see her, which meant he already *had* seen everything.

Her strangled cry brought his gaze flying back to her, and then he kept right on looking. She stood there, completely exposed, with no way to even pretend to hide herself.

He was too intense, too tall and too scruffy by far, standing erect on the shore, and it occurred to Jory that he could probably do whatever he wanted with her, and she couldn't stop him.

"Mr. Shaw?" She hated the quiver in her voice and crossed her arms defensively over herself trying to hide at least a few bits from view.

"Forgive me," he rasped, turning his back on her, but not making a move to leave.

"Mr. Shaw?" she asked again, though if pressed, she couldn't put into words what she was asking.

"You're to be a nun," he growled fiercely, without turning around. "Like it or not." And then he stalked away, back in the direction of their campsite, and Jory seethed with humiliation and more than a little anger.

Quite frankly, she'd had enough of men.

Men decided her future. They decided when she could stop and eat and sleep, and now they were deciding when she was allowed to be naked, or to be found desirable—or not—always, and forever on their terms, and no one else's.

Well, not anymore, not once she got back her money.

She waited until he was completely out of sight before emerging from the stream. Her cheeks, along with the rest of her, were positively aflame as though she was already burning in actual hell.

Finn had now seen every inch of her, and she hadn't meant for him to, but propriety and society and the Church would lay the blame solely on her, label her a whore, a wanton wastrel of a woman.

But it *wasn't* her fault, no matter how breathless it made her, watching him stand there watching her. Her cherrilets, already hard from the frigid water, had fairly ached at the sight of him, and a tingling warmth spread below her belly. His gaze seamed to scorch her skin, touching her, roving her with tender caresses until he ripped himself away and turned his back on her. As he turned, she caught the drape of his kilt standing slightly askew, not that she was looking.

And then he was gone.

It wasn't clear from his face whether he liked what he saw or was horrified by her imperfect form, whether he stared in admiration or disgust. He seemed angry, and now she would have to manage his feelings of shame alongside her own. She was exhausted already.

Dragging herself from the stream, she half-contemplated simply lying down and allowing it to carry her far away so she'd never have to face him again. But if she didn't warm up soon her feet might fall off and her fingers wouldn't be far behind.

And unless she was going to run off into the forest naked as the day she was born, she would have to face him. So, checking for spiders once more, she donned her skirts and plaid and then plodded back to the campsite, almost disappointed to remember the way.

FINN HAD WOKEN THE MINUTE THE LASS LEFT HIS SIDE. HE'D watched as she headed off towards the stream. What exactly had gotten it in his head to follow her?

On such a cool morning, he'd never expected to come upon her without so much as a fig leaf.

Her back had been turned—her lovely, round bottom on display for God and everyone—and he could have gotten away unseen. But when he turned to withdraw, he found her sgian dubh half buried in the mud, where it must have fallen when she stripped off all her clothes.

He'd meant only to retrieve it and then make a hasty retreat, but then she'd caught him there, and he ogled her like a lech.

She had looked so perfect, and so perfectly vulnerable, and oh, how he wanted to take her right there in the stream. Had the lass been put on earth to test him and his oath of celibacy as he'd never been tested? For even if she wanted a man, she was too good for the likes of him, with her keen mind and nurturing soul.

She would never be his to hold and protect until death.

But she was too beautiful and too headstrong by half. She'd insist on forging her own path through life, a pack of one—when she wasn't trying to heal the ills of the world—and it would make her all the more susceptible. He couldn't stand it. Those eejits back at the tavern wouldn't be the last to interfere with her.

When she finally appeared back at the campsite, fully dressed, thank Christ, he bellowed at her without preamble. "You must learn to defend yourself." Not exactly the apologetic greeting he'd planned.

The lass blinked. "What?"

"Ye need to learn to defend yourself," he repeated. "From danger. From attack."

She reached for her pocket. "I have my sgian dubh."

"That wee stinger? Ye could hardly fend off a badger."

She jutted out her chin defiantly, elongating her lovely neck. "You'd be surprised."

Finn swallowed. "I'm sure I would. Everything about you is one constant surprise after another. But ye didnae have it on you in the stream, did ye?" Blast it, he hadn't wanted to dredge that up.

Her eyes narrowed. "Was I in danger?"

"Aye, ye might have been. Had it not been me, but any other man came upon you looking like"—he gestured fervidly at her body—"that."

He hated himself for the verbal onslaught, words tumbling from his mouth without thought or precision, making it sound like he couldn't possibly find her attractive when what he meant was his vow to defend her virtue.

"Oh yes, any man except the great Finlay Shaw, who's too good to look at a woman so lowly as me."

Finn took a step closer to her, wanting to reach out and touch her cheek. "Ye need to learn to fight."

"I told you—" She reached in the pocket to get her little knife, but Finn caught her arm right below the elbow and held it fast.

"If a man bent on harm gets close enough for you to use it, mistress, it'll already be too late."

Anger surged through her whole body, darkening her face and

radiating from her like lightning. She tried to wrest her arm from his grip, but they both knew she couldn't.

"And if by some miracle you do get to use the thing, and you kill him? It'll be you hanged for murder—no matter what he was about to do." He'd seen it in his mind's eye from across the tavern the other night, and it still brought a roiling queasiness to his gut.

Her face fell once more, and though she was breathing hard, Finn thought she was beginning to see reason.

"Why do you care?" she whispered.

He relaxed his grip and rubbed his thumb up and down her arm in a way he hoped she'd recognize as a sort of apology. "You're in my charge," he said. But he had a feeling they both knew it was a lie. "And a lass as lovely..." His mouth went dry as she stared him down. "...and *obstinate* as you are, is sure to find herself in no end of scrapes."

She peered up at him, no longer shrinking from his gaze.

"What did you have in mind?"

He nodded and finally relaxed. "For starters, if a man comes at you from the front and tries to grab you, what d'ye do?" he asked, gripping her arm again, below the elbow like before.

She tried to jerk free, first pulling her arm in, then pushing it out.

"Nae, mistress. You have to take back the power."

"What power?" she scoffed.

"What's your left hand doing?" he asked.

She looked down at the appendage, as though seeing it for the first time, and then tried to pry his fingers off her arm.

"You know that willnae work."

"This is why I have the knife."

"Can you reach it now?" he asked, knowing she couldn't because her arm was pinned. "I have the power. You need to take hold of *my* wrist to take back that power."

She clapped her left hand around his wrist then, but he shook her off easily.

"How d'ye chop wood?"

"I don't."

"How *would* you chop it then?"

"With two hands." She clenched both fists to demonstrate.

"Aye, because two is stronger than one. Cover my hand."

Hesitantly, she covered his left hand with hers.

"Now push down until you can sweep back this way and grab my wrist."

She tried it, and this time her features softened with amazement when the move twisted Finn's arm backwards, forcing him away from her as she was able to grab him with her right hand and take control.

"Good," he grunted. "Now shove me down."

Following his instructions, she gingerly pushed him down as though she feared hurting him.

"And now you could take a kick and be on your way," he gasped, and she released him with a laugh.

"Where did you learn these moves?" she asked.

Her voice was warm with an admiration Finn had never heard directed his way before, and it did something to him, made him ache to hear more.

He pushed himself up off the ground and said, "I participated in a great many fights as a lad. Hamish, my father's right hand, taught me that more often than not, it's the fights you choose *not* to fight that matter most."

"To Hamish," she said with a tilt of her head. "Is he a Shaw?"

Finn swallowed. "Aye, he was. Now, say the man goes for your neck instead of your arm." He made a choking gesture with his two large hands. "May I?"

The lass licked her lips, but she lifted one shoulder and whispered, "I suppose."

He placed his hands gently around her neck pressing lightly on either side of her trachea. She licked her lips again, and he couldn't help but caress the delicate skin with his right thumb.

"Where's the weak point?" he asked.

"My throat."

He smiled. "Where's *my* weak point, mistress?"

She made to aim her knee at his bollocks and he laughed, which instantly relaxed her.

"You're not wrong. What else can ye do?"

She tried to pull his arms away and failing, made instead to claw at his face, but he was too far out of reach, so she went back to clawing at his hands, trying to pry his thumbs from her throat and beginning to panic.

"Stop, stop, stop, stop, stop," he said, and when he had her attention, he added, "Bend forward."

"Pardon?"

"You heard me, bend forward, avoiding my arms."

She did, and it forced his thumbs to break apart, allowing her to lurch sideways and duck under his arms to freedom, gasping for breath as though he'd actually been choking her.

"All right?" he asked, cupping her cheek, and suddenly he was seized with an urge to kiss her.

She nodded, still breathless from the exercise.

If Finn had been impressed with Jory's resourcefulness and determination before, he was overawed by her now.

He illustrated how to break free from a chokehold where the aggressor came in from behind, and in all honesty, he enjoyed every minute of being close enough to smell the river on her, at liberty to touch her almost anywhere he pleased.

But when he pinned her up against a nearby tree, a different sort of fire ignited in her eyes. He should have stopped to consider from her point of view how threatening the whole activity might feel. Instead, after she evaded another attack more easily than anticipated, he swept her legs so she tumbled to the ground, landing hard on her back, the wind knocked out of her.

Admittedly, she fell much harder than he'd intended, but didn't she need to be able to think clearly in such circumstances?

So instead of helping her to her feet, Finn straddled her belly, daring her to find her way free.

Much like their very first lesson, she panicked, flapping her arms at him and struggling instead of seeking out his weak spots.

"Calm down," he growled through gritted teeth as she landed a blow to his groin and squirmed beneath him in a way that threatened to tear him from stem to stern.

She bellowed something which sounded like a lot of unladylike curses and closed her eyes, breaths coming quick and shallow.

"Tuck in your arms, close to your sides," he said, but she ignored him and continued to flail. "Tuck yer arms and grab my wrist, mistress. And my upper arm wi' your other hand."

When she didn't even try to tuck in her arms or grab hold of his, he grew frustrated.

Apparently so did she, shrieking, "Get off me."

"Make me," he told her. It was a good job no one came upon them right then, or Finn would've been shot clean through.

"Get off, you bloody great oaf."

"Bring your knees up. One foot around my foot."

Finally she lifted her foot, but only to try ineffectively to kick him instead of following his instructions. The more she struggled, the tighter he held on.

"Ye cannae match me strength for strength."

She grunted in furious reply.

"Will ye not listen? Bring your—" And then he realized she wasn't simply wrestling with him.

Her nostrils flared and her cheeks flushed from holding back unshed tears. She wasn't there with Finn any longer, she was somewhere else entirely, fighting for real. "Go on then," he said softly. "You're powerful, Jory Mackintosh. Take back your power."

She screamed furiously, and he lurched back in surprise, providing the opening she needed to retrieve her sgian dubh and press it against his belly.

Finn held his breath, waiting for her to plunge the knife in between his ribs like a side of mutton. But she didn't. With the blade in her hand, she began to recover her senses and finally she flipped him off of her as he'd been trying to teach her to do. Then she stepped away from him, wrapping her arms tight around herself.

Chapter Eleven

Chest heaving, Jory smoothed her dress and tried to regain her composure. How ridiculous to have lost herself and reacted so. For his part, Finn remained deferentially on the ground. Had she actually hurt him?

"I'll admit you've a deft hand wi' a weapon, mistress. Have ye ever been taught the bow?"

So not hurt, then.

"No, Mr. Shaw," she said quietly, her back still facing him. "Bow and arrow were not considered suitable for young ladies."

"And blades were?"

"I have a knife. No one taught me to use it. Weapons of any kind are not ladylike."

"Reckon not. But I'll teach ye anyway."

Why did such a suggestion make tears spring to the surface?

"Oughtn't we resume our journey?" The sooner she was away from this confusing man, the better.

Finn raised up on one elbow, watching her. "Aye, we should. But if we catch a proper meal now, we needn't stop again before nightfall."

She bit her lip so it wouldn't quiver and attempted to inject levity into her voice, but it still sounded raspy to her ears. "A proper meal? More pine marten, do you mean?"

"Och, nae. Not this time of day. Though there might still be a rabbit or two about."

"You can hit a rabbit with an arrow?"

Finn rose and retrieved his weapons. "Aye, I can. But I'm a verra good shot."

He glanced back to where she stood with her arms folded defensively across her chest, and she thought she caught a flicker of regret in his face.

"What d'ye say? I think you've the makings of a fine marksman."

Jory rolled her eyes. "Oh, go on then." She followed him deeper into the forest muttering, "Marks*woman*," relieved he was willing to move on from what had happened without demanding answers, forcing her to relive it, or telling her how silly she'd behaved.

He led the way, allowing Jory to trail along behind, only looking back once to check on her, and she appreciated that, too. It gave her time to really settle herself. She hadn't meant to pull her knife on him. How completely humiliating.

But the moment he'd climbed astride her, she was no longer twenty-two-year-old Jory, and he was not Finlay Shaw of Tordarroch, her friend. Suddenly she was thirteen years old again, with Ellen's screams blocking out all other sound and Boyd Gordon's brother sitting on her chest 'til she could scarcely breathe.

It was how she thought of him: Boyd Gordon's brother. If they were ever properly introduced, it was Mister Gordon and young Master Boyd. She didn't recall his Christian name. How could she not remember such a detail, when she could see his face so clearly, right down to the tiny scar bisecting his eyebrow, the small mole upon his right cheek?

In that moment with Finn, Jory forgot everything he'd tried to teach her. She was ashamed of how upset she'd grown, but at least she stopped herself short of impaling him. It was his words that brought her back. *You're powerful, Jory Mackintosh. Take back your power.*

She didn't need a man to give her power, and he wasn't granting permission, he was reminding her she could take it. No one had ever spoken that way to her before, and when Finn said it, she almost believed. And now, despite what might have happened, he was going to trust her with yet another weapon.

Up ahead, he stopped and turned back towards her. He put a finger to his lips and then nodded his head to where the woods ended, opening into a sunny meadow. Jory joined him and he crouched inside the tree line and drew an arrow from his quiver. He demonstrated how to line the arrow up against its rest, how to pull back on the string, and then he handed the whole thing over to her.

It was somehow both lighter and heavier than she'd expected. She held it up, aiming out into the field where she could only see flowers and shadows from the slowly drifting clouds.

Finn moved behind her, and with his arms around her, he gently adjusted her hands so she held the bow with her left, just below the center of the arc. He adjusted the fingers of her right hand around the shaft of the arrow, a lovely thing with purplish feathers, almost too pretty to be an instrument of death.

"Both eyes open," he breathed into her ear, and it tickled across her scalp and all the way down her spine, warming her. Then he pointed to the middle of the meadow where a long-eared, russet-colored bunny sat upon its haunches, munching clover.

"Breathe in, pull back, release," Finn whispered.

But she didn't. She simply knelt there, watching the rabbit live its life. What had it done to deserve such an ending on this beautiful sunny day?

"It's all right lass, if ye miss, we'll find another, but he practically has a target painted on his rump."

Did she have one painted on hers too? "Can't we eat stale bannocks and cheese again?"

Finn looked at her like she was speaking in tongues. "I thought you'd be pleased after the marten. Don't ye like rabbit?"

Jory handed Finn back the bow and arrow. "I like it fine, but why does he deserve to become our luncheon?" She knew it was cowardly, but she had no appetite for it.

Finn sighed in exasperation. "How can ye expect to provide for yourself if ye cannae even kill a wee rabbit?"

She looked at him, then back at the fluffy creature. "The rabbit hasn't done anything to me," she said simply, standing up and walking away.

"But how will ye live?"

"I'll pretend to be a man, get a job. It's none of your concern."

As they resumed their journey, Jory regretted her words. She'd told him too much, and anyway what if she couldn't get a job? How far would her dowry stretch if she had to pay for every meal along with her rent?

In the end, she'd returned to the horses and rekindled the fire and eaten the rabbit Finn shot willingly enough. But it had been a quiet meal.

He kept eyeing her as they rode, attempting to be surreptitious, but she'd caught him three times already, and this time, she offered a wan smile she knew didn't quite touch her eyes. Still, he returned his own half-guarded smile.

"I know it's madness," she finally said. "That I'll gladly *eat* the rabbit, cook it, even skin it—but I can't bring myself to shoot it. I just..." She shook her head. Since when did words elude her?

"Dinna fash, mistress. You've a kind soul. There's none can find fault in that."

His words tugged at her, and she turned away so he wouldn't see her face. "A kind soul—until someone crosses me. Then I can be quite... unforgiving." She mimed shooting one of the arrows he'd stowed with her in case she wanted extra practice.

As though Nell was disturbed by her muttering, along with all the talk of dead animals, the mare stopped walking, flicking her ears from side to side.

"What is it, girl?" Jory asked, giving her a little kick to start her moving again, and Sparradh chuffed encouragement when he and Finn turned back to face them.

"All right?" Finn asked.

Like a drunk unable to walk a straight line, Nell stepped sideways into Sparradh. Had Jory been riding astride, her leg might have been crushed against Finn's. The Clydesdale snorted.

Finn reached out like he meant to take Jory's reins but thought better of it. "Perhaps she'd like a wee rest."

"I'm sure she's fine," Jory said, but the words had no sooner left her mouth than the traitorous old Nell reared up with a scream and then took off like a shot, as though bitten on the rump by a whole swarm of midges.

"Whoa," Jory called, trying to slow the beast, though her surprising gallop was far less terrifying than the breakneck ramble she'd taken with Sparradh mere days ago. But when she peered over her shoulder to see how far back they'd fallen, she was mostly blinded by her own long hair whipping in the breeze.

"Whoa, lassie," she tried again, imitating Finn's soothing tone.

Suddenly, five horsemen rode out from behind a small hillock, and Jory managed to turn Nell's head right at the last and veer off into the woods before coming to a stop. Back on the road, the riders closed ranks around Finn, forcing him to a halt as well.

From their kilts, she thought they must be more of the Watch, maybe even the same group they observed last evening which had left Finn so unnerved.

"Well, now, and who might you be?" the leader of the Watch asked, looking Finn up and down. He knew better than to offer too much, for any answer would be the wrong one. It was how the Black Watch worked.

Instead, he stared straight ahead, trying to make his gaze soft rather than searching, so they wouldn't notice him watching the lass skulking through the trees. Thank Christ the fool horse finally stopped.

"Were you harassing the young lady?" the leader asked.

"Not at all. She's my companion. Her mare was misbehaving."

The man snorted. "That old nag?"

"I'm as confounded as you. Perhaps she was frightened by a foul stench in the air." He couldn't resist one little barb.

The leader squinted at Finn. "You're not from these parts."

"We're not."

"And where might you be traveling to?"

"Aberdeenshire," Finn said, sticking to the truth as much as possible.

"What would you be going there for?" one of the others asked with a lascivious glint in his eye that made Finn's skin crawl, but a look from his leader made the lech shrink back into place.

"I don't like the look of you, Highlander."

"What a relief," Finn teased. "But the lady's under my protection. She's in no danger from me."

"Not your wife, then?"

The lass peeked around a boulder, sizing them up, plotting some kind of trouble, no doubt. Finn swallowed a growing lump in his throat and gave one sharp shake of his head to warn her off.

"You're trespassing on Gordon territory," the leader said, recapturing Finn's attention.

"Could say the same for you. Gordons haven't yet joined the Watch, last I heard, nor are ye meant to patrol the Lowlands."

" 'Tis true," the man agreed. "Though we patrol where we like, and being Grants, we've an... understanding with the Gordons."

A finger of dread slid down Finn's spine.

"What do they call you, Highlander?"

"Shaw."

"And have you hunted on these lands, Shaw? If you have, then you've stolen from the Gordon laird himself."

"A Shaw thief *and* a libertine. My, my," a third man spoke up.

"I'm no rake," Finn growled.

"What's the matter?" another asked. "Can't get it up, laddie, even for a pretty wee thing like her? Need us to show you how it's done?"

"Aye, it's in his blood. I heard stories about the Shaws at Preston back in '15."

Finn froze his features into stone and prayed their voices weren't loud enough to carry their words to Mistress Mackintosh's hiding place as they howled with laughter.

"D'ye need lessons in how to use it, is it?" the third one asked, clapping a fifth companion on the shoulder, and Finn realized there were only five of them. The sixth man from yesterday was missing.

Suddenly an arrow whizzed past the leader, barely missing Finn's shoulder before burying itself in the fifth man's saddlebag, causing his horse to jump sideways into Sparradh. Then they turned to see a burly brute of a man dragging the lass towards them, Finn's quiver slung over her left shoulder, his bow knocked to the ground and trampled under the sixth man's feet.

"You're making a mistake," she gasped as he tossed her forward like a sack of grain. "Mr. Shaw is escorting me to the coast. Why have you detained us?"

Finn was relieved to have her close again, hale and whole, but mercy the lass had a knack for turning things from bad to worse.

"Well now. I'd say the situation has changed," the leader said. "Looks like we've caught ourselves a couple of dangerous marauders."

She struggled breathlessly against her captor. "That's preposterous. I wouldn't have loosed the arrow if this oaf—"

"What's preposterous," the leader said to Finn, cutting Jory off, "is your lady friend coming at us with an arrow. Now, you can pay us for the damage—double. Or," he added, sidling up to the lass and running the back of his fingers down her cheek so her eye twitched. "Or we can take it out in trade."

Finn seethed with fury, but he held himself in check. "All the coin in my purse," he spat. "But you eejits will grant us safe passage from here to the coast."

The leader jerked his head towards Sparradh, and one of his companions moved to lighten the saddlebags, then he pointed to Finn's sporran, as well.

Sighing, Finn unbuckled and handed the pouch over. The leader emptied it of coin and examined the letter Angus had given him for a moment, as Finn's heart leapt to his throat.

"Bearradh Dearg?" the Watch leader asked, his face contorting into a wicked grin. "That's where you're taking her?"

The others began to guffaw, and their chortling rang in his ears long after they mounted up and rode away.

"Your bow," the lass whimpered.

"Aye?"

"I dropped it when that bloody great son of a boar grabbed hold of me, and I—I'm afraid it snapped in two." She held up the shards of yew.

Finn nodded. It was about the sort of luck he'd have. "Just as well. If ye cannae keep both eyes open, you've no business wielding a weapon."

It was cruel, and he knew it, but he'd been scared by their capture, and by his inability to protect her.

Mouth falling open in pouty protest, she said, "He surprised me."

"Aye. That's what people do. And you didnae do one single thing I taught you today. Didnae stay put, didnae keep *both* eyes open, and damn near took my head off, thank you. You didnae even attempt the move we rehearsed to break out of exactly the same hold that *bloody great son of a boar* put you in. You overthink every word from my mouth, but then when it matters, you dinnae listen to me at all!"

"Well I'm sorry I'm not some trained dancing bear for you to order about. Maybe if you spent less time trying to fix me and more time worrying about what's *out there*, then I wouldn't need to learn to fight!"

It was a blow to the gut—fix her?—but she climbed into the saddle before he'd had a second to argue, dug her heels in hard, and slapped the reins until poor Nell took off like a shot, and this time, Finn let her go. Was it trying to *fix her* to teach her the skills she'd need to survive? If so, then he wasn't a bit sorry.

Chapter Twelve

Jory had expected to hear the Clydesdale hot on her heels, but she soon realized there was no echoing answer to Nell's gallop, and a glance behind her only confirmed it. Everything was going wrong today, and she longed to be back in the cozy room above the tavern in Tomintoul.

She slowed Nell to a trot, and then a walk, but still there was no sign of Finn. Had the Watch come back with a taste for blood? Or was he ready to wash his hands of her and leave her out here to find her way to wherever she wanted to go alone? And where would she choose to go, with no money and no one to take her in, but on to Aberdeen?

When she reached a copse of trees, she led Nell off into the relative shelter and sat down to wait. But she didn't care for the solitude like she once thought she would while standing on the parapet contemplating her future. Unlike that morning, there was no cheerfulness to the quiet woods. It seemed dangerous—sinister—and Nell was still acting skittish and spooked. Surely Finn would come for her. Wouldn't he?

Not that she needed him. Only, she hated to part on angry

words, couldn't bear the thought he might believe her such a nuisance he'd give up on her now.

She didn't need him to fight her battles or take care of her, but in the quiet space between waking and dreaming, she didn't mind him wanting to do those things on her behalf. There was a difference.

And so she waited for what felt like hours, until she finally heard fast approaching hooves. By the time she summoned the courage to peek out of the trees, he'd dismounted and was studying the ground for her tracks. When he looked up, their eyes locked. His were a stormy shade she'd never seen before.

He held a small leather strap in his hand, tapping it against his leg as he approached, and she took a step backwards and then another, until she backed right into a rowan tree. Did he mean to hit her? Now, after everything else he'd tolerated? After he'd insisted to the Grants she'd nothing to fear from him?

"That's close enough," she warned in a wobbly voice, and he stopped.

She sighed with relief, but then he made up his mind to ignore her and stepped closer again. Out of habit, Jory reached into her pocket for her sgian dubh trying desperately to recall how to duck and pivot should he attempt to pin her against the tree, but her knife wasn't there! Only a hole where it ought to have been, and he was right. Now she had no protection at all.

She couldn't have said what she expected, but she was shocked when he grabbed a fistful of her skirts and shoved them up to expose her leg all the way to the thigh. She fought to push them back down but he held up the leather strap and she drew back, tensing her whole body in preparation for whatever he was about to do.

Then he grabbed hold of her leg and tied the leather strap to the thigh right above her knee.

It was most unexpected.

From his sporran, he withdrew her knife and slid it into the new sheath for a perfect fit, snug and secure against her leg. She could reach it easily through the hole in her pocket, and she wouldn't lose it now by accident.

He held her there for a moment, his body pressed close against hers. Her skirts were still raised indecently high, and his hands rested heavily on her thigh. Both of them were breathing hard and ragged, and a little angry.

And then he stepped back, lowering her leg and letting her skirts fall, before retreating to wait alongside Sparradh.

She should've grabbed his hand with both of hers—should have pushed and ducked and twisted and gotten him on his back on the ground. He'd had the power, and she let him have it, and she hated herself for surrendering it without a peep. Now he was waiting, all grim-faced and sweaty, but waiting just the same—giving her the power to choose to stay or choose to go, and she hated him a little for that too.

He kept his back to her, busying himself with the saddlebags and his recovered bow fragments, but he didn't mount. His posture was stiff, his head turned only slightly—listening for her, she realized. And so she caught up Nell's lead and went to him.

Finn took the reins and tethered Nell to his saddle, while Jory watched curiously.

"You'll ride wi' me," he said, his voice rough, as though his throat was chafed by grit.

A shiver ran through Jory, heating with anticipation. The skin above her knee still tingled from his calloused touch. "That isn't necessary, Mr. Shaw."

"You'll ride. Wi' me," he said again.

Finding she had no real desire to argue, she allowed him to assist her in swinging one leg over the massive Clydesdale and settling into the saddle, smoothing her skirts so they wouldn't bunch too terribly. Truthfully, she was glad he insisted. Still shaken from her encounter with the Watch, every rustling leaf and snapping twig made her jumpy. Waiting in the copse, her courage had begun to flag, but close to Finn she felt strong and capable, or at least she sensed the possibility of feeling so in the near future.

Finn didn't say a word as he gently slapped the reins and chirruped to the Clydesdale, who took off at a clip like he'd been wondering what they were waiting for.

It was strange, riding together again—always when he was irritated with her—his spearmint breath tickling her neck, his strong arms somehow protecting rather than imprisoning. Jory had rarely been so close to any man, certainly none for such an extended time, nor any she enjoyed. But try as she might, she didn't hate this.

Her back and neck typically ached terribly after only an hour in the saddle, but here with Finn she could melt into his warmth and rest those sore muscles. She took strength from his strength and enjoyed the scenery.

Without a list of things she needed to do, people to tend, or preparations to make, she allowed her mind to wander. Dangerous, perhaps, for where it wandered was back to Finn. Back to the day when they'd both been summoned by the Mackintosh of Borlum and that brief moment when she thought they'd be ordered to wed.

Jory had been despondent at the notion she'd be bartered off in marriage, and yet had things gone differently, might they have made a real go of it? She had little doubt the Highlander at her back would treat her with as much respect and kindness had they been linked by an unexpected, or even unwanted, betrothal. Much as she hated to admit it, she might get used to being bonded body and soul to the right person.

Still, as cozy as she felt there in Finn's arms, there was a distance between them which hadn't been there before. The silence hung as heavy as the air before a thunderstorm, and she couldn't quite work out whether his intensity was anger or something else altogether.

Surely if he were upset, he wouldn't have taken the time to

make a sheath for her sgian dubh, wouldn't have stroked the inside of her thigh with his thumb before letting her go. Enmity wouldn't elicit such stirrings, from her belly to the spot on her thigh, or the heat in her most private area where bouncing in the saddle now threatened to chafe her half to death as Sparradh vibrated beneath her.

And yet he seemed angry—bitter and closed off. Was doing her a kindness his way of tempering his temper? And if so, what would it look like when at last, she pushed him so far that his soldierly restraint finally snapped? The thought made her shiver.

"Are you cold, mistress?" he asked gently.

"A little," she answered, because it was easier than admitting the truth of what she'd been thinking.

He rubbed her arms, and more gooseflesh popped up than before he'd touched her, so he unfurled his plaid and wrapped her up, tightening his hold around her. "I've got ye," he whispered.

For a moment she allowed herself to imagine a future where they might stay like this forever, roving the countryside and... what? Gathering herbs and treating the crofters they encountered along the way? *What nonsense*. He'd be eager to get back to his brother, his land, his home. His future.

"I'm sorry," she said. "For..."

"Aye, me too."

She fit perfectly against him, where he could rest his chin atop her head. It was dangerous, such a comfortable fit.

"Did they hurt you?" he asked.

"No. You?"

"Och, nae. Takes more'n a handful of royalist bastards to hurt me. Dinna fash, mistress."

"You can call me Jory, you know."

"I know, mistress."

They had shared so much, but that one familiarity was a step too far? She sat up a little straighter so he couldn't rest his chin on her head comfortably any longer.

"Did they really not consult you before it was decided ye'd be a nun?" he asked, unfazed.

She laughed. How did he know so little about what it meant to be a woman?

"Did they consult you before deciding you'd be a soldier?"

"Nae, of course not."

"Well then."

"But it was decided when I was wee. Before I was born, really. I was the third son—"

"Of Tordarroch. Younger brother to the future chief. I know."

"So ye ken, it's different."

"Not so different. We both might have chosen elsewise, if it were ours to choose. Instead, we're both of us outcasts among our people for not being well suited to the roles they chose for us."

"Mayhaps. But then again, I'm a fair hand wi' a sword. It's what I was born for. I dinnae have the brains for much else."

Jory glanced over her shoulder at him, but all she could see was the stubble lining his jaw and his throat moving up and down as he swallowed. "And exactly who gave you such a notion, Finlay Shaw? You've taught me more than a few things on this journey."

He squeezed her tighter and then said, "And what makes you think ye're not cut out to be a nun? Or..." His breath was strained when he paused before adding, "or a wife?"

She shook her head. "My temperament."

He bent to look at her, an amused smile tugging at his lips. "Your temperament," he repeated. "Because marriage means war, aye?"

For a moment Jory thought he might kiss her.

For a moment she thought she might want him to.

But then Nell nickered, almost as though she could sense the rising tension and decided to play chaperone.

"Hush now, you old nag," Finn called to her affectionately. "We're not moving so very fast."

But the spell was broken, and they continued their journey in silence.

Though she didn't loathe sharing a saddle with Finn, after a few hours her bottom began to ache—and maybe she deserved it. A child would have been whipped for misusing him so appallingly and causing so much trouble. It should be her penance to endure the pain, but the thought made her wriggle in her seat.

She tried leaning forward, but that made her hip begin to throb. Then, when she settled back against him again, his sporran dug fiercely into her low back, almost seeming to throb itself.

"Should we make camp soon?" she asked.

"We'll stop at an inn tonight," he said, and his voice was tight —with exhaustion, no doubt, so she did her best to sit still and bear the ache.

When they finally reached the inn, Jory remembered. "But the Watch took all your money!"

"Not all of it," he smirked and withdrew a small pouch from his boot.

He counted out the coins for the innkeeper. There was only enough for one room.

"Och, not to worry. I'll bed down wi' the horses."

"The horses?" she asked, surprised he wouldn't insist on staying close.

He smiled sheepishly. "Ye'd prefer your privacy, aye? I trust ye well enough not to run again."

The nervous way he eyed her, Jory thought it might be more of a *desire* to trust than actual faith in her.

"But I'm afraid there's nothing left for a meal. Have ye any provisions still?"

"I'll make do," she said, though she'd finished the last of her stale bannocks and cheese earlier in the afternoon.

"Sneck the door, mind," he told her after depositing her

satchel in the room and bidding her good night, and she bolted it behind him.

It felt wrong, relegating him to the stable, but perhaps Sparradh's company and a pile of hay would be preferable to a night on the cold floor beside her bed. And solitude after so many days of constant companionship... it should be an absolute blessing, but after a few minutes alone with nothing but the sound of her own breathing, she missed his company. Every footstep in the hall, every flicker of light, every thud from a nearby room made her freeze and strain her ears.

When had she become such a faint-hearted child? She was the one who hummed lullabies and told Wee Ellen it would be all right. Had her bravado been mere illusion, or had Finn's succor these past days made her weak?

After an hour of restless pacing, she nearly jumped out of her skin when a light rapping sounded at her door, and she reached for her sgian dubh.

Then Finn's voice whispered, "Are ye awake, mistress?" and she threw her earasaid around her shoulders and beckoned him in.

"Thought you might be hungry for more'n scraps," he said, placing two bundles of heavenly smelling oak leaves on the mantle, along with a large handful of late season blackberries.

"Roasted fish?" she asked, her mouth watering at the smell.

"Aye some trout from the stream."

"Thank you."

He nodded and studied the floor, so shy after the intimacy of their shared saddle. "I'll bid ye good evening then."

He made a little bow and opened the door, but Jory couldn't let him leave. It was only polite to invite him to eat with her.

"Mr. Shaw?" she asked, reaching out to stop him. "There's more than enough. Will you not join me?"

He smiled and nodded, sitting alongside her on the floor before the fire to eat the delicious late-night meal.

"But how did you catch fish in the dark?" she asked, wiping deep purple berry juice from her chin.

"Moon's up now, and it's full bright."

"And you had fishing line?"

"I had my two hands," he said, rocking back on his heels and enjoying the impressed look that no doubt covered her face.

They grinned at each other, drunk on exhaustion and pleasantly full bellies, and when at last he prepared to go once more, Jory stopped him a second time. Weak she may be, but she was strong enough to admit she didn't want him to go.

"You could stay," she whispered, a little bit scandalized by her desire to keep him near, nestled chastely, as in the saddle. How would it be so very different from lying close together in the open air? He hadn't touched her thus far, despite many opportunities.

"D'ye want me to?" he whispered, and she nodded, breathless.

So he reached out for her plaid, and she bit her lip, allowing him to pull it away from her shoulders. But then he folded it like a blanket upon the floor, and she laid down alone, bereft, listening to the rise and fall of his breathing as he slept a few feet away.

She tossed and turned and trembled with a sort of hunger the trout had somehow awakened instead of satisfying. There was a tingling deep in her belly and parts further south, sort of like a sneeze that refuses to come. When she rolled first onto her stomach and then back supine, a certain slickness made her fear her courses had come early.

Reaching cautiously between her legs, she found it was not the blood of Eve but a clear dampness, immensely pleasurable to touch.

Absently, she found herself stroking up and down on the outside of her shift as the aching need grew stronger and her thoughts wandered over to Finn, to his broad shoulders and enormous biceps that could crush her as easily as cradle her like a robin's egg.

Her left hand migrated to her breast, where she circled the

delicate skin as he might have done when he stumbled up on her in the stream, and when the dampness began to soak through her shift, she allowed her fingers to venture back beneath the linen hem, to gently circle herself with long, tender strokes as her breath trembled and she grew swollen with need.

Jory imagined it was Finn who touched her, first with his fingers, but then with his tongue, tasting her as she had heard some men liked to do. Trying to stifle her breathy gasps lest he should hear, she traced the slick delicate skin faster, increasing the pressure until a trembling overtook her whole body and for a moment she pulsed and writhed in splendor, panting for breath.

What had just happened? Still thrumming with the pleasure, Jory curled lazily under the covers, breathing deeply and smiling to herself in the darkness. She of course had *some* notion of exactly what had happened, but she hadn't known it could be like that—all softness and ecstasy—or that she could manage it by herself. Rolling onto her stomach and pressing herself into the straw tick, she felt deliciously wicked, for surely such activity was frowned upon, and she already wanted to try it again.

She recalled some distant sermon railing against the vagaries of self-gratification, but it had gone rather over her head at the time. She hadn't quite been sure how it was meant to be achieved, and the warning seemed directed only at the congregation's men.

In retrospect, she thought perhaps men, and the women who serviced them, might all be much better off with a little less condemnation and a little more self-gratification.

Still and all, as much as she'd enjoyed it, she found herself quite baffled. It didn't fit her own self-image. She was a solitudinarian, quite immune from such stirrings. So what was it about Finlay Shaw that broke her to her very foundation and remade her as someone raw and needy?

Of course, even in her disinterest, she'd been curious. Men couldn't seem to stay away from the act. They used copulation for control, and she never wanted a man to have mastery over her.

But could the balance be tipped the other way? Could the mastery become hers instead?

You're powerful, Jory Mackintosh. Take back your power.

Setting power aside, he'd gone to her. Tender and attentive to a mere companion, willing to take direction, so what *would* he be like in bed? The thought alone set her tingling anew. It was going to be a very long few hours until dawn.

Chapter Thirteen

When she awoke the next morning, Jory still felt light and fluttery, a frenzied sort of exhaustion.

Finn had already stepped out, leaving a note that he'd gone to tend the horses, and it was a good thing, too, because she didn't think she could face him, lest she reveal the role he unwittingly played in her nocturnal wickedness.

Wanting to repay him, not only for last night's meal but all of his kindness, Jory slipped downstairs to see what she could barter for a breakfast. After some haggling, she traded all the willow bark in her satchel for a pot of tea, two bowls of piping hot porridge, and some fresh cream and strawberry preserves.

After five long days on the road, Finn's brows shot up when he saw the hearty breakfast, and he devoured every last savory morsel in minutes.

"I dinnae ken how ye did it, mistress, but thank you," he said. "I reckon that was the best parritch I ever et." And for some reason, Jory's heart began to swell.

Once on horseback, however, she felt fidgety. In the cold light of day, her behavior in bed last night felt all the more outrageous. Would Finn be disgusted if he knew? Or angry because she'd involved him without his consent, if only in her mind?

Obsessed with honor, would he laugh it off or consider it the ultimate betrayal, the straw to finally break him and make him lash out? After all, everyone had a point of no return. What was his?

"You're not ill, are ye, mistress?" he asked, peering at her as she bounced more than was strictly necessary in the saddle.

"Ill? No. Me? No," she answered too quickly, garnering a curious twitch of his lips, but he said nothing more.

She wasn't ill, though she did feel feverish. Wild. What she needed was to frolic, to run off some of her energy, to be chased—chastely—and maybe to be caught, too.

So when they stopped to water the horses and Finn was bent over inspecting Sparradh's new shoe, she snatched the woolen tam he'd donned at a jaunty angle.

"Och!" he exclaimed, but she jumped out of his reach and took off running before he could stop her.

"Get back here, you!"

He followed her across the shallow stream, up and around a yew tree. When she thought she'd lost him amongst some scrubby bushes, she doubled back, pulling the warm cap over her ears, and climbed up into the yew. She could see a fair distance from there and felt quite clever until he popped out from behind the other side of the massive trunk—how had he hidden himself so well?—and began to inch his way down the limb.

Straddling his perch, he lunged for her, and she squealed, reeling back so fast she lost her balance and wound up hanging from the wide branch with sweaty fingers quickly losing purchase.

"Hang on, I'll get ye," he laughed and swung down from the branch before dropping a short distance to the ground. He got to her just in time, as she lost her grip and fell into his outstretched arms.

The moment he set her on her feet though, she grinned at

him and took off running again with a giggle. He dove after her, but only succeeded in catching and loosing one of her ties. It felt incredibly naughty, teasing him, like something a girl Maggie's age might do if she hadn't been taught better manners. At the same time, it was completely and utterly liberating.

Splashing back across the stream, she half-wondered what he would do when he caught her. She couldn't outrun him forever and was already feeling a weary stiffness in muscles unused to their new alignment. For one breathless moment she imagined him pushing her up against a tree to seek his reward. She really must stop thinking that way.

Close on her heels, Finn kept pace with her as she darted in different directions like a madcap deer to stay ahead of his longer strides. When she glanced over her shoulder, she almost lost her footing because of the self-congratulatory smirk on his face. Turning back around she realized her way forward was blocked by the narrow opening of a small cave.

Jory was well and truly pinned now. He was probably tasting victory. She had nothing to fear from him, of course, but what might a less virtuous man do when he did finally win?

Finn took a step closer, arms reaching out to catch her should she try to slip past.

"Mr. Shaw," she nodded, as though she merely happened to encounter him on a Sunday stroll through her laird's parklands.

"Ye've got a mischievous streak, mistress."

"Have I?" she asked innocently, lifting her eyebrows to suggest nothing at all was amiss, despite her panting breath. Then she glanced up to where his cap still rested on her own smaller head, threatening to slip down clear to her nose and blind her, and she bit her lip. "Does mischief make you angry, Mr. Shaw?"

"Aye, verra angry. Someone should teach you a lesson," he teased, his voice low and raspy, and it did something to her stomach that she realized meant she was very much in danger of falling in love with the Highlander, and that was not something she could allow to happen. It was time for drastic measures to remind herself that men were still just men.

"But who would dare?" Jory pushed, and before a lecherous smile could spread too far across his face, she added, "Certainly not you. You're not man enough."

It was only a flicker, but she saw the hurt in his eyes, like the sun going down, and almost regretted her goading immediately.

Then it was gone, his tone still light. "Not man enough, am I?"

"You could have taught me a lesson so many times. But you're a gentle creature. Perhaps it's you should go to the convent."

He squinted at her. "Convents are for women."

She shrugged, as if to say, *Exactly*.

His frown deepened. "Have I done something to offend you?"

"You?" she scoffed.

"I thought we were getting on, but you've a cruel streak as well as a mischievous one. Another man would…"

"What?" she demanded. "Hit me? Go on then. Show us what a big man you are. Not man enough to take me when I'm standing naked in the stream."

He grabbed her then, each hand fully encircling an upper arm, and she licked her lips, heart pounding so hard she almost couldn't breathe as she stared him down. This was what she had wanted—to test his breaking point—but his fury only made her feel sick.

He gave her one jarring shake and then shoved her away from him. "Why d'ye provoke me?"

Bewildered by this response, Jory could only blink at him.

"Fickle woman. You've no response? Have I treated ye so badly? Tell me, why do you insist on pushing me so?"

The hurt and betrayal on his face made her feel terrible, and she shook her head. What answer could she give, except the truth?

"I suppose," she whispered, then stopped to chew her lip until her voice felt stronger. "I suppose, to see exactly when you'll snap."

"D'ye want me to snap?" he asked, his eyes as large and luminous as last night's moon.

She nodded, ashamed of her antics now.

"Why in God's name?"

"I suppose," she lifted her chin and looked him in the eye. "So I'll be ready when you do."

If it was possible to watch a man deflate, as though his body consisted of only skin and air, then that is exactly what Jory witnessed. As her words washed over him, Finn almost folded forward until he was squatting on the ground.

"Is this what my reputation has been reduced to, then? Nae simply the Shaw Wretch, but a man so impotent, ill-bred, and diffident of will he lashes out at irritating women without warning?"

Hells bells. Why did he think any of this had ought to do with him? Did he really know so little about his own kind? Or was it she who had it the wrong way round?

"Many men would. With less provocation."

Finn shook his head. Clearly she'd struck a nerve without actually meaning to.

No. That was a lie. She had very much meant to. Only his reaction was unexpected. Anyway, she had her answer, and now she had to somehow put it right.

She knelt down across from him but he wouldn't look at her, and just as well.

"Do you know the adder?" she asked hesitantly.

"The serpent, d'ye mean?" His voice was quiet, but strong.

"Yes. You know it?"

"I'm familiar, aye."

"Then you know it doesn't normally strike unless it's frightened or mishandled?" She rubbed her arms where he had grabbed hold of her and shaken her.

"Aye, that's true."

"Yes. And the red squirrel?"

Now he smiled a little, as though humoring her. "I've eaten more than I'd care to admit."

Jory wrinkled her nose in disgust. "Yes, please refrain from telling that particular story. But squirrels, you know, they'll take the cast-off skin of a snake and chew it up. Rub it in their fur to scare off the bigger animals, which would otherwise come after them."

His face was a mixture of pride and disbelief. "That's so?"

"Oh, yes. They don't mean any harm, neither of them. They're doing the best they can to stay alive. They can't bear to show their fear, you see, not to anyone."

He stared ahead thoughtfully, chewing the inside of his cheek. Jory hoped he understood the point she was trying to make—the apology on offer.

"Just to be clear, mistress," he said slowly. "Are you the squirrel, and I'm the adder?" His voice was even, but he still couldn't keep the teasing tug from his lips, and Jory burst out laughing.

How did he always do it?

Finn pushed himself to his feet and offered her a hand up. "We'd best get back. Sparradh and Nell will be wondering what's become of us," he said, offering her his elbow.

"Yes, of course," she said, handing back his tam.

He took it and smiled before pulling it snuggly over her ears instead. "Looks better on you."

Finn kept the pace slow and gentle, not like he was walking on eggshells afraid she'd bite—more like two lovers taking a morning stroll.

"How much farther?" she said, and he didn't need to ask what she meant.

He squinted up at the sun. "Bit more than a day's ride, I should think. No one should bat an eye that it took seven days instead of five. Or three," he added with a teasing smirk.

"Oh. Do you suppose we'll have the pleasure of encountering any additional members of the Watch?"

"I shouldnae think so. The Grants and the Gordons have always been friendly, mind, but—"

"Gordons?" she interrupted. Why would he bring them into it?

"Aye. But as they're running a secret convent, I wouldnae expect them to greatly encourage the Watch to hang around hereabouts."

Jory's blood ran cold. *Gordons* ran the convent?

"Mistress?"

"Sorry," she gasped. "Gordons, did you say?"

"Aye." His voice grew cautious and he shifted his stance to peer down into her face.

The air around her grew warm and swirling, like squinting through a fire. Finn patted Jory's arm, misinterpreting her fear.

"They know you're coming. They willnae wish to see you intercepted, not when they asked for you special."

She was fairly certain her lungs were pumping air in and out without actually using it. Gordons owned the convent. Gordons had asked for her by name.

"Gordons?" she croaked again. So finally, her sins would be paid in full.

THE LASS HAD UP AND FAINTED DEAD AWAY. ONE MINUTE SHE was perfectly fine, asking Finn questions, and the next—beads of perspiration broke out across her nose and forehead, her face went ashen, and she sagged to her knees.

She'd have hit the ground like a sack of grain had he not been holding her arm when she went down.

"Mistress?"

He didn't wait for a response before scooping her up and carrying her to the horses grazing by the bank of the stream.

"Mistress?" he called again as he laid her on the silty shore.

He hastily fetched a kerchief from his saddlebag, rinsed it in the cool, flowing water, then mopped her face and the back of her neck before placing it on her forehead and loosening her stays.

"You're all right. It's all right," he crooned softly, the same way he'd whisper Sparradh through a storm.

He had doubted what Angus told him of her frailty. She appeared as hale as any lass he'd ever met, and heartier than a few of the lads. But perhaps he'd been irresponsible, misjudged her stamina. Perhaps the morning's frivolity, after so many long and tiresome days, had all been too much.

It was foolhardy and selfish of him to play like she was hard to catch, and then to shake her like an angry child. When would he learn to harness his baser impulses? He knew well enough it was the inclinations that felt most innocent which could wreak the greatest havoc.

At last, her eyes fluttered open and she blinked into the sun.

"There ye are." He smiled down at her, taking up her freezing hand to rub some warmth back into it. Her fingernails were charmingly stained with mud from whatever plant she last harvested. "Ye gave me a wee fright."

"How embarrassing," she said, rubbing her face and trying to sit up until he squeezed her shoulder to stop her. "Forgive me, I..."

"Too much exertion, I expect."

She shook her head from side to side, holding it like it was splitting. "How ridiculous. You were saying—about the Gordons?"

"Does it mean something to you? I s'pose it would, for the Gordon benefactor to have heard about your piety and chosen you."

"Chose," she whispered, and she was fairly shaking now. She rolled onto her side and retched while Finn watched, helpless and confused. "Chose me? By name?" she asked, her stare piercing his soul.

"Aye. It's what the Borlum told Angus."

"What's the name of this Gordon?" she asked, searching his face like he held the answers to the mysteries of the world instead of useless dreams and a multitude of regrets. "Boyd? Is it Boyd Gordon?"

He shook his head again, more regret. "I'm sorry, mistress, truly. I wasnae told his name, only the name of his keep—Bear-radh Dearg."

Finn helped her sit up, propped against a tree, and returned to the stream to freshen his kerchief. She stared through him as though she were lost in another world when he placed it once more upon her forehead. But she caught his wrist and gave it a tiny squeeze that he dared to imagine meant more than simple gratitude.

"I suppose I'll have to explain."

"I think you better had," he agreed.

But she didn't. Instead she kept staring out at the water, or the trees along the opposite bank, or at who knew what—different trees on a different bank in some different, far-off place, maybe.

So Finn lifted her feet into his lap because elevation could help with swooning, and because he needed to be closer, needed to touch whatever part of her he could get away with. He unlaced her boots, drawing her gaze back as she watched, detached, while he freed first one and then the other ice-cold foot.

He held the left in both hands for a moment to warm it, and then began to rub the length of it, pressing into the tender spots along her arch, circling from heel to ankle, stretching out each toe, focusing on her foot rather than the walls still separating the two of them.

"I was bested once by a Gordon," he said, concentrating on her foot so he wouldn't have to meet her perceptive eyes. "During the '15. Some of their number claimed to support the Stuarts, you see. Others were ardently opposed. It proved difficult to judge the truth of who was who."

It had been his greatest ignominy. If he were more clever, more discerning, his eldest brother might still be alive. He had only himself to blame for what happened at Preston, and shoulder the blame he did. He wasn't one to hide from or deny his responsibility. He wore his shame upon his face like the severed ear of a thief. But in the deepest part of his heart, when he was all alone, he burned with hatred—and yes, some amount of recrimination—for one man: Long Thomas Gordon.

"You were young," she said, attempting to absolve him of the sin that could not be forgiven.

"We were all younger then," he growled.

"We were children," she argued forcefully.

"I was a *soldier*. Or anyway, I dressed up like one and pretended to be—until I met Long Thomas Gordon."

Jory shivered.

Twice Finn opened his mouth to say more about how Gordon had tricked him, about what his failure had cost them in battle—what it had cost Rob and her father.

But he couldn't bring himself to admit what he'd done.

"I take it this Long Thomas Gordon did not support the cause?"

"He did not."

Finn slipped Jory's shoes back on.

"And that's why they call you the Shaw Wretch?"

He nodded. "I lost my brother, my family, my name."

"Hardly fair."

"A name is earned by word and deed."

"If that were true, then they'd have long since changed my name."

But Jory—Marjorie—Marsali in the Gaelic—meant warrior, and Finn doubted anyone could argue with it.

She'd given him permission to use her name, but if he allowed himself such familiarity, he might forget she wanted to be alone. And then he would begin to hope as he could not allow himself to hope, that he might someday become more than a wretched escort to the lass who fit so perfectly in his arms.

No, he would wrap her name up in soft wool and keep it safely in his sporran, but in waking hours, he must at least strive to maintain the wall between them, so he might wash away his guilt by delivering her safely to the convent as ordered.

Chapter Fourteen

The years of shame wafted off Finn like a cloud of midges in the dusk of a hot summer day. They were both outcasts thanks to a Gordon, this Long Thomas and Boyd's brother.

And now she was to be handed over to them to make amends for her deep shame. Her sin was too great, she was beyond hope. But Finn—he could be redeemed. Unless she got in the way.

"I know why the Gordons want me, why my uncle would have agreed to it and kept it from me. But why does the Tordarroch care?"

Finn sighed and drew his knees up. "My brother fancies himself a great strategist. We're all of us pawns in his game."

"No. You're a knight, Mr. Shaw. You may come and go on your own horse, move in unusual directions. You may wage battle with the pawns." She glanced up, forcing him to look at her. "Or a with bishop."

Finn caught her eye, and with it, her meaning.

"What's at stake?" she asked.

"A treaty. This Gordon claims to control a portion of the Watch through an old clan alliance."

Up to now, Jory saw Finn as nothing more than a courier, delivering her to her fate. She knew his brother might be embarrassed if he failed, but she hadn't thought or cared about the consequences for him personally, beyond the shadowy specter of honor.

"But what does it mean for *you*?" she pressed.

"Fortunately, mistress, ye cannae be banished twice. If Angus is in a right wee temper, I suppose he'll have me drawn and quartered and served for Christmas dinner. But like as not, I'll be fine." He was chewing the inside of his cheek again, though he shrugged, pretending not to care. "I always land on my feet. Are ye ashamed of me?" he whispered. "For being duped by a Gordon, as if I were a wean fresh off the pap?"

"No, of course not." *I could never be*, she wanted to add.

Before her tenth birthday, the Mackintoshes had attended Mrs. Shaw's funeral along with the rest of the clans. She'd watched him walk resolutely behind the casket, determined not to cry. *Protect his left side.* His mother's words rang in Jory's ears back then, as they still did today, as though she were willing him unto Jory's keeping. She only wished she could have gone with him to Preston, to protect him from whatever had gone wrong there.

He offered her a dried strawberry from the seemingly endless stash inside his sporran, because of course he did. Until the moment the first morsel touched her tongue, she hadn't realized she was hungry. If only they could stay there by the little stream forever, frozen in time like tales of Brig O' Doon.

"If you take me there, your quest is complete. Will they blame you if I leave? Will it come back on you? If I find my dowry and run away?"

Finn leaned his head back against the tree and looked up at a woodpecker, hammering obliviously into the bark. "S'pose that's between you and the priest."

Was he giving her permission? Setting her free to choose without concern for his future?

That morning Jory's plan had been to enter the convent as a soon-to-be nun, find her dowry or its equivalent, and await the most opportune time to steal away into the night. She had planned to do it on her own, but the revelation that the convent was a Gordon stronghold... perhaps, this once, she needed to ask for help from a man—from this man.

The price of failure was much too high. She couldn't allow herself to be caught in the clutches of any Gordon, not even— maybe especially not—a pious one who knew her name.

But the cost to Finn was too great as well. He was so close to being vanquished, to repaying a debt his brother should never have demanded, no matter what Finn believed. Could she really take all that away from him? It wouldn't only be between her and the priest. No Gordon would hold up his end after being double-crossed, not any more than a Mackintosh would.

As though he sensed the question, he bumped her shoulder and then stayed there pressed against her, confusing her resolve. "Berry for yer thoughts?" he asked, holding out another piece of dried fruit.

"Would you help me? If I asked you to? Would you help me steal back my fortune and vanish? Even knowing—"

"Aye," he said simply, and she turned to look at him, to search the deep, mossy fields of his eyes for truth.

"Even if it means—"

"Aye," he said again, not allowing her to finish, as though the full weight of the consequence she was trying to remind him of was too final and too heavy to bear.

He agreed without hesitation, without demand, without even the knowledge she withheld of her dealings with one particular Gordon.

She asked, and he said yes. It was so simple. Who in her life had ever offered her as much?

"JUST LIKE THAT?" THE LASS ASKED, HER FACE A PERFECT picture of surprise, and somehow, for Finn, her gratitude made it all worth anything that might come later.

Angus would be livid, no doubt, and would lay the blame solely on Finn when the plan failed. But then he would have anyway, even with the lass locked away in Bearradh Dearg, because what was really in it for the Watch?

The world wasn't ready for Mistress Mackintosh, indeed it didn't deserve her, but when had the world ever gotten what it deserved? She was everything, but to all of them—the Mackintoshes and the Gordons—she was simply one more mouth to feed, whose dowry would eventually run dry.

Aye, Finn would sacrifice it all for her, and it would be no sacrifice at all, because he was starting to think he might be in love with her. And in a choice between the lass who'd never once called him a wretch, and a brother who despised him, well...

"Whatever you need."

A tear slipped down her cheek. "Do you still want to know? Why I hate them, why..."

Finn wanted to know more than anything else, but he said, "Dinna fash. Ye needn't tell me if ye'd rather hold your peace."

She chewed her lip fiercely and Finn chastised himself for again wishing it was *his* lip she was chewing. This was hardly the time for such things.

"It was the year after the Rising," she began, and for some reason his blood ran cold. "A Gordon and his sons were visiting my uncle in Inverness. Ellen and I were playing with some kittens in the stable when they found us."

She blinked back tears, still chewing that lip.

"I can guess the rest lass," he said softly, to let them both off the hook.

"No. You can't, not all of it. At first I wasn't going to fight. I was afraid, and I meant to let them do what they wanted. Get it over with. When the older one went for me, Wee Ellen tried to run for help, but the younger brother, Boyd, stopped her.

"She started to scream. The sound filled my ears—it was all I could hear."

Finn couldn't imagine it, the silent wee cousin making any sort of stramash. He shifted uncomfortably and ran his hands over his face and hair, but he didn't interrupt again.

"You've never heard such a chilling keen, but no one came. I couldn't see—he'd managed to get my skirts up over my head, but rather than the mortal shame any decent girl should have felt, I could only think of getting to Ellen. Protecting her so she wouldn't have to scream.

"He was a big boy, a man, really, all legs and arms, but no match for my flailing." She laughed bitterly and then took a deep, tremulous breath. "He went for his belt, I knew because he was only fighting me with one hand, and I tried to stop him, but instead of his buckle, my fingers latched onto a little knife tucked into the belt. I managed to get hold of it and started swinging it around, slicing it frantically in every direction until I felt it pierce something, and then I just yanked it down and pulled it out and waved it around some more."

Finn grimaced because he could easily imagine Jory fighting so hard, and now so much of the past week made sense. A hot, sour bile rose up his throat as he recalled her fear the other night when he'd taken her to that inn, the fear—of him—when he took the self-defense lessons too far. He should have heeded Angus's warning and treated her far more gently.

"I gutted him, Mr. Shaw. And when he slumped over on top of me half dead, I crawled out from under him and ran to Ellen. I grabbed the younger Gordon by the hair though he was a few inches taller than me, and I held his brother's bloody knife to his throat and told him to get out of there or he'd be next. Ellen and I hid the rest of the day and night under our bed. Uncle and the

Gordons left in a hurry and they took the dead son away with them. I don't know what my uncle had to bribe him with to keep him quiet about what I'd done."

"What *you'd* done?"

"I killed a man that day, and I will burn in hell for it as sure as I will not repent."

Her words were like the knife gutting *him*. Not only because of what the Gordon had tried to do, but because the bastard had forced her into this guilt narrative simply for fighting back.

The lass was trembling, and Finn wanted to pull her close, but he was afraid to touch her in such a state. "There now. It wasnae your fault... and you're in good company. Julian the Hospitaller was a murderer, and they made him a saint."

She smiled sadly. "Yes. But he was sorry."

"I suppose. He was also French." He made a disgusted face, and this time, she really did laugh.

"You said yourself the knife would be my undoing. That it wouldn't matter what I was defending myself from, not to the law."

Finn reached for her face, and she let him tilt her chin up to look at him.

"Maybe not in the eyes of the law. But the law could frequently do wi' a good pair of spectacles."

She smiled again, and he realized for the first time in his life he knew his favorite color, and it was the color of an early pine cone at dawn, of gingerbread fresh from the hearth, the sparkling brown of her irises when the sunlight caught them, shining through the trees.

"You needn't keep your promise," she said. "It's enough you'd be willing, but I know what it would cost you."

"Don't even think it. To have carried that inside yourself for so long, and here was me blubbering on about my *honor*."

He shook his head at himself and she almost laughed. Jory

sagged into him and he tucked her under his arm, smoothing her hair and resting his chin atop her head.

"I promised Ellen I would take it to my grave."

Finn didn't understand why it would matter to the cousin when by Jory's account she'd not been hurt nor involved in the killing, but he squeezed her and said, "Then Wee Ellen has my word as well. Which is almost the same."

The lass leaned her head against his shoulder.

"You're safe, ye ken?" he murmured. "It'll never happen again."

"Don't make promises you can't keep," she whispered.

She was right, of course. There was very little certainty in the world, but especially for a woman alone in it.

"I swear," he murmured, "on the graves of my forefathers, the cross of my Lord Jesus Christ, and the blessed iron that I keep ever at my side. I may be a Shaw, but I pledge *you* my fealty, Marjorie Mackintosh. And whomsoever dares to raise a hand against you, may God have mercy on their souls, because I most assuredly will not."

Chapter Fifteen

For years Jory had been surprised she'd faced no reckoning after felling the Gordon. In the first weeks, even months, she'd expected the rival clan to appear on her uncle's doorstep, demanding her surrender, or to set upon her in the streets or drag her out of her bedroom by the hair. Every rumble of hoof beats had made her freeze, the quick stride of a boot had made her flinch and search for a place to hide.

She was in no hurry to recover her stolen dowry now. A Gordon convent in a Gordon castle, run by Gordons who'd asked for her by name? Hell, maybe she should let them keep her dowry as a blood fine and never go near the place herself. So when Finn suggested another hunting excursion, getting meat in her belly to restore her strength, she agreed.

He was a skilled hunter. Aside from yesterday when he tried to teach her the bow, she'd had little opportunity to observe him—the way his tall, lithe body moved silently through the bracken like a long-legged cat; the way the muscles in his calves rippled when he squatted down to peer through the scrub, holding the position for what felt like hours; the way he tilted his head to the side as though he could see better with the one eye than the other, and then righted it, no doubt chided by a voice from his childhood, not unlike the one he'd used when instructing her to keep both eyes open.

And then there was his seemingly endless supply of patience. Someday he'd make a wonderful husband and father to some lucky family, and Jory burned with envy for his future wife. Sure, she could sit for hours at the bed of the sick, alert to any change, or not, as the body alone could determine. But waiting and watching, crouched down in the grass, ignoring the biting midges, anticipating the most subtle flick of movement to betray her quarry and spring her into action—she found it so tedious she almost wanted to scream, like trying to remove a whisker-thin splinter from your own finger or thread a needle with the frayed end of a spool.

Finn, though, clearly reveled in it, at one with his newly fashioned bow, proving that quietude could breed strength.

After an eternity he glanced at her, put a finger to his lips, and beckoned her to join him. She crept as quietly as she could, but a twig snapped beneath her boot and she froze, her focus shooting to Finn. Even after all this time, she expected an angry impatience in his countenance, but only his lips twitched.

When she finally reached him, he helped position her so she could see what he saw: a gorgeous buck browsing in some tall grass. Jory marveled at the sight, until Finn handed her the bow.

"You need the practice, aye?" he answered her unasked question in barely a whisper, his lips brushing the tiny hairs of her cheek, sending a jolt through her stomach and directly to her lower parts as well.

With no opportunity to protest, she found his arms around her reminding her how to hold the bow, where to place her hands, and how to aim.

"Both eyes open," he breathed into her neck, almost inaudibly, sending another wave of shivers right through her, and Lord but they were lucky she didn't accidentally shoot the arrow straight up only to impale them both on its way back down.

Finn helped her draw back the bowstring, her heart hammering in her ears so loud he could probably hear it too. Then he took his hands away, but she could still feel the touch of his gaze, watching her instead of the buck.

She aimed at the deer, then closed her eyes and loosed the arrow.

"Well done, mistress, aside from closing your eyes there at the last," Finn teased, rubbing Jory's arms before moving away from her to confirm the deer was dead.

"You mean I actually hit it?" she asked, incredulous. She'd closed her eyes thinking surely the arrow would be wasted in the scrub, the deer bounding deep into the forest like a flash.

"Aye, knew ye could, and a nice shot too, perfectly behind the shoulder. Couldnae have done better myself, eyes open."

"But why'd you let me shoot it?" Jory asked, her voice rising to a higher pitch. "I thought it was only for practice."

"Och, ye need the meat. You're practically skin and bone."

"But I couldn't eat a whole deer if I started now and went 'til doomsday," she protested. "What'll we do with it all?"

Finn removed the inner loin and fixed the rest onto the back of his saddle for transport. "It can be dried and smoked, traded and shared. It willnae go to waste."

They roasted the tender cut and shared it between them, juicy and earthy, and divine. Sometimes in moments like these, Jory could forget they were on a journey, forget that soon Finn must return home to pay the piper, and she would start life over on her own.

"You're very good with your weapon, Mr. Shaw," she said, because she didn't want to think about separations or goodbyes.

He tried to suppress a snicker at the compliment. "Wasnae always. My first hunting trip was almost a disaster, in point of fact."

"Do tell." She was eager to hear more stories of young Finn.

"I was a wee nipper—couldnae have been more than eight—and the whole family went out for a sennight. It was right before Mam's troubles began, ye see.

"At home, my da was always the Tordarroch. Tough and demanding, as a laird must be. But out there in the forest, he was different." Finn smiled at the memory, and Jory found herself joining him.

"Even Rob kept Angus off my back. But I was always last, ye ken? Born last, and trying to catch up and measure up ever since."

His words brought a twinge to Jory's heart. She was fair certain he wasn't only referring to hunting.

"I was the last to spot the quarry, slowest on the draw. My aim, well, it left something to be desired. By the last night, I hadn't wounded so much as a tree."

"It was your first time," she conceded, but Finn shook his head, not interested in excuses.

"Next morning, I woke early and slipped away on my own. In the misty dawn I spotted them—a whole field of deer grazing in a clearing. It was almost a shame to disturb them. I knew I had one shot, and then they'd scatter to the wind. But Angus's taunts still rang fresh in my ears."

Jory could imagine him, a miniature of himself this very day, aiming practice arrows at an apple on a fence.

"I slowed my breathing, closed one eye and then the other to see how the field altered—but opened them again," he added, shooting her a look that made her shiver. "I fired a single arrow at the nearest young buck."

Shaking his head, Finn tore his gaze from his reverie and looked Jory in the eye. "My hit wasnae as clean as yours. I had to slit the poor beast's throat, nearly emptied my stomach then and there. But I did my duty, and I didnae cry."

"Eight years old, what on earth did you do with it?"

"Och, I was a braw little lad. Managed to get it up on my shoulders and stagger back to our camp."

Jory could picture the scene, how proud Finn must have been, fit to bursting.

"My mother's face looked a bit like yours does now."

Then he turned away, rather pleased with himself, she thought, as a scarlet flush covered his neck and ears.

THE MEAL RESTORED THE LASS ENOUGH TO CONTINUE THEIR journey. But as the day wore on, and the miles between them and the Gordon convent slowly fell away, she grew less and less settled, wiggling in her saddle and fidgeting with the reins.

She kept looking around with narrowed eyes and turning her face towards the sun as though for the last time, before tossing surreptitious glances Finn's way.

"We need a plan," she finally announced. "We'll be there soon. If we've any hope for success, we need a good, solid scheme."

"Aye," Finn answered cautiously. "S'pose we do at that."

He'd been dreading such a conversation from the moment he promised to help her, though he'd hoped to delay it if he could.

"Perhaps if we dressed as peddlers..."

He gave her a sidelong look showing precisely what he thought of *that* idea.

"A prospective nun, then?"

"You *are* a prospective nun."

"A different one. I could be your sister—"

" 'Twould never work!" he exclaimed in a strangled voice.

"Hear me out. We could ask for a tour to get the lay of the place. How are you at petty theft? Maybe we could lift a key."

"Or we could kick down the door and take it."

"Kick the door in?" Jory exclaimed. "That won't do much for the clan relations."

"But stealing from them in the dead of night will?"

"Ideally they wouldn't know it was us."

Finn sighed. " 'Tis a convent, aye? How well protected can it be? A display of force, take what's yours, high-tail it back to the Highlands—or wherever it is ye want to go. I s'pose *not* back to the Highlands, aye?"

"I suppose not," she said, and he wished again she'd tell him her own plan to survive. "I don't... mean to be critical but... we don't know what to expect inside, do we? They're Gordons after all. We can't assume them to be unarmed. It was a fortress once, even if it's meant to be a convent now."

"So you'd rather use deceit?"

The lass inclined her head to indicate she would.

"As ye say, they're Gordons. Ye cannae trick a trickster, mistress. That's the first law of deception."

"But if we're clever enough—"

"We're not," he cut her off, darkly. "There's a reason, d'ye ken, it was me they sent wi' ye and not someone else. It's because I've no head for strategy or subterfuge. They cannae spare a single man from their planning to disrupt His Majesty's roads and bridges, but they *can* spare me. Because I am worse than useless to them. I'm a bloody hindrance.

"I won't believe that," she said, and his heart warmed bitterly at her staunch defense.

"Matters little if you do," he said, but what he didn't say was it mattered very much to him.

"They sent you to protect me."

"They'd no notion you'd warrant much defense."

She frowned but held her peace, perhaps finally coming to understand the wretchedness of Finlay Shaw, until she said, "Perhaps you should cut out the deer's entrails and hide me inside the carcass as a peace offering to the convent?"

"And you thought I smelled bad?" he asked, slyly. "When ye find yourself roasting over a spit, mistress? What'll you do then?"

The lass gave Nell's neck a gentle pat. "Well, then I suppose I'll have more to worry about than any dowry."

Finn laughed out loud, a deep barking guffaw—because that was what Jory made him do, even when all the world felt hopeless.

THEY RODE SOUTH UNTIL THE STARS CAME OUT AND HE BEGAN to fear he'd misjudged the distance or forgotten the way.

Like their first night on the road, she looked up in fascination at the stars, their twinkling light softening her features.

"Scorpius," he said when he followed her gaze to the hook-tailed constellation sitting low in the night sky.

"How does the story go then?" she asked.

"It's a scorpion, innit," Finn explained. "A vicious wee beastie wi' a powerful, venomous stinger in its tail."

"In its tail?" Jory asked, looking up again with wonder.

"Aye. It follows the hunter Orion—that's him there, wi' a dirk hanging from his belt. Ye see, Orion boasted to be such a fierce hunter he would kill every animal in the whole of the world."

"Rather extreme."

Finn could imagine she was rolling her eyes as she said it. "The goddess thought so too."

"Goddess?"

He knew she'd be intrigued by that detail, and her reaction didn't disappoint. Her wide eyes were lit up by starlight.

"Goddess Gaia. So she sent Scorpius to find and stop Orion before he could go on his murderous spree."

"The hunter became the hunted," she marveled, "because a *goddess* decided."

"Aye, just so. And after Scorpius stung Orion, Gaia set the little fella in place, permanently guarding the night sky from the overzealous woodsman."

"Forever hunting," she said. "And forever hunted." Her tone turned very solemn.

Was she thinking of herself as Orion, doomed to look over her shoulder for the rest of her life if she took back her dowry from the Gordons? It was the same fear that plagued Finn night and day, how to help her without making everything worse?

"Ought we to stop?" she asked with a shiver.

"Nae, mistress. We're close enough now."

"Close? To where?" Then in a strangled voice, "Aberdeen?"

"To a village. Not even a village, a croft where we can pass the night. Would ye like to get down and walk awhile?" he asked, and when she agreed, he helped her down so they could walk side by side if not quite arm in arm.

"Are ye going to tell me your version?" He nodded towards the constellation.

"What makes you think I have one?"

"I dare say ye have a story for all of them."

She nudged him playfully, and his whole side tingled when they touched. "Well, it's a fishhook, isn't it?"

Finn shook his head. "Nice try, mistress. I know there's more to it than that."

"You think you know me so well?"

She turned to him, and he wanted to cup her face in his hands and kiss her until time stood still. "Aye. I believe I do," he answered, a little breathless.

Jory grinned, though she quickly tried to flatten her mouth so he wouldn't see.

"There was a young fisherman desperately in love with a beautiful lady with long, flowing, raven-colored locks and eyes of the deepest brown," she began. "The lady was rumored to be a selkie, and even though the fisherman might have easily found her seal skin, he couldn't bear to force her to stay as his prisoner, so he loved her from afar.

"But a cruel man did find her skin and did force her to marry him, though everyone knew he was incapable of love. He boasted throughout the village how he'd hidden her skin so she nor anyone else would ever find it, amused by the notion she would even try.

"Every day, the young fisherman searched high and low for the selkie's missing skin. Then one day, he pulled in his line and there it was, caught up by his fishing hook. He mended it and whilst the husband was drinking in the tavern, he took it to her so she might be free.

"She changed back into a seal at once and returned to the brine, escaping her cruel husband at last. The young man was, of course, devastated to see her go. But at night, when he was sleeping, he could hear her singing and calling to him from the shore."

Finn was enraptured by her story, lost in her words, so at first he didn't notice she'd gone silent. "And she haunted him forever after?" he asked pitifully, thinking how he'd face the same sorrowful end after saying farewell to Mistress Mackintosh.

"She haunted him for a time," she whispered. "Until he stopped resisting her call. Until finally he took his boat out one late evening and followed her across the sea to a land far away where they could be together. For she knew he'd never try to trick her or trap her, and he never did try to take her skin. And though she would sometimes go back to the water, she always returned to him. And they were happy."

They'd stopped walking and turned towards each other, the starlight sprinkling her face with shadows. Her back must be hurting, for the high shoulder pinched practically up to her ear. He could almost be content to stand there in the road havering with her until the end of his days, but she smiled up at him, a soft, tender smile, and he was overcome once more with the urge to close the distance between his lips and hers.

"Mistress Mackintosh," he breathed.

Her smile disappeared as she swallowed and whispered, "Yes, Mr. Shaw?"

She was so beautiful. Christ, how he longed to kiss her. But it wouldn't be right, even if she wasn't going to be a nun. He was a destroyer of beautiful things, and then there was his penitential vow of celibacy after the '15.

"Mistress," he sighed again, bending his neck so his forehead rested against hers.

She shifted her weight and his heart stuttered in anticipation of her lips, for he knew they'd be soft upon his own.

And then suddenly his legs were swept from under him and he landed on the ground, with the wind knocked from his lungs.

"Bloody hell," he wheezed. The back of his head throbbed where it hit the road and even the silence surrounding them roared mightily. Was it the Watch come upon them unawares?

Her weight settled itself across his middle, the point of her dastardly little sgian dubh pressing against his throat.

"The truth, Mr. Shaw?"

"The truth of what, you miserable minx?" he moaned, wanting to roll her off of him, but unnerved by the proximity of the dagger now he knew her history with a blade.

"Do you think me stupid? We've been riding south, not east, for most of the day. Clearly we're not headed to the coast."

She had him there. He'd tried to be subtle about the shift in direction, knowing she'd need convincing of this particular plan. But it would be easier to explain himself without the cold edge of her blade against his chugging pulse.

Chapter Sixteen

Jory shifted uncomfortably, not realizing she'd sat directly on Finn's sporran. How could it be so hard?

As she squirmed, her knee knocked the sporran at his side. But then what...?

Glancing down at her lap, she quickly looked up to meet his gaze. When he turned away, a red tide flooding out across his cheeks, she realized exactly *what,* and scrambled off him.

"Do you deny changing course?" she demanded.

"I do not," he said to the ground. His candor surprised her.

"Is this why you were unwilling to discuss a serious plan?"

He shook his head.

"Tell me, Mr. Shaw. I will have the truth."

He sighed and pushed himself to his feet, so she took a step back, sgian dubh at the ready.

"We cannae storm the castle just the two of us. It would be a fool's errand."

"I never took you for a coward."

"It isn't cowardice," he growled. "To recognize when you're beaten before you've begun is good sense. Hope and desire aren't the same thing as a half-decent strategy."

"I have a strategy."

"D'ye mind?" he asked, gesturing at her knife, and she sheathed it and folded her arms. "Pardon me for saying, but you have an idea, mistress. A dream. If gumption alone was all that's required, I ken ye wouldn't need me. But it isnae. I'm sorry, but it's not."

Jory wanted to argue, but he wasn't wrong. It was why she'd pressed him to help her come up with a real plan. But the idea of quitting galled her when she'd come so far, even if the Gordons deserved recompense for the life she'd taken.

Finn busied himself, straightening his kilt and sporran, brushing off the dust and crunchy leaves. "We need more men," he said.

Her head snapped up, even as she shook it. "Absolutely not."

He reached out to remove a leaf from her hair and it silenced her. "I've a friend, name of Leask, lives not far from here."

"No."

"He's a good man. I trust him wi' my life."

"Well, I don't trust him with mine."

Anguish cut a jagged edge across Finn's brow. She supposed he was equating her lack of trust in this stranger to a lack of trust in him. Could he not see how it was different?

"This morning you said *you* would help me."

"I will."

"*You*. Not some other men."

"Bringing them is me helping you."

"We don't need them. We can do it ourselves, you and me against the world."

Finn shook his head. "It's not enough."

Not enough. Her plan wasn't enough—*she* wasn't enough. Sure, and how many times had she heard that over the years? It was why her dowry was so large, after all, because without it she would never be enough. "You think I'm small. And weak," she said. It wasn't a question. What had happened to *You're powerful, Jory*

Mackintosh? But then that was days ago—before. "Because of the fainting?" she asked. "Were you ever going to help me at all?"

The flex in his jaw as he tried to think of an answer was all the answer she needed. Crestfallen, she mounted Nell and waited for Finn and Sparradh to proceed.

After at least another hour in the saddle—who could really tell once the sun went down, when an hour felt as long as an entire day?—they finally arrived at a clearing where a small stone cottage was nestled against the forest's edge, a stable set off to one side.

The lights were out because all decent folk would be in bed at such an hour, but a candle flickered to life and a curtain was drawn aside as they approached. Then Finn whistled a call like a tawny owl, and before Jory could finish begrudgingly admiring his skill, the door was thrown open.

"What in God's name are you doing here, ye dirty wee bastard?"

Mr. Leask was a stout man closer to Jory's height than Finn's, with bronze skin and a trim beard, and a great wide smile when he spoke. His wife almost towered over him, her long, golden-red mane plated and tied off with blue thread hung over the front of her shoulder.

They welcomed Finn and Jory into their home in the dead of night with a warm embrace and no further questions, not even, *Would you be needing supper?* Mrs. Leask simply set about heating it on the hob while Mr. Leask poured them each a warming dram, and Jory couldn't remember ever feeling quite so cared for, outside of Finn's ministrations or Wee Ellen's embrace.

There was rabbit stew with soft, fresh bannocks and hearty ale. Despite the large venison lunch, Jory tucked in, conflicted by the unexpected warmth exuding from this couple and her crushing disappointment in Finn.

The husband saved her the need to speak. He kept up a one-sided conversation as she and Finn ate, leaning back in his chair with his hands folded across his belly expounding on news about couples recently wed and bairns nearly born, and who had gone to Edinburgh, to sea, or to the grave.

Finn nodded and grunted appropriately, still as frustrated with Jory as she was with him.

The wife watched them both a little too closely, only looking away from Jory long enough to glance at Finn and back again, until finally their bowls were clean and she gave Mr. Leask a knowing glance. "You should see to the horses."

"Too right," her husband replied, slapping the table. "Too right, we should, and here's me been monopolizing all the conversation. Come, lad, you can fill me in on what news you bring."

Finn nodded and rose from the table, kissing Mrs. Leask on the cheek as he followed her husband out the door without a backward glance at Jory, who neither wished to chase after him nor to be left alone with her hostess.

It was all she could do not to wither under the woman's discerning eye. "So..." Mrs. Leask began. "Are you with child?"

Jory balked for a moment before answering. "Will you believe me if I say I'm not?"

"Dinnae ken," Mrs. Leask said.

"Then what's the point talking about it?"

It was close and hot in the Leask cottage, and the peat smoke and sage made her tired eyes feel as gritty as ground barley. They ached, and she ached to close them, maybe never open them again.

"He's taking you from Moy to Aberdeen, so you've been on the road for what, four days now?"

"Six, actually."

"Six days! And you've only now arrived?"

Jory looked up, realizing too late she was only helping cast doubt on her character. "There were... complications."

Mrs. Leask raised an eyebrow. "Is that what they call it now? You can be honest with me, lass. I'm not your ma. Can ye be sure you're not with child?"

How angry would Finn be if she threatened their hostess with her sgian dubh? "I assure you, there's no possible concern." She took a swig of tea, mostly to do something with her hands, but the drink had long since gone cold.

"D'you not like men?"

She spluttered at the question, choking and spraying tea everywhere. Mrs. Leask blinked and leaned back in her seat. "Our Finn's a braw lad, anyone can see. There's none finer than him, and I include my own late sons, God rest their souls, as well as my nephew, still living."

Jory's curiosity was piqued. "Yes," she coughed. "He's very gentlemanlike. Even to ladies who don't care for the species."

"Aye, I suppose he would be. Even after nearly a week alone with a bonnie lass."

Warming at the unexpected compliment, Jory attempted to turn the course of conversation. "How long have you known him?"

Suddenly Mrs. Leask rose from the table and became very busy rummaging through a small cupboard, her back to Jory.

"It's only, you said 'our Finn,' but I know of no family connection between Shaws and Leasks. You're not part of the Chattan Confederation, are you?"

"No. But we're on the same side of things. And we've known Finn a long time. Longer than a week."

"Since the '15, do you mean? Did he and Mr. Leask fight together?"

"Och. You can hardly call what happened to that lad at Preston a fight. I imagine he's told you?"

She returned to the table with a plate of fresh-baked shortbread and offered it to Jory before taking a large flaky biscuit for herself.

"Bits and pieces," Jory fibbed, accepting the rich, buttery treat and allowing it to dissolve on her tongue. It was maybe the best thing she'd ever tasted.

"Well, ye'll have heard the expression, 'the enemy's enemy is a friend,' aye?"

Jory nodded, though she never had.

"The Gordons were an enemy to us both. Before and after Preston. When Finn needed saving, Himself got the lad out of it, and when we needed help with the harvest, he was there at our side. He's been like our own son these last ten years, and that's all I'll say on the matter."

"In that case, Mrs. Leask," Jory said, "then I suppose we're to be friends, as well, you and I."

"So?" Leask said, managing to imbue the word with a dozen layers of meaning like he always did.

Finn glanced at him and then turned back to focus on the long even strokes he brushed across Sparradh's back and down his flank. "She's to be a nun. I'm escorting her. Nothing more."

His old friend had the decency not to laugh or audibly roll his eyes. "Catholic convents are illegal."

"Aye. This one's secret. Surely you've heard of it."

"Ye cannae mean the Red Cliff."

Even the crickets seemed to stop churring, as though the chill running through Finn was cold enough to finish them off for the season. He searched Leask's face with narrowed eyes. "Bearradh Dearg, aye. Why?"

"The Gordon castle?"

Finn nodded. "What have you heard?"

Leask leaned back against a stall rail and shook his head. "Rumors."

Suddenly Finn's dinner sat like a boulder in his belly. "Tell me."

"Ye willnae like it."

"It's to do wi' the Gordons. You could tell me they call water wet, and I wouldnae like it."

Leask laughed and then sighed. "The story goes the keep was transferred to Long Thomas Gordon some years past."

His friend was right. Finn didn't like it. "Long Thomas? Christ, did he trick them out of it?"

Leask grinned. "Aye, maybe so. 'Tis said they had some notion it could keep him out of trouble."

"Bloody hell."

"The story goes, families who send their daughters to be brides of Christ never hear from them again. The girls don't write. They don't visit for Hogmanay. It's as though they vanish."

Finn was clutching the curry comb as hard as he clenched his jaw, like he was trying to crush Long Thomas Gordon into dust, but he felt as though he were falling down a well.

"But," Leask went on, lifting his arms in surrender. "You and I both know the value of a rumor."

"If you mean they're rooted in truth..."

The older man brought over a sack of oats for Sparradh and began to brush down Nell. "So why did you bring her here? Because you're in love with her?"

Finn shrugged. What was the point of protesting, really? "She doesnae want to be a nun."

"No?"

"A dowry was paid. By rights it's hers. We mean to take it back."

Nodding Leask said, "And ye'll be needing help."

"I wanted to leave her here wi' Alys where she'll be safe."

"So that's what the cold shoulder was about."

For a moment Finn was taken aback by Leask's perceptiveness, and his friend smirked at him. It was a comfort, finally being back among folk who who understood without explanation.

"That woman..." He shook his head.

"Aye. All women."

"Will you help?"

"You know I will." Leask finished brushing Nell and gave her a helping of oats. "What's your plan?"

The question made Finn snort. "At the moment? Kick the door in and if it is indeed Long Thomas on the other side, separate his head from his shoulders wi' a broadsword."

"Well. It's something. Though ye'd be hard pressed to call it a plan."

Finn patted Sparradh's rump and tossed the brush away. "You know I'm no great hand at such things."

"You're also not fifteen anymore."

Finn glared at the man. *Then why does it feel like I still am?*

He took a seat on a barrel opposite Leask, leaning back against the stable wall, arms crossed over his chest.

Leask lit a pipe and asked, "We know what Long Tom is like. Any chance it's a trick?"

"In weaker moments I've questioned whether Angus might set me up to fail. But if it's a trick, the Borlum's ignorant of it, and I cannae think Angus would double-cross him after the man helped smuggle him back from his servitude in the Virginia colony."

"Surely the rumors have reached the Highlands. Why would they take the risk?"

"If they have, I dinnae ken it. Angus is eager for an alliance to muzzle the Watch."

"Angus is grasping at faerie dust."

"Aye."

"And the lass?"

Finn rubbed his hands over his face, trying to chase away the exhaustion as well as the nerves. "They said the priest asked for her by name. She reckons it's some kind of revenge. But... she's canny. If the Mackintoshes did have doubts, maybe that's why they let her go first."

Suddenly he recalled the parchments Angus had given him to be signed, and retrieved them from his saddlebag, gazing at his brother's wax seal.

"Let's see it, lad."

He handed it over, and Leask held his pipe to the seal until it warmed enough to peel carefully away.

After scanning the first page, Finn handed it off to his friend and began reading the second, noticing the name of young Margaret Mackintosh, Jory's youngest cousin, before moving on to the third, which named his own niece Lilith, who was then but ten years old.

"A promise," Finn growled. "A steady stream of future Highland lasses, bound for the convent on the coast."

Leask shook his head, reading each page as Finn handed it to him.

" 'Tis only rumors, aye?" Finn asked.

The older man sighed. "My cousin Abel, ye remember him?"

"Aye."

"Before Preston he sired six daughters."

Finn whistled, both impressed and slightly horrified.

"He couldnae afford six dowries, so he split one amongst the younger four girls and sent them to the convent."

"And?" Finn leaned forward, desperate to hear a good outcome.

"They didnae write."

"Is that all? Perhaps they were angry."

"Verra likely. When his great uncle died, he came into a small inheritance, so he hitched up a cart and took his wife to Bearradh Dearg. They meant to see the girls and give them an option—the convent could keep three for the price of four, and one could return home and be married.

"Solomon's choice?"

Leask raised a hand in concession.

"What happened?"

"They were barred entry and forbidden to see the girls. The youngest was but twelve. They were told the nuns were at prayer, and it would upset them to be so freshly reminded of the lives they'd left behind."

Finn scoffed. The dark feelings he already had about the lass's plan to infiltrate the convent were now growing colder and more jagged by the moment. He would have to tell her. Maybe then she'd see reason and agree to stay behind.

"So THE CONVENT'S BENEFACTOR," THE LASS BEGAN, "IS THE same Gordon who..."

"Double-crossed me at Preston, aye."

She paced back and forth the full length of the stable as he filled her in on what he'd learned.

"And I'm but the first of many sacrificial Chattan lambs off to slaughter, to be handed over and never seen nor heard from again?"

"For what it's worth, I don't think either your uncle or my brother knew."

She rounded on him. "And that's supposed to make it better, is it? Knowing so little, they would hand us over to sworn enemies in the hopes that our sacrifice would keep the Watch at bay?"

"It wasnae *my* idea."

She stopped pacing and leaned over, hands on Finn's bare knees, looking him in the eye. "How did you not know which Gordon you were taking me to?"

"Angus didn't mention—"

"And you didn't ask."

"Because it's one and the same, can't ye understand? Every Gordon is Long Thomas to me, and at the same time, I never expected to lay eyes on the bastard again."

She, out of anyone, had to understand. They were the same, she and Finn.

Staring off into the distance, she nodded like she understood exactly what he meant, and the knot in Finn's chest eased.

"So when do we leave? Did Mr. Leask have a better plan?"

"Mistress..." he shook his head, the knot tightening again like a noose.

"You can't still mean to leave me here."

"Ye cannae really expect to come—"

"It's my fight."

"It's too dangerous."

"It's not for you to decide, you're not my husband!" she shouted, and for a second Finn wondered how quickly that might be rectified, then at least she'd have to listen.

Who was he kidding? *Snap out of it, Wretch.*

"This isnae only about you, ye selfish woman," he said, feeling a little bit bad, but wasn't she selfish? "Maybe Angus *does* know what Gordon's about—maybe the price for freedom from the Watch is your dowry and all the others' too. Maybe the lasses don't return because the price has been paid. Maybe I'm about to blow up all of it, taking something which by rights isnae mine nor yours anymore."

"It's wrong!" she said, throwing her hands in the air.

"I ken, but sometimes that's the way of the world. Sometimes, as I said, we're but pawns in other men's games."

"Yes, but—"

"I have so much to gain by doing as my brother asks—my whole life, hell, my birthright. And I am willing to cast all of it aside, for *you*, so will ye please just heed me and stay here?"

They stared at each other, both breathing hard, but she still wasn't hearing him.

"You need me to get in. But I don't need you. I can handle myself with a Gordon without your thirst for revenge getting in my way."

Thirst for revenge, was it? He stepped closer, his face a breath away from hers. "You asked for my help. Ye dinnae believe I'm only here for revenge."

She shook her head, but said, "I do."

He stepped back. "Ye dinnae ken this Gordon. Long Thomas befriended me. He pretended to be a Jacobite, pretended to be an ardent supporter of our cause. I was meant to be on watch the eve before the Battle of Preston. We had a plan, my brothers and me —*my plan*—for how I was to lie in wait for the royalists, then send word of their arrival before slipping behind their ranks to assess their cannonry. But I allowed Long Thomas to lure me away from my post with nothing more than the promise of a few bannocks, a swig of ale, and the attentions of a pretty lass."

Jory rolled her eyes indignantly, no doubt thinking he deserved whatever he got. And she was right.

"He slipped something into my ale, stripped me naked, and tied me up. Then sent word on my behalf that all was quiet. Had I remained at my post, would things have been different? Dinnae ken. I might've warned them of the plan to burn the village, or that surrender had been negotiated without their knowing it.

"Would we have won the battle? I can never know because I wasnae where I was supposed to be. So do I want revenge? Aye, mistress. Because while I was trussed up like a piglet, men died, my father among them. My brothers and my countrymen were rounded up and imprisoned in squalor. My brother Rob, heir to my father's land, died in the filthy place. So yes, I do want revenge, and I willnae trust Long Thomas Gordon within arm's reach of ye."

His chest heaved. He'd flayed himself before her, and if she continued to insist, he had no walls left to resist her.

Instead, she turned on her heel and stormed back towards the cottage.

"Aye, fine, go, run away. It's what you do, isn't it?" he called after her. Then, thinking better of his words, he added, "Mind ye stay there."

Chapter Seventeen

Whether it was right or wrong to be angry with Finn, Jory had stormed off, and she couldn't exactly go back to the stable now. Especially not given what his foster mother kept insinuating. She also couldn't bear to go inside the cottage and pass the night under the woman's unrelenting gaze, so she remained outside, drawing her earasaid tight against the creeping cold, turning her back on Finn in the stable and on the Leasks within their cottage, as well.

Run away, he'd said. *It's what you do.* Maybe so, but if she'd been smart, she'd have done it years ago, before the Shaw boy ever became the *Shaw Wretch*, each of them somehow charged with the other's keeping. Whether his dying mother had intended to give him unto Jory or not, she couldn't let him destroy himself and his future for a cause which wasn't his—so she lied, pretending to believe he wanted only revenge.

Long Thomas Gordon nearly destroyed Finn once. She couldn't allow him to do it again in pursuit of her thirty pieces of silver.

If she left now, and did it on her own, Angus couldn't blame

Finn. She'd faced down one Gordon on her own. She could do it again, with both eyes open.

Perhaps the convent was Long Thomas's penance for his behavior at Preston, this alliance his reparation. The other girls rumored to have disappeared may not have spoken to their families because they felt forsaken. She could certainly understand that. Maybe they, too, were sent away for being outcasts to begin with. Regardless, it was time to go.

White-hot tears stung the back of her eyes as she realized she might never see him again, but she shook her head, pushing them away before they could even taste the night air. Once she had her dowry back, and a place to call her own in Edinburgh, she would write to him, and he would forgive her.

She could do this. She was Jory Mackintosh, her mother's daughter, and she was strong. It was time to take back her power.

Hours later, Jory felt certain she knew what it would be like to be thrown from a horse and then ground between two mill stones. Every single part of her throbbed with pain. She'd walked for ages with only Polaris to guide her before deciding to stop and nestle down beneath some shrubs until morning. But without a fire, she was far too cold, and there was no flint to start one.

All she could do to stay warm was resume walking. After some time, a blanket of fog rolled in, shrouding her in the blackest night.

She hadn't seen the tree branch until she smacked into it, nearly decapitating herself and leaving the skin around her right eye and cheek scraped and swollen. Nor had she seen the ground drop away until she was rolling down a steep embankment, flailing and whumping, down, down, down until she landed at the bottom with her feet in the air, a tangle of skirts and plaid, and a cold breeze freezing her nethers.

Deciding enough was enough, she burrowed down into her plaid right where she landed and went to sleep. Perhaps she'd freeze to death, and it would serve Finn right if he cried when he found her. Would it be possible to come back as a ghost through the sheer malicious will to haunt someone and make their life a living torment?

Miraculously, she'd survived the remainder of the night, and her first thought upon waking was, *I can't be a ghost because being dead wouldn't hurt this badly*.

Her second thought was in the form of her stomach rumbling and a curse of regret that she hadn't at least packed some of Alys Leask's delicious shortbread.

There was nothing for it but to keep moving forward.

She struggled to her feet and set off once more, stumbling towards the rising sun.

Run away. It's what you do, Finn had yelled after her. She couldn't very well argue he was wrong.

If she had awoken as a ghost, she'd have found him and apologized, and then punished him for the rest of his life for being right.

But this time was different. She wasn't running away—she was running *to*. Her mistake was not in leaving but in asking for his help to begin with. She knew better than to rely on anyone but herself, and besides, a more selfish request had never been uttered. He'd agreed without hesitation, but he had named that part of her character correctly, too.

Once again, in the harsh light of day, her actions appeared much more foolish and impulsive than when she'd conjured them. Continuing east would certainly bring her to the Aberdeenshire coast eventually, but not today. And then what?

She was cold, and hungry, caked with mud and reeking of mildew and every foul thing. Even with the adjustment to her boot, her right knee and hip were tight enough to cause a limp that would only worsen with each plodding step, and the hairs on the back of her neck would not lie flat for the constant sensation of being watched.

It would only be Finn, of course, coming to her rescue once more, for who else could it possibly be? And what would she say to him when he finally did appear? Was it worth the risk to tell him the truth, that she loved him and wanted to spare him the pain and humiliation of falling lower in his clan's esteem? Love had made her stupid and reckless, and—

She froze.

On the ground before her lay the splintered shaft of half an arrow. Two of three fletchings still attached, it was notable because of the goose feathers' unusual, almost-purple hue.

Jory knelt down and when she ran her finger along a silky feather it came off in her hand. She'd only seen such feathers once before, in the fletchings of Finn's arrows, like the one she had fired at the leader of the Black Watch. Shivering, she realized exactly who had been following her, and she dropped the feather in her pocket as she glanced around herself for somewhere— anywhere—to hide, but she stood in an open glade, completely exposed.

With a rumbling of hooves they surrounded her, all six members of the Watch. Surely they'd been following her long enough to know she was completely alone, that no one was coming to her aid.

"Well, well, well," the one with the broken front tooth said, peering down at her from his horse. "What do we have here?"

"Gentlemen," Jory greeted them, hoping at least one of them actually was a gentleman. "I'm so relieved you've found me."

"Where's your companion?"

"I—I don't quite know. We were separated, and I was thrown from my horse," she lied, hoping her disheveled state was enough to lend credence to the story.

The ringleader of the group jumped down from his midnight black stallion and grabbed Jory's chin, tipping her head up roughly to inspect her swollen eye. "Did he assault you?"

She forced herself to laugh. "No. That happened when I was thrown."

He kept her chin tilted uncomfortably for much longer than necessary before releasing her. "I'm very pleased to hear it. Are you in need of assistance?"

She considered saying yes, asking them to take her on to the convent, but the thought of traveling with them made her feel physically ill. "No." She pasted on what she hoped looked like a smile. "I'm perfectly well. Thank you for the offer."

He tilted his head in acquiescence. "Is it true you're on your way to Bearradh Dearg?"

A shiver ran down her back, urging her to run.

"Yes."

"To pledge yourself a novice?" he asked, and now the shiver was replaced by sweaty dread. Wasn't the convent supposed to be a secret? If Protestant members of the Watch knew, who else did?

"I go because I was invited."

The man leered at her.

"You'll have to come with us," he said, taking her firmly by the arm. "This is dangerous country for anyone to wander, but especially a lady of virtue like yourself."

She tried to think of an excuse or retort, but nothing came to mind, and there was no point even attempting the moves Finn had shown her, not with six of them on horseback, and no hope of ever outrunning them all. Before she could reply, she was hoisted into a saddle as the horses cantered in circles once more, then split into three groups, each heading off in a different direction.

FINN HAD LAIN AWAKE MOST OF THE NIGHT, PLAYING THE argument with Mistress Mackintosh over in his head. He had finally revealed the scars of his past, but not in the way he wanted to, not tenderly, but brandished in a torrent of angry words intended to shock and prove his point.

It was the first time he'd shared his story with anyone save the Leasks. When he returned to the shelter of their croft after Rob's death and Angus's transportation to the New World, the whole miserable affair had spilled out of him over the course of many drams and more than a little shortbread.

Confessing to the lass, his words sounded as ugly as they had so many years ago when he was nothing but a wee bairn pretending to be a man. And what was he now, but the very same? Running around, trying to prove his worth to Angus, to Chattan. To her. She didn't need *him*, she needed a warrior—cunning like Angus and strategic like Rob, not some hapless whelp led astray by a rumbling belly and a hardening cock. She needed someone else—anyone else—but she was stuck with him, and God help him if he bungled this up and lost her too, the same way he'd lost his brother.

When at last the sun awoke to light the edges of the day, and Leask's cow grew restless and began to low, Finn roused himself from his nest in the hay and stretched his aching back, hoping she'd fared better inside. Then he settled onto the milking stool like old times, finding peace in the alternating rhythm and the splash of pure white milk.

"Ye didnae have to do that, son. Was she too loud?" Leask whispered, when he arrived to do the chore himself.

"Nae, I didnae sleep over much," Finn replied, handing over the full bucket. "And I'm always happy to earn my keep, you know that."

"Tapadh leat, a mhic," Leask said, accepting the warm, frothy milk. "She slept out here wi' you then?" he added softly with all but a wink in his eye as he peered over his shoulder and around the stable.

"The cow?"

"The lassie."

The heat Finn had worked up in milking evaporated from his skin all at once, leaving him with nothing but a cold, damp sweat. "Nae. She spent the night in the cottage with you."

Leask raised his eyebrows in surprise.

"Didn't she?"

"Dinnae think so. She was outside for a bit, muttering to herself after your scrap, but then I fell asleep before ever hearing her come in and there's no one there now but Alys."

"You're certain?" Finn asked. It was a ridiculous question, but he was unable to stop himself from asking it anyway. "Could she be in the privy?"

Leask shook his head. "I've come straight from there."

Clicking his tongue for Sparradh, Finn reached for his sporran and cap, but his friend held out a hand to still him.

"Go steady, lad. She's a lass who knows her mind if ever there was one. If ye mean to follow her, ye need a full belly and a plan."

"Not hungry," Finn said, his childish tone ringing in his ears.

"Maybe not." Leask ignored the tone. "But if she's injured or elsewise you might need help. And I require breakfast. Ten minutes. Kettle's already warming on the hob."

Everything in Finn wanted to go, go, go. But in his heart, he knew Leask was right. "Ten minutes," he agreed.

An hour later, they'd found and lost her tracks a dozen times or more.

"She should be easier to follow," Finn grumbled. "The weight of her left foot leaves a distinctive mark, and there's a 'V' etched into the heel of her boot."

"Whatever for?" Leask asked.

Finn gestured at the world around him.

"Ah. So she's done this before?"

"Aye."

"And where did she go then?"

"Straight into a bog, the wee hoyden."

They'd managed to pick up her trail even after she tumbled down a ravine, but now the lass appeared to be walking herself in circles, when they could find a trace of her at all.

"D'ye think she means to hoof it all the way to the coast?" Leask asked, still contemplating the ground. He pointed, finding the next visible footprint.

"I dinnae think she thinks at all." Finn sighed. It was his fault she'd taken off this time. He'd practically dared her to go with his parting shot.

He'd been relieved when they found the spot where she most likely passed the night—even more relieved she wasn't still there, frozen to death. She was maddening and headstrong and exhilarating and infuriating and—

"You should tell her," Leask said.

His head snapped up. Had he been thinking out loud? "Tell who what?"

Leask tried to smirk at him, but his expression was sad and far too sympathetic. "When we find the lass, ye must tell her how ye feel."

Finn looked away. Hadn't he told her a thousand times already in a thousand different ways?

"Am I wrong?"

"Nah," Finn said, moving to inspect a snapped twig. "But it doesnae matter."

"And why not? You said she didnae wish to be a nun."

"She doesnae wish to have a husband, either."

"Maybe she doesn't know what she wants."

"To all who know me, I'm still 'the Shaw Wretch,' nothing more, and always will be."

Leask made a sound of disbelief, low and gravelly in his throat. "Mmphm. Not to them who *know* you."

"She deserves a king."

Now his friend chuckled. "Aye, lad, certainly every woman does. But she, an orphaned daughter of a soldier, the ward of a—now what did Alys tell me? A tutor? She's no higher prospects, so why *not* you?"

"Her father was at Preston."

"We were all at Preston."

"He was kind to me. Tolerated me more than many a man. He would spar wi' me sometimes—humoring me, I'm sure."

"So ye carry *him* now too, is it? Right alongside Rob and the rest of them?"

Finn nodded.

"Laddie," Leask began, but he knew well enough Finn wouldn't hear whatever excuse he might make for his fifteen-year-old self, so he cut himself off and clapped Finn on the shoulder.

Before stepping forward to find the next footprint, however, he said, "If she feels an ounce for you as you feel for her, then it willnae matter what's in the past."

"And if it does matter, I shall find myself unable to face another day."

Finn knew what it was to lose a parent at too young an age—knew, too, what it was to become an orphan at any age—and he alone had done that to her.

He'd wanted to murder the physician for the mere sin of being unable to save his mother's life, though it was no one's fault. But his carelessness had taken her father from her. Once she put two and two together, how could she ever forgive him?

He could swear he caught a hint of lilac on the breeze, like the air itself was taunting him, as though he'd missed the lass by mere moments. "There," he said, pointing to a splintered arrow shaft, one of his, but missing two fletchings, and there the trail went cold, trampled over by half a dozen horses before shooting out to the north, south, and west, but none in the direction she'd been walking all day.

"It has to be the Watch," Finn said.

"You don't know that. She may have encountered some helpful horsemen who are at this very moment ferrying her straight back to the croft safe and sound."

"Nah," Finn argued. "It's the Watch. The same ones we met two days ago."

"Ye cannae know that, Finlay Shaw. Not for certain."

"This," he held up the splintered shaft. "This is mine."

"What, a broken stick with one good fletching?"

"It's *my* arrow."

"It's *an* arrow.

"It's the very same one she fired straight into the Watch fella's saddle." Finn shoved the arrow in his old friend's face. "How many times have you seen a goose feather of such quality? Such hue?"

Leask squinted at the feather under his nose, then extended his arm out to its full length, inspecting the fletching's bluish tint.

"But once," he finally admitted. "The quill you sent Alys could be its double."

"Aye," Finn agreed. It was his arrow, which meant the Watch had passed this way. Jory had stood here as well, the slightly heavier heel print evident right next to where he'd spotted the arrow. She'd found it too, recognized it, and then vanished leaving only her scent.

"They have her," Finn growled, jumping into the saddle. "They must."

"Whoa, there, young buck. Don't go jumping to conclusions. Even if they have her, what'll you do?"

"Get her the hell back."

"Ye said yourself the tracks go in three different directions. There's only the two of us."

Leask was right of course. Much as it pained Finn, he couldn't run off like an eejit, not and have a prayer of finding her. But even the mention of a delay made his heart pound in terror.

"We dinnae have time for a plan."

"There's always time."

"They could be violating her this minute."

"Lungs like hers, I imagine we'd hear her scream." Leask leaned over to pat Finn's shoulder from astride his own mount. "Come lad. If it *is* the Watch, they're not likely to harm her before she reaches Long Thomas. We need to do this right, and that means we're going to need another man or two."

Finn turned Sparradh in a circle, imagining the scene. Six riders came upon Mistress Mackintosh as she stooped to examine the broken arrow. She heard them before she saw them, a ferocious whirlwind of beating hooves. Heart in her throat, chill bumps rising on her arms and neck, she knew at once they were the Watch.

Did she call out? Scream? Nae, she laughed at them and scolded them, attempting to send them on their way.

But they took her, he had no doubt. The horses ran both windward and leeward, surrounding her from opposite directions, trampling their own prints, stamping them into oblivion. Then one of the riders forced her onto his saddle.

The thought made Finn's chest tight with anguish.

Did the brigand clutch her closely to himself, basking in the scent of lilac, leaving his own dank musk in its place? Did he take liberties and grope her, while she bit her lip and silently endured? After Finn had promised her...

He should have known better than to promise.

Two riders initially headed south, two north, and two west, the direction from which he and Leask had approached, which meant they'd likely all doubled back, regrouping to continue their journey further along.

"We must find her," Finn said. "If I follow these two riders, and you follow those, I'd give my eye teeth we'll meet within a mile upon the road."

"Six riders? What are our odds, d'ye think, the two of us, outnumbered three times over?"

"Better than theirs would be," Finn growled.

"With no pistol or sword? Think, lad."

"You want to waste time, it's yours to waste. I'll find her myself." He had to. Like Perseus, his wasted heart would follow her to the ends of the earth and fight away the monsters in his path.

Leask rode around in front of him so he had to look up. "Damn it, use your head, Finlay Shaw. Or else what good is having it attached to your neck?"

Finn blew steamy breath out through his nose. He wasn't a child. If he wanted to fly off half-cocked without a plan, then that's what he'd do.

"You go after her now, like this, sure as not, you'll both wind up dead."

"Like Rob, d'ye mean?"

"You know I didn't."

Finn peeled the last remaining feather from his arrow and placed it gently in his sporran, tossing the broken wood to the ground once more. "Ye've a plan, have you?"

"Aye. We go home. Bring in a few extra lads. And come up wi' a plan."

"Meantime, she could be——"

"Meantime, trust her to keep herself alive."

Leask was right, he was always right, but Finn couldn't bear to ride back the way they'd come, putting even more distance between himself and the lass.

"These men of the Black Watch—they'll not be working for Long Thomas? Angus had a notion he might be able to control them, but Thomas is not the laird now, is he?"

"No, lad. The Gordon laird is one of his cousins. Thomas

stood to inherit his uncle's castle, but when his father died, the clan elected his cousin. They wouldnae follow Thomas."

Finn nodded. That, at least, was the first decent thing he'd ever heard about the Gordons.

"But then, this arrangement—it's with the wrong Gordon?"

Leask tilted his head in silent agreement.

Chapter Eighteen

Ramrod straight and stone-faced, Jory sat with thighs that ached from being clamped around the unfamiliar horse as it careened across the hills and dales at break-neck speed, somehow far more terrifying than her attempted escape on the back of Sparradh. She hadn't realized it then, but she'd trusted the Clydesdale as well as his master.

She shared the saddle of a man called Digger, who smelled as though he'd possibly bathed sometimes in the past year, and who thoughtfully kept her secure upon the thundering beast by cupping one hand over her breast at all times. Though her skin crawled as they zigzagged across fields of heather, Jory didn't have much time to dwell on her fear or humiliation. She was too busy imagining all manner of retaliation: an arrow to the throat, a sgian dubh to the eye.

At last Digger and his companion, the leader of their small band, rejoined the rest of their party, turning eastward. Jory reminded herself bitterly that it was, after all, the direction she'd had in mind when she set out on foot the night before—an excursion she was now regretting with all her heart.

She'd been right to try and protect Finn, but she should've let her dowry go and found another means to begin her life in Edinburgh. Pride may goeth before destruction, but surely greed was also lifted up before a fall.

"How much farther?" she asked Digger once they slowed enough that she needn't shout.

He grunted an indiscernible reply so she looked to the man in charge, who she'd learned was called Baen. "Bearradh Dearg? Is the cliff really red?" she asked.

"Stained with the blood of sailors whose ships have crashed into the rocks below," he replied with a wink.

Jory shuddered but said, "I understood it was less than a day's ride from this part of the country."

Baen sniggered. "In a hurry, are we?"

Something in his laugh shot a chill right down her spine. "Thomas is expecting me."

He laughed again.

"Long Thomas?" she repeated, but he ignored her, riding off to share a joke with one of the others.

None of the men said another word to her until they stopped to water the horses by a stream. Jory knelt down to splash her dusty face, and Digger shoved an empty water skin in front of her.

When she looked up at him askance, he shook it at her, finally grunting, "Fill it."

"I'm neither your wife nor your mother," she replied, offering a respectful bow and stepping away.

Before she knew what was happening, he'd grabbed a fistful of her hair and forced her to her knees, submerging her whole head under the freezing current.

She closed her eyes tight against the rocky bottom, her head aching with a cold which trickled from her ears into the deepest parts of her throat and then to her brain. She held her breath until bubbles forced themselves out her nose and mouth like individual cries for help that no one would ever hear.

Then she was yanked back out of the water and set on her feet like a soggy rag doll. Without a word, Digger slapped her hard across the mouth with the back of his hand, catching her lip with the edge of his ring. A stony indifference glinted in his dark, soulless stare. He placed the water skin in her hands.

Jaw aching, lip stinging, she looked around at the other men. Most were still engaged in their own activities, as though nothing had happened at all. Only Baen was watching, curious to see what she would do next, but not inclined to intercede on her behalf.

Take back your power, Finn's words rang in her ears once more, but perhaps his own judgment had been clouded by his good and gentle nature. Jory had been able to knock him down, her knife at his throat, because he let her, because there were lines he wouldn't cross. She wouldn't be able to gain the same advantage as a prisoner of these men.

For now, the safest course was the path of least resistance, and so, shaking far more than she cared to admit, she knelt to collect the brute's water.

When they resumed their ride, she was placed in front of Baen, a small mercy, she supposed, to escape Digger. As they approached a fork in the road, her hand went to her pocket, to the feather from Finn's broken arrow. At the movement, Baen stroked her arm in a lazy way.

She tried to sit stock still, ignoring his breath as it hit the exposed part of her high shoulder in an uncomfortable, clammy way. Goodness knew she didn't want to do anything to encourage the throbbing creature digging into her lower back—most assuredly not a sporran, she was horrified to realize, when she felt it twitch against her. Instead, she tried to focus on making this one an ally.

"I want to thank you and your men for escorting me," she said.

When he didn't respond, she added, "I hope the coast is not so very far out of your way."

Still no answer.

"Do you work for Long Thomas Gordon?"

They obviously knew something of the not-so-secret convent, and perhaps the rumors surrounding it, as well.

Baen snorted a derisive laugh.

"What's funny now?" Digger asked, staring openly at Jory's currently unmolested bosom.

"Do we work for Long Thomas, Dig?" Baen repeated.

Now it was Digger who snorted. "Work for Scarface?"

A chill ran through Jory despite Baen's hot breath and sweaty torso.

"I'm not sure he pays well enough to call it work, madam," Baen answered. "We scratch his back time to time and accept what he offers in exchange."

"Scarface?" Jory asked, hardly breathing.

Digger burst into a full-bodied guffaw. "Aye, Long Tom survived Preston only to fall on his own wee knife, didn't he? Cut hisself from cheek to jowl. Right ugly bastard, Long Tom Gordon."

The other riders all began to laugh and pass a flask between them, almost as though they were toasting their dislike of the fellow they called Scarface.

And as for Jory, every last thought fled her mind, leaving it filled only with the image of a young man drenched in his own blood.

FINN AND LEASK PAUSED ON THEIR RETURN TO THE CROFT AND asked Leask's cousin Roddie to ride out and summon his son, also called Roddie. As soon as the four of them rode into the yard an hour later, Alys was ready with bowls of venison stew made from the deer he and the lass had brought.

"Why have the Watch strayed so far from the Highlands?" Finn asked.

"Nasty bastards," Roddie Junior said.

"They do as they please," his father agreed.

"They seemed to know of the convent when we met the other day. But why would they? If Long Thomas isnae the Gordon laird, and they're not working for him, why take her at all?"

"Does he really need chapter and verse as to the *why*?" Roddie Junior asked, and Leask elbowed him.

Finn glowered at the table, and Alys rubbed his shoulder before setting out fresh bannocks and filling his bowl. "Eat," she demanded, and though he had no appetite, he did as he was bidden, every bite reminding him of the lass's ecstatic face as she tasted the roast loin but one day ago.

"Dragging a woman along merely to take their pleasure would be a liability," Roddie Senior said. "Extra mouth, extra weight."

"She's more than all that, for Christ's sake," Finn growled, and the two Roddies raised their eyebrows at each other.

"They'll be taking her to the convent for the reward," Alys told them, and all four men turned towards her in surprise.

"Reward?" Finn asked.

"Of course. All those tales of girls gone missing? You think Long Thomas went out and scrounged them up on his own like the Rat Catcher of Hamelin?"

"I thought they were sent by their families," Finn said, and the others all grew suddenly very interested in their food. "Isn't it meant to be secret? From Protestants at least, from the Watch if no one else?"

"Sure, and three can keep a secret if two be away."

"What reward though?"

"Enough, Alys." Leask turned to Finn. "It's idle hearsay."

"Gossip or not, doesn't make it any less true," Alys argued, and Leask put up his hands in surrender so she slid onto the bench across from Finn. "Every town, every village, up and down the coast and from here to Aberdeen has a story of a girl gone missing. She went to gather wood in the forest or clover down the stream. She was searching out lost lambs up the hill, taking the air along the shore, collecting shells. One after another, they disappeared. Some had sweethearts. Some, elderly kin. One was raising her dead sister's bairn. They didn't all simply run away or wander off and get snatched up by the faeries."

"So you think..." Finn began, but he couldn't bring himself to finish the thought.

"Who better to kidnap a lass against her will than the Watch? Respectable. Trustworthy. Ordained by a Protestant God and the King himself."

Roddie Senior and Leask scoffed, though the latter turned his dismay into a cough at a sharp look from his wife.

"They come upon her. Offer her a ride. Next thing she knows, she's praying matins at Bearradh Dearg. You can bet your boots they're paid upon delivery, and handsomely too. They'd have to be, else why do it?"

"She has a point," Finn said to Leask, and Roddie Junior rolled his eyes.

"Or," Roddie Senior suggested, "Protestant hysteria is sweeping the district at the notion of a Catholic convent. It hasn't been so many years since the Catholic churches burned in these parts. Them as heard about it will be afeared for their own lands should the crown find out."

"Guilt by association," Junior agreed.

It may be a stretch, assuming they'd taken her to the convent. But the alternative, that they might have taken her *anywhere* in the world to do whatever they pleased—it didn't bear thinking about.

Leask rose from the table and shoved his wife's rocking chair aside. Then he pulled up several loose floorboards, revealing a priest hole filled with swords and pistols. He glanced at Alys who nodded grimly, before distributing the weapons to Finn and the Roddies.

Outside, Finn rehearsed moves as familiar as breathing. Traveling as much as he had these last ten years, he'd seldom held a sword since Preston, but muscles have memories which don't soon forget.

The group knelt in a semicircle behind the house watching Finn scratch out a map in the dirt. There was one road east to Aberdeen and another south to Edinburgh.

"What if they don't take the road?" Roddie Senior asked.

"The road's faster, and they'll not think they've any reason to hide."

He marked Aberdeen on his makeshift map. "They should make it no further than this area by nightfall." He placed an X along the route between the spot where they'd found the arrow and the coastal town.

"*If* they've headed east..." Roddie Junior trailed off.

Finn nodded. "She might wish to go to Edinburgh eventually. But what reason would they have to take her there?"

"Flesh market?" Junior suggested tentatively.

"If what Alys suggests is true, the convent will pay more," Senior replied.

Finn's stomach roiled at the notion of Jory being auctioned off before a salivating crowd. He never thought he'd live to believe Long Thomas Gordon might be the lesser of two evils.

"We must be certain," Finn said. "The tracks split off in three directions. We should ride back to the point where the horsemen split. Senior, me, and Leask," he said, looking from one older man to the other. "We each follow a set of tracks, and I ken we'll reconvene on the low road."

"And me?"

"Is it true you've a herd of cattle?" Finn asked Roddie Junior.

"Aye," he answered, with a slightly dubious scowl.

"How many?"

Junior studied him. "Enough."

"In that case, I've an idea."

. . .

THE MEN RODE BACK TO THE MEADOW FROM WHICH THE LASS was abducted, and Finn had been right. All three trails did indeed reconvene on the low road and turn east. He sent Roddie Senior on ahead to help Junior deal with the cattle while he and Leask continued to follow the trail.

At least riding gave him something productive to do, otherwise he'd have long since run mad with guilt, replaying their last conversation over and over. *Ye're selfish. Run away.* He would take it back tenfold given the chance.

"She'll be all right," Leask said, as though reading his thoughts. "It's in their best interest, ye ken, to deliver her intact."

"As a nun, sure," Finn rasped. "But what if we're wrong? I cannae understand the disappearances," he confessed. "I see the value in tricking desperate fathers out of meager dowries. But why pay out for those who'll only cost you?"

"I didnae tell ye all the rumors," Leask said grimly.

"What? Why?"

"Because. I cannae be certain they're not *only* rumors, and I willnae be breaking bread in other people's houses."

"Speak plain, old man."

"Every lass who's been taken has been *innocent*."

"Innocent?"

"Unmarried and untouched. Jesus, lad, ye ken well enough what I mean."

"Nuns are supposed to be—"

But Leask shook his head. "Nuns are supposed to remain chaste, aye. The rumor is they don't after they arrive."

Finn was exhausted. His head felt sludgy, like over-cooked parritch. "Who?"

"Sailors, most like. Lured by the siren song of... well... virgins."

Cheeks burning, Finn looked away, hoping Leask wouldn't notice the flame climbing his neck and face.

"So the rumor goes, there *is* no convent," he said seeking affirmation.

"Aye."

"But Abel's four daughters." Finn shook his head. "How can he leave them there?"

" 'Tis a recent story, and shame does funny things to a man." Leask gave him a meaningful look, and didn't Finn well know it.

"Are you sure it's not a fabrication to keep the Protestants away?"

His friend shrugged and went silent, leaving Finn's imagination to roil like an over-heated kettle. Which was more likely? An elaborate hoax to hide a brothel or one to hide a convent? The castle was ideally perched near the sea, although sailors would have to make their way up a long and winding road, else scale the steep cliff. Either way, he had to get to the lass before she reached it.

When they came to a crossroads, he stopped and closed his eyes, trying to sense her, to smell once more a lingering hint of lilac, to feel which way she passed, for there were prints heading down both roads.

"You go right, I'll go left?" he suggested to his companion, but not twenty paces along, he stopped Sparradh and called Leask back when something on the trail caught his eye.

Before his feet touched the ground, he knew what it was. Finn plucked the blue-violet feather out of the dirt and held it up to the sunlight for them to examine together. From his sporran he removed its twin. There was no mistaking them.

"You clever, clever lass," he marveled, beaming up at Leask, knowing perhaps it might be a mere accident or coincidence but choosing to believe she wanted him to find her.

Chapter Nineteen

As though watching herself from outside her own body, Jory no longer felt the horse beneath her. Could it be possible that Long Thomas Gordon, the man who had brought about all of Finn's unhappiness, *Scarface* to those who knew him, was in fact the very architect of her own undoing? Being chosen by name wasn't merely a matter of recompense between two clans. It was far more personal than that.

Plenty of men had scars, she reminded herself, trying to catch her breath. There was no way the Gordon who attacked her and Ellen nine years ago, whom she blindly stabbed, had not actually perished as she'd always believed.

There had been too much blood. It haunted her at night when darkness overtook the world—blood on the straw, on her skirt, on her hands. But had she ever heard anyone actually say Boyd Gordon's brother was dead? It was never discussed outright with her. He'd simply vanished, the stable scrubbed clean.

Was it within the realm of possibility he was not only alive, but in fact heir to a castle-turned-convent, a castle to which she'd been summoned in order to serve her long overdue purgatory?

If it was true, if Long Thomas was the Gordon she tried to

kill, nine years older and marked for life, then her dowry was lost to her forever. She needed to disappear. Immediately. But how?

Jory didn't want help from anyone. She never had. Still and all, as the sun sank closer to the western hills, she'd thought Finn would come for her. That he hadn't spoke volumes about the bond she'd imagined they shared.

He'd told her she was powerful, but she couldn't overtake six men at full strength. Not on her own. Overnight they might tie her up, and who knew what else. She would have to try and escape. Some part of her must still be the same little girl who flew into the fray all gnashing teeth and flailing claws, and if Finn wouldn't be there to fight on her other side, well, then she'd have to fight both sides by herself, and this time, she would do better to remember the defensive moves he'd taught her.

When they stopped for the night, she hung back, away from the stream, watching as the others fell into well-established roles. Three of the men set to fishing, while Digger built a fire, but it was Baen's icy stare which most unnerved her.

Jory sat alone on a log, trying to think of a plan for her escape, when Digger approached shoving their catch in her face. She sympathized with the fish and their glassy-eyed stares.

"Cook them," Digger said.

And this time, she didn't dare argue. She cleaned them and set them by the fire to roast, memories of the trout and wild berries Finn had brought giving her an idea, and she slipped off to forage along the tree line.

"Where do you think you're going?" Baen called after her.

"To find some wild garlic to season your dinner."

Baen nodded but kept a close eye on her as she went. "Not too far," he warned.

She was, of course, not looking for garlic. The men could eat their fish flavored with piss and wind for all she cared. She hoped instead to find something more useful.

First she spied a raspberry thicket, heavy with full, ripe

berries, and she gobbled them hungrily, straight from the branch, the juice dripping down her chin. Finn would have laughed at her sheepishly trying to wipe it away before he could see. Appetite merely whetted, she found what she was looking for—caps which ignorant foragers sometimes mistook for chanterelles.

Jory glanced back at Baen and then scurried over. The fungi were dark orange, different from actual chanterelles in both shape and brightness. Nowhere near as quick or certain as a death cap or a destroying angel, the deadly webcap was not to be trifled with either. She picked a heaping mound of them to go with the fish. It was a risk if any of the men knew their flora, but based on their teeth, she wouldn't lay odds.

Humming to herself, she returned to the fire, trying to put on the demeanor of a woman in her natural environment, finally accepting her lot and role.

And when she invited the men to partake, they came with gusto, though more than one eyed the mushrooms suspiciously.

"What's this then?" Digger asked, holding one up to study it more closely.

"Chanterelle," Jory lied. "They're quite tasty, and very good for you."

She'd grown used to the idea of going to hell for murdering the Gordon. Now that he might not be dead, it didn't faze her to blacken her conscience for real.

"Fungus, innit? I've heard if you eat them then they'll start to sprout between your toes and out your ears," said Roston, the younger man with the dead, jagged tooth.

"You're filthy enough I don't doubt it, whether you eat these or not," Jory said, and he lifted his hand like he might smack her. "But chanterelles will help you stay strong and healthy," she went on. "Good for the teeth, or so I've heard."

The last might have been a bit much, but Roston sniffed one of the mushrooms and lifted it to his mouth.

"Stop," Baen said with quiet authority, and all the men did at once. "You eat one."

Five heads turned to face Jory as she considered Baen's demand. Would just one bite make her sick enough to prevent her leaving?

When she didn't respond right away, Baen added, "Chanterelles are a lighter orange, I believe."

At his pronouncement, every plate was thrown to the ground and Jory took off running.

Her legs were stiff and uncooperative after so many hours riding astride, on top of the hours spent walking, but she forced them to move as fast as they could go.

After making it less than a furlong, rough hands scratched at her, catching and ripping strands of her hair. She managed to get her knife unsheathed before one of them dove at her legs, knocking her to the ground. Her cheek smashed painfully into tiny pebbles and bracken as grit burned her vision. Then he rolled her over and slapped her, yanking at her skirts. It was Roston, and Jory momentarily delighted in his shocked face when she brandished her weapon.

Then he forced her wrist to the ground one-handed, while the filthy fingers of his other hand squeezed her throat until she could neither draw breath nor make a sound. Everything started to go black, before muffled shouting brought Jory back, and she opened her eyes to see Roston and his yellow teeth being pulled off her.

"An innocent mistake I'm sure," Baen said, hauling Jory's attacker back by his sark and swinging him away from her. Then he noticed her reaching for her knife, and he laughed.

The moment he was released, Roston lunged for her again and Jory snatched up the sgian dubh and swung it at both of them, but Baen kicked the other man away and caught her wrist, wresting the knife from her fingers.

"Come on, Baen. The bitch tried to kill us!"

"Peace. Don't you recognize her blade? Scarface pulled it on all of us more than once as lads. Look," he said, holding it aloft to show the hilt, where her thumb had not quite rubbed away the last of the Gordon crest. "You can still make out the stag he was so proud of." Then his face broke into a grotesque grin and his laughter bellowed across the clearing. "I always knew the story of how he got that scar wasn't true."

Jory looked up into the faces of Baen, Digger, and Roston while the other three lurked behind them. Roston's hand was on his belt buckle, moments from dropping his breeches but Baen yanked his rotten-toothed companion back by the scruff of his neck, clenching Jory's knife in his other fist.

"I've told ye a hundred times, Scarface tests their virtue himself, and he won't pay if we bring him one's not a virgin. Besides—this one's special, or have you not been listening?"

Jory swallowed back the sickly, sour taste of raspberries and balled her hands to keep them from shaking. She couldn't see any way out of it now.

"She don't look special to me," Digger protested. "She's all crooked and hobbledehoy. Seen her shoes?"

"Oh, you're special, aren't you?" Baen asked softly, and Jory shook her head. "How old could you have possibly been when you maimed him with his own knife?"

She swallowed, though her throat was completely dry.

"Aye, she's special, lads. Ole Scarface'll pay twice," he wagged his eyebrows, "three times," he wagged them again, "for the chance with this one."

Roston shook his head and leaned towards her again, and again Baen shoved him back.

"She tried to poison us, Baen. We can't let her get away with it!"

"Beat her if you must, but you'll not take her maidenhead. And try not to mess up her face too much."

He released Roston then and the man lurched at her with Digger egging him on.

Jory skittered backwards until she hit a tree, with the stream to her right, and nowhere else to go.

He lunged for her again and she tried to kick him, but he grabbed her leg and yanked her towards him, slamming her head against the ground as she lost her balance. She wriggled onto her stomach, still kicking with her free leg, praying to make contact with his face or his groin. She wasn't picky. Expecting him to pull her back again by the leg, she shifted her weight, the better to kick him, but instead he caught a fistful of her hair and wrapped it around his hand.

As he dragged her along towards a fallen log, bracken from the forest floor scraped her legs and stung her eyes. She clawed at his hand, stumbling along so the hair wouldn't be fully ripped from her scalp. Grunting, but biting her lip to keep from crying out, she was well and truly the chained maiden from Finn's story now.

When Roston threw her against the log, it knocked the wind out of her. His belt buckle jangled again despite Baen's order. But this time, he didn't shove up her skirts.

With the flick of his blade, he sliced through the laces tying her stays, then ripped open her top layers, bearing her back to the cold evening air.

When the full weight of his belt landed across her back the shock made her scream. Then she clenched her jaw and held tight to the tree, waiting for the searing pain to end. If God was truly merciful, perhaps she would soon black out.

⊶━━

"It's getting late," Finn complained. "I didn't time it right. They'll be stopping for the night soon if they havnae already."

"Good."

Trust Leask to remain calm and even keeled.

"Give us a chance to properly catch them up."

"But the coos."

"It's a good plan, lad. Solid. No less so if we wind up modifying it. The coos will come in handy as ye thought."

"If they're here in time," he moped.

It was a small comfort that Leask still had confidence in the plan—Finn's plan, for all intents and purposes. They'd thought through every scenario and contingency, except the ones they'd never imagined, and in the moment the plan had felt right. But Finn couldn't climb out from the shadow of certain disaster. The boulder he was forever pushing uphill now sat squarely on his chest, threatening suffocation.

"It's a good plan."

He nodded.

"Lad. It's been ten years since Preston. Isn't it time you stopped flogging yourself over a boy's mistake?"

"When does one stop being punished for murder?"

"Murder? Ye didnae kill anyone, lad, how could ye, trussed up wi' the pigs?"

"Is the man who drops the torch and burns the house down any less guilty than the one who sets fires on purpose?"

"Aye, obviously, the difference being what's in here." Leask pummeled his own chest. "Anyway, ten years is long enough to spend in hell. If the good Lord sees fit, he'll send ye there when the time comes. Why add to your sentence on earth?"

Finn had no answer.

"I didnae ken Rob well, but I dinnae think he'd want you to let one terrible night define ye. Now you listen to me. Are ye listening, soldier?"

"Aye," Finn rasped.

"It's a good plan," Leask repeated once more, and this time he allowed himself to believe.

It had better be a good plan anyway. Because if it went wrong and, God forbid, something happened to her, he would never forgive or trust himself again, not in ten years' time nor in a hundred.

"If the lass doesnae want to be a nun—" Leask began cautiously.

"She doesnae wish to be a wife either." Finn reminded him.

"Bit unusual, innit?"

"She's... different. She's..." he searched for a word that could possibly do her justice. "Exceptional."

"Well," Leask replied, studying him. "Maybe she'd want a husband if he made a habit of telling her so."

Finn snorted and shook his head. He wasn't sure there was enough luck left in the world to allow him to hope.

Minutes later, the night was rent by a scream—quickly muffled. Finn recognized her voice immediately. "Find the damn coos," he whispered to Leask before urging Sparradh as fast as he could go. The Clydesdale needed no encouragement, as though he also recognized his mistress's cry.

"Don't be a fool. Wait for the rest of us," Leask called after him, but his words might as well have been the wind.

Finn slowed Sparradh when he reached a clearing along the side of the road and snuck through the trees until he could see the damnable Watch. Four of them stood laughing and horsing around while a fifth thrashed Jory against a fallen tree. Only the sixth had the decency to look shame-faced as he kicked at pebbles near the river.

Finn's ears rang with a rage the likes of which he'd never known, hungry to wipe them all from the face of the earth, and their lecherous smirks along with them. His pistol would be more lethal, but guns were noisy and took time to reload, when what Finn required was stealth and speed, so he took up his bow instead.

Picking his mark carefully, Finn fired an arrow straight into the back of one of the bystanders. When the other three spun around in confusion and then ducked for cover, Finn took careful aim and fired once more, catching her assailant right through the throat so he fell with his arm still raised for another lash. Then he leaped into the saddle and flew into the camp, sword flashing to meet any weapon they might draw.

The lass slumped against her log, clinging to it with one arm to keep herself upright. He might have to dismount to get her. Damn, he should have waited for Leask. What was he thinking, trying to take them all on alone, and his mistress's life hanging in the balance?

The shame-faced one fled into the forest, but the other three surged on Finn. They brandished their own swords but none of Finn's fury. He spun and whirled, broadsword clashing with each in turn. Soon as he knocked one back another came at him as he fought his way closer to the lass, desperate to reach her, to see she was all right, desperate to kiss her wounds away if he was being honest, but he kept his back to her fearing one look would cleave him in two.

And then suddenly Leask was there, galloping into the clearing, giving Finn a moment's breath. When he turned, he found her watching, delicate brows knit together as she tried to smile at him.

He gazed at her, wanting to say too much but unable to utter a word, and she stared at him, choking back tears. Then her expression turned to horror, and he spun around to meet his next attacker with the full might of his sword.

It worried Finn that she wasn't trying to fight them all off single-handedly, swinging her little knife or wielding a stick like a sword. Had the Watch managed to break her? And could it be undone?

When he finally dispatched his assailant he turned back to her, searching her face for a clue.

"You came," she breathed.

He took her face in his hands—needing to taste her lips, to know she was real—but then he remembered himself and stopped short. "I will always come for ye," he said against her lips, and instead of kissing her, he lifted her onto Sparradh and galloped past Leask who followed him up onto the road and away, the thundering and mooing of Roddie Junior's fluffy, ginger cows clogging the road behind them so the bastards couldn't follow.

Chapter Twenty

Hunching rigidly in front of Finn, Jory's ruined clothes threatened to expose even more of her, but her back was too raw to sink against his chest and her nerves too frayed to relax. She could smell the Watch on her, sour and vile, as though still imprisoned on one of their horses. But he had come for her. She'd thought he was going to kiss her—what utter foolishness—but he *had* come for her. She was safe. For now.

None of them spoke a word as they galloped into the creeping darkness. Eventually a third man caught them up to confirm something about cows being a success, his father and son still half-heartedly trying to round them up and unblock the road for the Black Watch riders—what was left of them.

"The way should be clear by morning. If ye've still a mind to go east," he added, eyeing Jory, and she was too exhausted to spare much worry about who he was or what he knew.

"I suppose you're still intent on retrieving your dowry?" Finn asked her gruffly.

She stiffened more, leaning further away from him, and when she spoke it was hoarse and strained, a stranger's voice. "It's not about that now."

"No?"

"That place... the Red Cliff... it's not a place where God is welcomed."

"What did ye hear?" Finn asked. "What did they say?"

She didn't want to talk about it or think about it ever again. But Maggie's name was on the list, and Finn's young niece, as well. And how many others were already there?

"Long Thomas, he..." She shuddered and Finn pulled her close though she immediately leaned forward again, away from him. "He tests their virtue."

"I'll kill him," the young man with the cows said.

"Get in line," Finn growled.

Jory faded in and out of fitful sleep, as the men made hushed and hasty plans for how they might rescue the girls of Bearradh Dearg. Two men named Roddie would hide a wagon in the woods below the castle. They'd create a distraction so Finn and Leask might gain entry, and then usher the women out, one by one if they had to, before spiriting them all away.

"You'll need me to go in as bait," Jory said, knowing they thought her deaf to their scheming.

"The hell you will. Ye'll stay at the croft wi' Alys," Finn argued.

"While you do what? Storm the castle? The pair of you?"

Finn spluttered.

"There's no need for a diversion. He's expecting me. It's an easy and obvious choice. I must go."

She didn't like it either, but it would help. It made sense. It was the right and only option.

"Have ye forgotten I just killed two members of the Black Watch to free you?" he hissed.

"No," she insisted, though she shivered when he said it. "I haven't forgotten. All the more reason to make sure we succeed. And now we have a cover story. I was kidnapped by a band of ruffians, and you, my sworn protector, liberated me so we might continue our journey. He shouldn't suspect aught's amiss."

"Perhaps not, but he's a schemer himself. I willnae risk it."

"It's not your decision."

"It bloody well is my decision. I swore a vow to protect ye, even unto death—"

"The lass is right," Mr. Leask interrupted grimly, and it was such a relief to have someone take her side. "I don't like it any better than you do, lad, but she's our ticket in. This is bigger than all of us now."

"I don't care about the other girls, d'ye understand? If it's a choice between them and her—"

"I don't believe you," Jory said. "You can't walk away now any more than I can."

Behind her, Finn stilled, trying to formulate another argument, but there was none to be had.

"It's settled then," Jory said. "We'll go at dawn."

"I'll make arrangements," the stranger said, turning his horse and peeling away from them, back the way he'd come.

The rest of the journey was silent. When they reached the cottage, it was empty despite the late hour. Even Mr. Leask looked confused not to find his wife knitting by the hearth with warm food and too many questions.

A note lay on the table, and Finn handed it to his friend, eyebrows raised in question.

"My niece's babe has come early. Alys's gone to help. I should follow." He raised his eyebrows at Finn before adding, "Eat what ye can find." He gestured around helpless and sorry for it. "I'll be back by morning."

"Thank you," Jory said, but the words which held so much feeling came out as a whisper, so she kissed his cheek instead. Blushing, he nodded at her and shook Finn's hand, then left them standing awkwardly alone.

She pulled her plaid tighter around her shoulders, not wanting to be touched, and yet desperate for Finn to wrap his arms around her and never let go. He stood with his back to her, and she wanted him to look at her, and she was glad when he didn't try.

"Did you do it on purpose?" he finally asked.

"Get caught? By a band of foul, odious reavers?"

"Gòrach," he whispered, shaking his head.

"Stupid am I? Well, and maybe I am for thinking I could walk all the way there on my own. Naive at least." But was it fair to call her stupid? Maybe so, but to assume she'd gotten herself caught by the Watch on purpose, even she wasn't that stupid. "Did you know they call him Scarface?" she asked.

"Who?" Finn finally turned to face her.

"Long Thomas. Because of an accident in 1716, they call him Scarface."

He shook his head but then turned pale. "You said ye killed him. Gutted him, you said." He took a step closer and she stumbled back, stopping him in his tracks.

It was an involuntary reaction, she didn't mean to push him away.

"I couldn't see. I thought I *had* killed him. It turns out I may have only sliced up his face. And now he's arranged... after all this time, he's arranged for his vengeance."

Finn swallowed as his eyes darted around the room processing her words. It was the first time during the entire ordeal that her tears were so close to the surface, and Jory began to shake. She leaned back against the wall, immediately springing forward again, wincing as the pain shot up her back like she'd been touched with hot iron.

Finn strode towards her, but again stopped himself. She had thought he was going to kiss her when he looked at her in the glade, but always, always he held back and turned away.

"Are you hungry?" he asked with a helpless look on his face that said he knew it was a ludicrous question.

"No."

"Whisky then?"

"No. Thank you."

"What can I do?" he asked, his own eyes glistening like dew-covered moss.

Jory searched aimlessly around the cottage, looking but not seeing, trying to think what to say to make him feel better enough to leave her alone and stop trying to make *her* feel better. When her gaze landed on a large bathtub in the corner, she sighed.

He followed her glance. "A bath?" he asked, and she nodded.

So he guided her to sit on a bench beside the fire as he heated a large kettle for the tub. And when it was ready, he turned his back so she could slip into the bath unseen.

The moment she did, however, the warm, comforting water loosed something in her and she pitched forward, hugging her knees as she attempted to stifle her gasping sobs. What an absolute and utter fool, to be mewling like an infant now when she was safe from harm.

Finn whirled around to face her, and she ought to cover herself, but she'd brought her hands to her mouth to try to stifle the sound of her cries, as her whole body shook with weeping. Angry stripes across her back burned at the touch of water and air, and she embraced the pain, letting it tether her to the moment.

"Is it too hot?" Finn exclaimed, looking for a bucket to fetch some cold water and cool it down at her say-so.

"No," she gasped. "It's perfect."

"Then what...?" he stopped himself, but his tenderness only made her cry harder. She wanted him to hold her. She wanted to be left alone.

Finn took up a sponge and a cake of soap and leaned over the tub shushing her and kissing the top of her head, cradling her against his chest as she cried. Her hair spilled down her back in a tangle of ringlets, and he swept it over her shoulder to hide the curve of a breast peeking under where her arms encircled her knees. Then, more gently than any touch she'd ever known, he lathered the sponge across her shoulders and down her wretched back.

When her breathing was finally under control, she peeked at him, puffy-eyed, over her low right shoulder, and he smiled sympathetically, but it didn't stretch beyond his lips.

"Are you angry with me?" she whispered.

"Aye. Verra angry indeed. You shouldnae have left like that. Making me chase after ye, and all the while feart ye'd be furious wi' me for doing so." But there was no animosity in his voice, and Jory felt the knot in her stomach loosen a tiny bit.

"I am," she said, even though she didn't mean it. She turned away from him, hiding the bruises on her face. "I didn't need your help. I had it under control."

"So I saw."

"Thank you for coming," she whispered.

"I told ye. I will always come for you, mistress." He sat back on his heels, fiddling with the soapy sponge and it slipped from his fingers into the water.

Jory looked down where it had fallen and then up into his face, his eyes so fiercely green she thought he might weep emeralds instead of tears.

"Don't you know that?" he asked, pouting his lips, and Lord, how she wished he would kiss her.

She nodded and licked her own lips, drawing his attention to the swelling where Digger had slapped her mouth. His pupils dilated as he cupped her cheek, tracing soapy bubbles across her lip with his thumb. She turned her face into his touch and pressed a kiss against the inside of his wrist. Then his face bent to meet hers, and he kissed her softly, but with a surprising hunger.

When he pulled back to examine her, she followed him, leaning up, out of the tub. Her kiss was far less gentle than his had been, tasting his lips and tongue to let him know they were the only things she hungered for in all the world, embracing the pain in her swollen lip, because the pain reminded her it was all real.

A draft caused her to shiver, and Finn pulled away again, as though suddenly realizing precisely what he'd been on the verge of doing, and he shook his head.

Jory hadn't once felt exposed until that moment, when he backed away from her as though she were the serpent in the garden. His kiss had been like everything she'd never imagined, his touch, what she'd always known but been unable to name. But now his look of horror and revulsion sent her reeling. She had never felt more vulnerable or ashamed.

He stumbled away and turned his back on her once more, running a hand through his wild ginger mane. "I should see to the horses," he said, though he made no move for the door.

"Truly?" She forced anger into her voice to mask the heartbreak lurking there. "Am I so repugnant you'd rather sleep with Sparradh?"

She shouldn't be hurt, she kept reminding herself. He'd made her no vow, nor been offered her hand. And yet she had thought he felt something for her, something deeper than duty or honor.

"Rather—?" He whirled on her, and his whole face went beet red when he saw her standing naked. He spun back around and then groped for a sheet of linen on the nearby bench and handed it to her. "Can you not see that ye—I'm trying to—it's my sworn duty to protect your virtue, mistress," he finally groaned.

"Perhaps it's not yours to protect."

She snatched the linen from him to dry herself and then wrapped it around for decency's sake, whatever decency could still be salvaged. "Look at me, Mr. Shaw."

He dipped his head but didn't look or turn around.

"Have the courage to face me when you reject me, damn you." Her voice wobbled and broke and she hated herself for it, but he turned around, hangdog, unable to meet her eyes.

"Reject you? Is that what ye think?"

"I know that my face may be pleasing enough, but my body is not desirable. Even Perseus wouldn't—"

"Perseus?" he asked, confused.

"I'm sure you must have been with a great many more perfect women."

Finn put a finger to her lips to silence her. "I havnae."

"Are you going to be a poet and tell me no such woman exists?"

"Aye, nor would I have bedded her if she did."

"Please, Mr. Shaw, we agreed to be honest with each other. Do not lie to me now. I don't hold it against you. You're a man, the son and brother of a laird, handsome and strong, and—"

He looked up, and for a moment she thought she saw hope, but then she blinked and it was anguish.

"I've no expectation—" she stammered, but he cut her off.

"Stop. Christ, please just stop," he begged, and so she did, her heart rending with each labored breath she drew.

Finn reached out with a trembling hand, and then faltered as he always faltered. It was the pause that made her tears start afresh, and she turned her head away. Then he caught her cheek, wiped the tear with his thumb, let his fingers stroke the side of her neck.

"My sins of lust and wantonness left me tied up like swine and my brother dead. I've spent the last ten years trying to atone for that night of weakness, for those sins, so as not to accrue any further black marks against my soul. I havnae lain wi' any woman."

His agonized confession brought her to tears once more. How she wished she could have been there for him back then, protected him from himself if that was what he needed to prevent whatever senseless, self-imposed chastity he'd pledged.

She reached out, tentatively, sweeping a wild ginger lock back into place, and he closed his eyes. "How can it be a sin if I want you to?"

His throat worked up and down to form a reply. "Dinnae ken," he finally whispered.

"I could die tomorrow."

He shook his head, then pressed his forehead to hers.

"I do not wish to die a virgin, nor do I—"

"Ye willnae die."

She drew a tremulous breath. "Nor do I wish to have stolen what I will not freely give. I was sent here at the request of a man who tried to take it when I was hardly yet a woman, who now seeks payment for *my* sins. I may not have control of my dowry, my future, or in many cases my own body, but this one thing ought to be mine to give."

"Of course it should."

"And yet..."

He took a step back, but the glint in his eye set her skin on fire.

Jory bit her lip to stop herself from blurting out that she loved him. It was the only explanation for her feelings, wanting him by her side at all times, and—though she wouldn't admit it—needing him, feeling stronger simply because he was there.

"Christ have mercy on my soul," he whispered, springing back to her like a coil and taking her face in both his hands to kiss her deeply, like a dying man receiving a drink. He pressed her back against the wall, kissing her jaw, her throat, her neck as she ran her fingers through his thick, wavy hair.

"Are you certain?" he paused long enough to ask, and when she nodded, he took her hand and led her to the bed, her damp towel falling forgotten to the floor.

His face flushed as he allowed himself to scan every inch of her, dropping his kilt, and at her insistence, slipping his sark off over his head as well. He kissed her cheeks, her ears, her temple, murmuring, "Marsali, Marsali," and her Gaelic name had never sounded more truly hers.

He kissed his way down her body, softly, gently, but hurriedly and with need, as though he'd been wanting to taste her every minute of every day they'd spent together, and when he finally returned to kiss her parched lips once more, his ferocious urgency set her tingling down to her core and beyond.

Finn trailed a thousand kisses and caresses down her belly and back up again until the ache in her back had vanished and she felt only the touch of his lips and the cool air upon her skin, until she squirmed with need and could feel him hard against her.

She lost herself in a swirl of sensation, of touch and temperature, his whispers tickling her ear and across her breasts as he called her beautiful, perfect, lovely.

"Sure?" he finally asked one last time, and she nodded and pulled him up to kiss her as he entered her, both of them gasping a little, and then she lost herself completely.

All night long, she lay curled against his side, breathing in the heady scent of him until his manhood found new life and began nuzzling her leg like an over-eager puppy. Then he eased back, and she rolled onto her side, smiling at him and trailing tentative fingers down his thigh until he caught her wrist to stop her, kissing her before whispering directly in her ear, "Any closer, and it'll all be over, mistress."

His tone sent a shiver straight to her most private parts, and Jory retracted her hand and climbed on top of him.

She straddled him, marveling at the way she could make his chest judder in barely rhythmic breaths. Even after touching herself, she'd never imagined joining together could be so... otherworldly. She'd never dared to hope he'd be equally as uninitiated as she was, that they could learn it all together. She wanted to torture him, to make him gasp and squirm for relief as he'd done to her, but she wasn't sure how much his confusing anatomy could endure.

Kissing his chest, she twisted the coarse reddish hairs in her fingers, enjoying the thunderous thudding of his heartbeat, until she realized it was her own heartbeat, pulsing in the vein of her neck and rushing in her ears, but it beat in perfect harmony with his own.

"Marsali," he whispered again, and she knew he was right. She was no longer Jory. He had changed her, remade her, and somehow, like her name, she was now whole.

Much slower than the first time, she eased onto him, and he nuzzled into her neck. In the morning they could worry about dowries and brothers and the future of the world. Tonight, there was only them and this and a hundred different sensations stealing her breath as she moved against him like an oar pulling water as he caressed her and kissed her, and they rowed right over a cliff together. She couldn't even distinguish their voices as they both cried out in passion and clung to each other to keep from drowning.

Chapter Twenty-One

The singing of a dotterel roused Jory before dawn. Lying prone and facing Finn, she felt sore in new places and a little bit shy. He was awake and watching her, his head propped up with one hand. Her whole body burned under his intense gaze, but she resisted the urge to bury her face in the bed-clothes.

He reached out, tracing feather-light patterns along her low shoulder and spine. He didn't seem repulsed by her crookedness, merely an eager lover looking for any excuse to touch skin, searing every inch he touched and leaving a chill in his wake.

"We have to leave soon," she whispered.

"Aye, we do," he breathed in her ear, kissing her tenderly, first her lobe and then her cheek, and then her neck, where it met her shoulder.

"Or we could stay here forever. Your friends could find somewhere else to live."

"D'ye think they'd mind?" he teased, and she couldn't help but giggle, which in turn made him grin. "I love it when ye laugh."

This time, she did bury her face, right up against his chest where the hairs tickled her nose. He continued tracing invisible shapes across her skin, his fingers nearly but not quite touching the edges of a stripe left behind by Roston's belt, and she couldn't help it when she flinched.

"Does it hurt verra much?" he asked.

She shook her head, though he wouldn't believe her.

Finn rolled off the bed taking his heat with him.

After rummaging in the cupboards, he returned a moment later with a small pot of ointment smelling of arnica and comfrey.

"May I?" he asked, holding it out. "I meant to last night, but..." He grinned sheepishly and raked a hand through his delightfully disheveled hair in a way that made Jory want to forgo the salve and wrap her legs around him again. Instead she nodded, and Finn sat down alongside her and began to rub the salve into her sore back. His touch was achingly tender, and she unclenched muscles in her stomach she hadn't realized were tensed.

It reminded her of the last time they'd met before the war. As usual, she was watching from a window as he sparred with Angus in the yard, this time using real swords. The elder brother had been in a fierce temper, giving the younger everything he had, though even from above, Jory could see Finn holding back. Angus landed blow after heavy blow on Finn's targe, and then when he managed to knock the shield from his little brother's hand, he landed blow after blow on Finn himself with the flat part of the sword.

At the time, Jory had been astonished Finn didn't shout for mercy, merely grunting as he absorbed each strike.

When Angus had finally worn himself out, Finn limped away to the stable to lick his wounds. Jory flew down to the kitchen and collected a bowl of water and clean linen, before following him.

He didn't acknowledge her, but neither did he tell her to go, and afraid of breaking some magical spell, she remained silent as well. She cleaned his bloodied knuckles and a few minor cuts, placed leaches around his swelling eye, and rubbed a balm into his back and arms, much like the one Finn was using on her now.

When she finished, he hung his head in defeat, unable to look her in the eye, but he had squeezed her hand—all the thanks she would ever need.

It was strange, Jory realized. Even at twelve she'd had no use for men, because what use had they ever had for her? And yet she was always fascinated by Finn, drawn to him. They were kindred spirits, motherless and lonely. She'd always wanted to be a safe harbor for his soul.

A few weeks later, he was off with the rest of the Shaws and Mackintoshes—her father included—and she hadn't seen him again for years. When he finally returned it was as the *Shaw Wretch*, lurking on the fringes of the occasional gathering, but mostly keeping out of sight.

He finished with the salve as the sun began to rise, and Jory could sense an invitation to mount him one last time but he was interrupted by the rumble of hooves, of Mr. Leask returning home as promised.

"We have to go," she whispered again, and he kissed her cheek. She hoped desperately that it wouldn't be for the last time.

"Aye," he whispered. "Aye, mo chridhe, we do."

Mr. Leask seemed to take more time than necessary before entering, enough so Jory was dressed in Mrs. Leask's spare shift and laces and Finn was securing his kilt when the older man finally came inside. He nodded to each, refraining from eye contact or comment on Jory's flushed cheeks or the satisfaction pouring off them both.

"Maidainn mhath," Finn said, and Mr. Leask grunted, offering them bannocks for the road.

Finn grew somber as he saddled Sparradh and Nell, causing his foster father to clap him on the shoulder.

Jory wished he would make some excuse for her to ride with

him, but rationally they needed as many horses as possible, since they had no idea how many girls were inside.

"If we're separated—" he began.

"Don't worry about me. Get those girls out," Jory said.

"Aye, but if we're separated make for the chapel, ye ken? I'll find ye there."

Jory nodded. They would certainly be separated and the chapel was as good a place as any to reunite.

"It's a good plan, lad," Leask said.

"Aye," Finn sighed, and Jory nodded her encouragement. It *was* a good plan, and besides, it was the plan they had, and the time for fretting about it was past.

They rode east in silence, across the fields instead of by the road, lest they encounter the remainder of the Watch again. The thought made Jory's bowels feel loose, and she took slow, deep breaths to settle them.

Sparradh and Nell kept pace side by side while Mr. Leask's roan steed pulled up the rear. Periodically Finn would glance at her, and she'd catch his eye and her nerve endings would crackle like a lit fuse heading for a crate of black powder.

As they drew nearer to the coast and the air grew tinged with brine and the cry of gulls, Jory began to feel like she was buzzing on the inside, vibrating with anticipation of what was to come.

When at last the silhouette of Bearradh Dearg loomed into view, Mr. Leask peeled off toward the nearby forest, and they continued up the path, the two of them alone.

Finn grew extremely fidgety, matching how Jory felt on the inside. "I've something to tell ye," he finally said.

"What—now?" she asked. She wasn't ready for deep conversation or proclamations of any kind.

"Aye, now. It's only—your da, he was with us at Preston."

Her... father? He wanted to speak of her father? "I know," she said swallowing back the disappointed relief that threatened to choke her.

"Then ye ken I'm responsible for making you an orphan."

"Why? Did you shoot him in the back?"

"No, I—"

"Then stop talking nonsense." She kicked Nell to continue up the path without him.

"But—"

"People die in battle Mr. Shaw." Jory turned the horse to face him, he looked so sad she couldn't stand it. "You were a soldier, you knew the risks. So did he."

"Not all the risks, maybe."

"He never got over her, you know. He mourned my mother every day for twelve years. Sometimes I think he went chasing after war hoping it would afford him the chance to see her again." She wanted to ride back to him, to kiss him and wipe his guilt away. But she was meant to be a nun, and out here, anyone could see.

A Gordon clansman met them at the door and gruffly allowed them to enter the empty Hall. Jory's breath quickened and she fidgeted with the folds of her skirt. Finn touched her elbow and offered her an attempt at a bolstering smile. She nodded, her breath returning to normal at least.

After several agonizing minutes, Boyd Gordon's brother appeared.

She recognized him immediately, though he was nine years more haggard, with wrinkles and sun spots marking his once pale skin. Still the same straight blond hair and aristocratic nose, his once-perfect features were marred only by the thick, ropey scar circumnavigating his visage.

Long Thomas swept an assessing gaze from Finn's boots to his face and down again. His left eye twitched as though he distantly remembered but was unable to place him. Then he turned his beady, adder-like stare on Jory. She felt weak, her legs starting to go, but Finn stepped close to accept her weight without her having to lean at all.

"At last," Long Thomas almost hissed, and Jory fought a tremor which might have given her away. "Mackintosh, was it?"

Perhaps it was her imagination, but she thought she discerned a momentary flicker of recognition. It took everything in her to smile and not throw up.

Her lips moved, but the words sounded far away, the voice not her own. "Mr. Gordon. My apologies for our delayed arrival."

"Nonsense." Long Thomas let his gaze roam her body.

At her side, Finn flexed his sword hand.

"Let me show you around your new home."

"There's papers to be signed," Finn interjected as Long Thomas reached for her elbow.

"Of course." He retracted his hand.

"You're the laird of Clan Gordon?" Finn asked.

"I'm the laird of this castle."

Finn took the papers from his sporran. The wax had been replaced as though he and Mr. Leask had never read its contents.

"But you sign the alliance on behalf of Clan Gordon?"

Long Thomas smirked, glancing down at the papers before studying Finn's face for the first time. "Ah, but the Chattan clans didn't make an agreement with Clan Gordon. They made it with my own emissary. My men and I will be the best of friends to the Mackintoshes and the rest."

"And the Watch?" Finn asked.

Long Thomas shrugged. "I'll have a word."

"What more could we ask?" Finn said in a tone perhaps only Jory would recognize as sarcasm.

The Gordon shrugged and then called to an unseen servant, "Bring me a quill and ink."

But Finn extracted both from his sporran, as well.

"You're quite prepared."

"Quite."

Long Thomas held the papers against the wall and scribbled a blotchy signature before shoving them back at Finn. " 'Tis an arduous journey. Thank you for delivering such precious cargo," he added, tossing him a coin in dismissal, but Finn let it fall to the ground untouched.

"An arduous journey, yes," Jory agreed, finding her voice in the strength of Finn's rebellion. "One he'll be eager to reverse *tomorrow*."

Even though he wasn't really leaving her behind, it all felt too real, and she wasn't ready to let him go yet. She swallowed back bile, and then turned her most charming smile on Long Thomas Gordon. "Surely you mean to invite him to sup?"

Gordon didn't miss a beat. He smirked condescendingly at them both. "I'm sure the kitchen maid can find something for you while I give our new sister a tour."

He extended his elbow and placed Jory's hand in the crook, covering it with his other palm, trapping her. With a tight smile, she felt rather than saw Finn take a step towards them, and so she turned back to him with a warning in her eye.

"Good sir," she said, "I do hope we meet again before you depart back home. But in case we do not, please allow me to say..."

Her mind went blank because she had so many things still left unsaid, and her throat grew tight with tears that couldn't possibly be shed.

"Allow me to say that your loyalty and chivalry throughout this journey—well, I am forever indebted and grateful."

She extricated her hand from Gordon with a tug, meaning to shake Finn's, but he took it and pressed his lips to the back without ever breaking his steadfast lock upon her eyes. For the second time in as many minutes, she couldn't breathe, but this time it was for all the right reasons, and from his touch she tried to draw every last ounce of strength and courage.

"It has been my honor, mistress."

Then Gordon put his arm around her and moved her away.

Jory tried not to shudder or retreat from his touch, but when his hand drifted to the small of her back, she couldn't help it.

He looked at her askance.

"I should love to see the chapel," she said.

"Of course." Gordon led her through the Great Hall, past tapestries depicting biblical scenes. Pointing to a corner exit, he called over his shoulder to Finn, "The kitchen is through there. And the laundry, as well," he added for Jory's benefit. "The sisters take their meals here in the Hall, and those with the skill help cook."

To the left was a small vestibule, boasting a stained-glass scene of St. Andrew in ornate shades of scarlet and sea-toned blues. The rows of wooden benches and small stone altar were covered in a fine layer of dust from infrequent use, but the gruesome depiction of the crucified fisherman helped to steel Jory's resolve.

"There's no perpetual adoration?"

He smiled quickly. "Not yet."

A tabernacle stood on the otherwise barren altar, and the door was not quite shut. "But where are all the sisters?" she asked, turning her focus to Gordon.

His glance flicked to the tabernacle and then back to her.

"They're engaged in silent reflection. Now," he guided her towards the bastion, where dark stairs led both up and down, and he gestured for her to climb up. She thought she might suffocate inside the stuffy turret, waiting for him to attack her from behind, but he merely followed a little too closely. It was almost hysterical how everything was upside-down, as she ascended to the depths of hell. He led her down a winding corridor surprisingly empty of fire and brimstone, to a room off by itself.

"My quarters?" Jory asked.

"In due time." He opened the door to what was clearly his public chamber, fitted with a large desk, a chair, and slightly out of place in one corner, a divan.

"Where is the priest? Father...?" she babbled, because to keep him talking felt safest.

"On an errand. Please, have a seat." He offered her the armchair and leaned back upon his desk, allowing the sunshine to properly light his face for the first time.

The scar, though not quite as pronounced as Digger had intimated, bisected the same brow which had once held a childhood scar and stretched from his left temple all the way down his neck, where it disappeared into his collar. Even as he stared at her, Jory couldn't decide if the eye was still functional or not.

Studying him properly in the light prompted a visceral memory of stabbing wildly with the sgian dubh, and Jory could feel her hand dragging it down the length of his face, leaving behind a permanent reminder of what he tried to do.

"Now tell me, madam, have you any skills?"

She blinked, coming back to the present. "Skills?"

"Our community grows larger day by day. Everyone must contribute to keep it running."

"Do the sisters work in the community then? Helping the poor?" Jory asked, feigning interest. "How many of us are there?"

"Not nearly enough." He laughed. "Would you care for some claret?"

Without waiting for an answer, Gordon selected a decanter and two crystal goblets from a shelf in the corner of his chamber, near the window.

"No. Thank you." Jory smiled demurely. "I've so many questions. How will I occupy my days? When will I take my orders?"

"All in good time." His words filled her with dread. How long would it take Finn to find the missing girls, and how much time had passed so far?

"Have you a little garden? With herbs and the like? Or a patch of soil for planting one perhaps?"

"Are you nervous?" he asked, the barely concealed smirk returning to his lips.

Jory opened and then closed her mouth. "Excited," she finally said with a shrug.

He came and stood before her, too close, belt buckle and the arousal barely constrained by his breeches right there at eye level. "Good."

She forced a smile that she was certain he would know was fake, even with one good eye.

"You're to be a nun," he said in a soft, almost seductive way and acid rushed up the back of her throat once more. *You're the tutor's ward*, he had said the first time.

"Yes," she replied.

"Nuns must be chaste."

"That does seem to be standard."

"Such a waste," he lamented. "And are you?"

"A waste, sir?"

"Chaste, madam."

She didn't know how to react. Should she pretend to be surprised? Affronted? Horrified? Frightened? He was waiting for a response, so it was too late to pretend to be anything but repelled. "My uncle would not have sent me here otherwise."

He laughed, sharp, quick, humorless. "I'm sure he believes so. You understand of course, I cannot take chances, I can't simply take your word for it."

"Is it not between myself and the Lord, sir?"

Another short laugh. Jory reminded herself to take slow, even breaths, counting them as she went.

"Perhaps it should be between the three of us, with God as witness."

"I don't understand," she lied. Somehow she had not expected him to get down to the business of things quite so immediately.

He sneered at her again, then turned away to pace before the window, and Jory feared he might see too much, if Finn's mission was in progress.

"I feel quite faint," she said, standing suddenly. "Perhaps I should have that glass of wine."

"Perhaps you should."

His attention successfully diverted back to Jory and the wine, she looked around the room as he poured it. Perhaps her dowry was here in his chamber. There was no trunk, no saddlebag, no chest of any kind. And then she spied the sgian dubh lying upon his desk. *Her* sgian dubh. Or more accurately, the one she'd carried since winning it off him nine years ago—until she lost it to Baen yesterday. Which meant the rent collectors had beaten her here.

She snuck a look at Gordon. He was watching her intently. He knew she'd seen it. He'd left it there for her to see—a test—and her reaction had proven without a doubt who she was. She held his gaze for a moment as he held the wine, and then they both lunged for the knife.

FINN WAS SICK WITH DREAD AT LETTING JORY GO OFF WITH THE vermin Long Thomas. It was the right thing, he supposed, all according to plan. He had to let her go so they could carry out the rest, but he didn't have to like it.

As soon as Gordon led her into the chapel, Finn slipped across to the opposite stairs.

The place was deathly quiet—too quiet for a convent, he thought. But perhaps not for a brothel at this time of day, late enough the sailors had stumbled back from their shore leave, and anyone else had returned to town. He came to a chamber and pressed his ear against the door to hear the muffled murmurs on the other side, then opened the door and stepped in.

Three women stared back at him, and then flew at him with a broom and an iron poker from the fire. "Peace!" he whispered, holding up both hands in surrender. "Peace."

"Who are you?" asked the oldest, a raven-haired lass with the darkest eyes he'd ever seen, like a selkie straight out of Jory's tale.

"My name's Finlay Shaw. I've come to rescue you, if that's what you need."

"Shaw?" she repeated.

"Rescue?" the youngest asked, no more than fifteen.

"Aye. Unless you really are brides of Christ or... anything else, and happy about it. Are you Abel's wee girl?"

She nodded back at him eagerly.

"I've come to return you to your da."

The third woman threw herself at his feet sobbing.

"Is this a trick?" the dark-haired one asked. "Do you expect payment? We've nothing to our names."

"No, I swear it." Finn crossed to the tiny window and looked out, attempting to get his bearings though it was hardly large enough. "How many of you are there?"

"About thirty, I suppose."

He stifled a gasp. "And guards?"

"At least half a dozen. Always in and out of the place, never the same ones for long."

"Could be useful," Finn speculated.

"Are you alone?" the youngest asked, opening the door to peek into the corridor for a moment.

"My friends are in the woodland to the west. Are ye allowed outside?"

"Not often," the first replied. "We tend a garden inside the walls, and occasionally we go down to the shore to gather mussels and clams."

It might be possible to sneak a few of the girls out under the auspices of a beach combing party, but not all of them. He'd have to think of something else.

"Is there a dungeon?" he asked.

"Aye," the girl who had wept at his feet volunteered. "I found it once... I've never been able to summon the courage to go back. There's a door down there, but it's locked."

It would likely be a one-way drop outside the castle walls, meant for waste disposal. From there they'd have to take their chances crossing the meadow to the woods, but it was apt to be the safest bet.

"You remember the way?" he asked, and she nodded. "Good lass. Can you spread the word to the others?"

The youngest bobbed her head, eager to duck out of the chamber.

"If Long Thomas was storing money—gold or even jewels— where would it be hidden?" he asked the others.

"The payments you mean? He splits them with the priest. Some of it they take away, but until they do, Scarface hides it in the chapel, doesn't he?" the raven-haired lass asked her companion who nodded vigorously.

"All right then. We go quick and quiet-like, and then you don't stop until you see three fellas wi' a wagon hiding right inside the trees."

He sent them down the stairs in groups of two and three, listening for footsteps between each group. Surely Long Thomas would arrive upstairs with Jory soon, and he urged them to hurry.

With more than a little distress over following the orders of a strange man, the lasses of Bearradh Dearg eventually assembled in the bowels of the keep.

There were whispered demands as to why the one had never mentioned finding the door before, and skepticism that they wouldn't all perish on the other side, but Finn ignored them, tugging against the rusted chain until it threatened to rip the hide clean off his palms. The fear of being found by a guard and imprisoned, of never seeing Jory again, outweighed the risk of noise, and he finally gave up and smashed the lock with his sword before prying the creaky door open.

Then he froze at the sound of footsteps on the stairs, a finger to his lips as the girls gasped and huddled closer together. Light and fast the footsteps came and his heart leapt in his throat, waiting for Jory to emerge, but it was a brunette who had stayed behind to make sure everyone got out.

One by one he helped the lasses lower themselves down, giving them explicit directions on keeping low to the ground and running as quickly as possible to Leask and the Roddies awaiting them in the forest.

Near the back of the line, a blonde with an already tear-streaked face began to blubber that she couldn't possibly go through the rank hole into the unknown below. As her cries grew louder, and her refusal more certain, Finn thought he might have to knock her out or gag her, but there was no one left to help drag her to the forest once she was outside.

He took her scrawny shoulders in each of his hands, startling her into silence. "What's the most beautiful thing ye can think of?"

"My kitten," she whispered in surprise.

Finn nodded. "And just think how many kittens are on the other side of that door. So verra many."

Finally the lass nodded and followed the others through.

By rights, he should have gone with them to fight off any Gordons who may try to follow. But what could he really do, one sitting duck with a sword in a meadow, against guards who might watch from the battlements with pistols or bows? Precious little. The girls would have to take their chances as Jory was doing even now, for he would not leave her behind, no matter the plan.

As soon as he saw the last girl safely out of the castle, he crept back up to the main floor and crossed the Hall to the chapel, but there was no sign of Jory yet.

It really was a lovely chamber, reminiscent of the chapel from Finn's childhood at Tordarroch, except for the grandeur of the stained glass. The carven statuary was of a similar style, though, and as he gazed upon the crucifix for a moment, he thought sheepishly back to his coupling with Jory, the unrivaled ecstasy of it, like two hands fitting perfectly together. Had everything he'd been taught of abstinence and self-recrimination been wrong?

Then he shook himself out of his reverie, straining his ears for footsteps. He'd give her five more minutes, but if the lass didn't turn up then, he'd have to go find her. He didn't even want to give her that long, but she'd have his bollocks for breakfast if he wrecked the plan now.

In the meantime, he began to search for the treasure the girls had said was often stored here. There were no obvious hiding places. Perhaps a loose stone hid the loot, but when he traced the mortar between them with his fingers, nothing could be pried loose.

Then steel scraped across steel as behind him, a sword was unmistakably drawn.

Finn drew his own, and it fairly sang with life after being buried in Leask's cellar for so long. He turned to face the entrance before flinging himself down behind the feeble protection of a wooden bench.

It was one lone guard, the same one who let them in and then stood lurking in the shadows when they first arrived.

"Lost?" the guard asked.

"I... verra much enjoy the... architecture and masonry of castle chapels. I came in to admire the stonework and... fell asleep," he lied half-heartedly.

"Chapels have that effect. And then ye woke up and thought ye'd have a poke around?" the guard asked, stepping closer.

Satisfied there was only one man, Finn found his feet and edged himself along the side wall towards the door the guard had vacated in order to follow him. "Wouldn't anyone?"

"Appeared you might be looking for something."

Finn shrugged. "Had to try my luck, didn't I?" He held out the silver coin he'd picked up after Long Thomas left with Jory. "Eight days' trouble. I fought off bandits and chased after an ungrateful and uncooperative wench. She nearly gutted me for my trouble, and your master gave me this. I hope your wage is less of an insult."

"He'll pay me handsome enough when I tell him I've castrated a thief." The guard grinned, showing two missing incisors from a row of jagged teeth.

Then he lunged. Their swords clanged, the vibrations carrying all the way down Finn's arm and into his heart, which pumped them right back out again as blood charged with the heat of battle. But the guard had the better position, wedged as Finn was between benches and wall, more worn out than he'd realized after last night's activities.

He countered the guard blow for blow and thrust for thrust, until Finn tried to throw him off by stepping forward, pushing his sword up to give himself room to slip away. It was a beginner's mistake, which he wouldn't have made on more sleep. The guard lost no time, hooking Finn's raised hands with the cross guard, forcing his arms higher until he could bash his pommel into Finn's chin.

He landed like a sack of grain, hitting a wooden bench on his way down. Lucky that, or they'd be wiping his brains up off the polished stone.

Laughing, the guard flipped Finn onto his stomach and pressed a knee into his back to hold him still while he garroted his wrists and snatched his dirk. It was every shameful failure of Finlay Shaw's entire life rolled into one, exactly what he'd feared would happen, and what he had sworn an oath to prevent. He couldn't help Jory now. He was no use to her—no use to anyone.

Every good and right thing he'd ever done couldn't possibly make up for letting her down now.

"I know of a treasure," he gasped as the guard dragged him to his feet. "The dowry of the lass I brought. Free me. Help me find it, and I'll share it wi' ye."

The guard ignored him, shoving Finn so he stumbled out of the chapel and towards the stairs leading to the dungeons below.

"Let me go and it's yours. Every last coin."

The guard simply shoved him harder.

At a different set of descending stairs, they were met by another guard. Finn thrashed and swung like a wild boar, like a prehistoric bear, like madness itself untethered. He would not let them chain him below without a fight.

Together they tumbled down the stairs, and on the landing Finn scrambled to his feet, using his full height and weight to fight them both together, with no sword or dirk to help him. Every time they got near him, he threw them off again like fleas, snarling and gnashing his teeth to appear all the more fearsome— and take off a finger if they came too close.

Twisting around, he gained the advantage, maneuvering his bound hands over the smaller guard's throat. But a punch to the gut from the other guard freed his comrade, and together the two crowded Finn backwards, away from the safety of the stairs, away from Jory, wherever she may be.

Between the two of them, they got his right hand manacled to the wall before he managed to claw one guard off with his left, leaving a streak of blood across his cheek. Thus restrained, though, they had an easy time finishing the job. He almost managed to bite one guard's ear when he bent down to perform a final weapons check.

So this was how he would die, chained to a wall and left to imagine a room above where Long Thomas must surely be violating the woman he loved.

And he did love her.

What an absolute failure of a man.

He howled in fury, and then the guard who caught him in the chapel raised the hilt of his sword and bashed Finn in the head, and the world went sideways and then dark.

Chapter Twenty-Two

Gordon's filthy fingernails reached the knife seconds ahead of Jory, knocking the hilt as he tried to grab it, so it skittered across the desk. Her last hope of self-defense dashed, Jory altered course and backed up, unable to look away from the scar, bulging and angry-red near his ear, fading to a hot, more furious white as it roped its way down past his chin.

His mouth broke into a jagged sneer causing the scar to writhe across his face like a snake attempting to shed its dried-up old skin. "I knew the priest could persuade them to send you," he said.

In one stride he closed the distance between them, grabbing her shoulders in both of his hands and shoving her against the wall and down onto the divan. "Do you remember me? Do you think on me each day as I have thought on you each time I looked in a mirror, each time I scratch an itch that can't be reached?"

He stroked her face, tracing the shape of his own scar upon her skin with his fingernail, down to the neckline of her dress, which he clutched in his fist like he meant to rip it away. Jory held perfectly still, not breathing, as though his very touch were venomous and ready to sink sharp fangs into her flesh.

"Each time another dares gape at me and cannot hide their disgust—oh yes, I have thought of you every day, the little bird that would not be caught, the filly that would not be tamed."

He studied her from top to bottom, the full length of her, and Jory could not have felt more exposed were she stripped bare before a thousand witnesses.

"And now look at you. Little Miss Mackintosh all grown up. It's time for you to repay your debt."

He drew a deep breath as though he were inhaling the essence of her, and Jory felt her mind beginning to separate itself from her body. She had no weapon, no hope of escape from this madman, and Finn was busy trying to rescue the innocent ones. He couldn't help her this time.

"I will have what's owed to me," Gordon practically purred.

"You have my dowry already. Surely it more than settles any debt."

"It does not."

She closed her eyes, trying not to smell his putrid breath, ripe with decay, or feel it on her neck. And in the stillness she heard Finn's voice. *You are powerful, Jory Mackintosh. Take back your power.*

She forced a laugh she didn't feel and relished the shock that flickered across his face. "I bested you as a girl. Do you really think you're man enough to take me now?"

Gordon slammed his hands around her throat, knocking her head against the wall so hard her eyes watered.

She whispered Finn's words to herself, though no sound could escape her lips.

"What was that?" Gordon asked, easing his stranglehold a tiny bit.

"I take back my power," she growled.

Then she tucked her chin, grabbed his forearms, and pulled him towards her. It caught him off balance like Finn said it would, and she brought up her knee right into his groin. He crumpled to the ground, rocking and clutching himself and gasping for breath as tears leaked from the corners of his eyes.

Not wasting any time, Jory leaped over his writhing form to scoop up her knife from the far edge of his desk, when a ruby ring on the bookcase caught her eye. She leaned over the desk, stretching to snatch it up, dropped it into her pocket, then raced to the door.

Gordon reached out to catch her leg in a last attempt to stop her, and she paused long enough to swipe a ring of keys from his loosened belt and kick him again between the legs so he curled onto his side, retching.

She flew down the stairs, nearly tripping and rolling the whole way. When she reached the main level, she could hear footsteps approaching from below so she raced out of the turret and across the Great Hall. If she couldn't seek a moment's sanctuary in the chapel, then what was even the point of God?

Inside the chapel, benches had been overturned all helter-skelter. The tabernacle door still stood slightly ajar. Hastening to the decorative vessel, she crossed herself and then opened it. There she found, not the holy sacrament, but a plain burlap sack filled with money. Hers or not, she snatched it and closed the door, then she turned her back on the altar to take in the rest of the scene.

There'd been some sort of scuffle by the look of it, but where had everyone gone?

A sword glinted on the floor between a bench and the wall, and when Jory stepped closer, she found a dark puddle of blood, and she sucked in her breath. Finn had planned to meet her here, and he'd surely come, but was it his blood or someone else's? And would he return?

She was absolutely going to be sick.

Dropping heavily onto a bench, she set the bag beside her and took the stolen ring from her pocket. It was her father's ring.

What would he do if he were here now? Should she take it on faith that Finn got out, and make her own way to the forest? Should she search for him or wait here obediently for his return?

That would make her father laugh. She'd never been one for obedience.

She peeked at the bloody floor again. Could a real physician tell whose was whose just by looking? Shuddering, she pulled her gaze away, and there, by her foot, was a silver brooch she recognized immediately as belonging to a Shaw, the words FIDE ET FORTITUDINE circled a dexter arm holding a dagger. Fide et Fortitudine, faithfulness and courage, and who in her life had ever shown her the meaning of those words but the *Shaw Wretch*? She had to find him. She scooped up the brooch, nestling it and her father's ring inside the sack for safekeeping, and then crept to the doorway.

Scarcely breathing, Jory listened for more footsteps, but only silence met her ears. If those heavy masculine steps had sought out their master, they'd have found him by now.

Outside the chapel, the Hall was deserted, the exit unbarred. The guards could have been down in the dungeons for anything, but somehow she knew—like an invisible fishing line directly through her heart was guiding her into the dim passage leading down into the bowels of the earth.

FINN'S HEAD ACHED AS THOUGH IT HAD BEEN REPEATEDLY trampled by a team of fully grown Clydesdales. In the blurred shadows he could swear he saw her, Jory, floating before him like an angel in a white shift.

When he shook his head, she vanished. For a moment, he tried to slip back into semiconsciousness to see her one last time, kiss her full lips, smell her, and remember what it meant to be alive. But then, as though bitten by a flea, he realized if he ever wanted to see her again—and should he be very lucky, kiss her as well—then he must get free.

He pulled himself to his feet with the help of his chains, and yanked on each one with all his strength, but it was no use. There was no escaping the iron manacles that bound him, short of gnawing off his own arm. Would Leask and the others come looking for him? Or, as he'd instructed, the moment the last girl settled into the wagon, would they head for the safety of Aberdeen?

And what of Jory?

The vision of Long Thomas slithering sweaty fingers down her bosom enraged him enough to try again—to almost believe he could dislodge the entire wall with the pure force of his hatred—but the stones were solid, and he howled once more in frustration. If only the guards had left his dirk, he imagined he might have been able to pull off some impossible feat of flexibility and cut off his hand. He could fight with one if he had to.

Would Angus laugh at his demise? Or shake his head in disgust—one more in a long string of failures? What hubris, to hope any plan of his might actually succeed.

"There you are. Just hanging around leaving me to do all the work?"

His apparition had returned, and this time she stood before him with disheveled hair, one hand on her hip, not angelic at all but feisty and full of spark, exactly the way he liked her best.

In this dream, she carried his sword, like an archangel straight from battling Lucifer. She propped it against the wall, and he marveled at the sound of steel against stone.

The phantom scanned his bruised and bloodied face in the flickering torchlight, and he tried not to wither under her gaze.

"Thank you for coming back to me. I didnae wish to die wi' out imagining your face one last time," he gasped.

"Die? You're not going to die."

Frowning, she shifted a sack hanging over her shoulder, and she no longer had the soft look of a dream about her.

Finn blinked. "Are ye real then?"

"I hope so. What did they do to you? Have you been drugged?"

"Nah." He shook his head, aggravating the pain, causing the dungeon walls to swim around him. "Ye must get out, mistress. Save yourself. There's a door—I dinnae ken if it can be reached from here, but on the opposite side of the dungeon, there's a door. Ye must find it. It'll drop ye outside the castle walls."

"You can show me," she whispered, withdrawing a ring of iron keys from her pocket.

Finn sagged with relief, tipping his head back to laugh, but even to his ears it sounded like weeping.

Waiting was its own fresh torture, smelling her hair as she fumbled through six wrong keys, trying each one unsuccessfully before finally clicking the left manacle open. He didn't give her a chance to unlock his right hand before cupping her face, stroking her hair, pulling her in for a kiss that made him dizzy again.

She dropped the keys.

"Control yourself, Mr. Shaw. I shall have to start all over now."

She bent to pick them up as he murmured, "Worth it," for he wanted nothing more than to kiss her and keep kissing, fiercely, battling his tongue against hers and assuring himself she was whole.

"The girls?" she asked, as she tried each key over again.

"I got them safely out of the keep and came straight back in for you. Had a notion your dowry might be hid in the wee chapel. You found it?"

"Found something. But I appreciate your foolish risk all the same."

"I made a vow. Did he hurt ye?"

"No. Not much. He tried to choke me, but he was little match for your tutelage." She glanced up at him with a small smile, and Finn reached out to touch her again.

She tried another key, and his manacle slipped off, and Finn took her face in both hands to kiss her properly.

"We must go now," she whispered.

Chapter Twenty-Three

When Jory offered Finn his sword, her hand brushed against his, sending a thrill up her arm. Their eyes met for a moment, and she saw the light from all the stars in the night sky and all the stories to go with them. "Come," she murmured, snatching one of the torches from its sconce on the wall.

They hurried along the dungeon corridor, but came up short—only three more cells, reeking of human excrement and God knew what else. There was no door, no drop to the outside, not even a waste chute or tunnel from this dungeon to the one from which Finn had helped the girls escape.

"We'll have to go up."

"The main door was unguarded just now," Jory said, but she should've held her tongue for when they emerged into the Hall, they found the biggest, burliest guard she'd ever seen. He almost made Finn look like a child.

Jory retreated into the shadows of the turret, as did Finn, nearly treading on her feet in his haste. "Up then," she whispered, but it was too late.

"We've been spotted." He nodded toward the guard, who was advancing on them, cat-like despite his bulk, sword at the ready.

"What do we do?"

"Keep to the edges along the tapestries. Make your way to the door, slow as you can until you're beyond his seeing. I'll distract him. When you reach the door, for Christ's sake, run."

"What about you?" She doubted there was time to bring Leask and the Roddies to help.

"Forget about me."

There was a resignation in the way he said it which Jory didn't like, as though while chained he'd made up his mind to die and hadn't quite gotten over it.

"It's no good," she said, stamping her foot. "Think of a better plan."

"Go," Finn ordered, every ounce the commander he didn't believe himself capable of being, and somehow Jory couldn't refuse. One glance at his pleading look, and she found herself slowly edging her way along the tapestries, which up close and in the torchlight proved the furthest thing from biblical—scenes of debauchery of every fathomable kind.

She ripped her gaze away from the woven horror at the sound of Finn grunting as he held off the giant. Each echo of steel meeting steel made her flinch. As when she was a child, she couldn't ignore the certain knowledge that he was disadvantaged in this fight.

She stood there, frozen, caught between his order to run and a higher order to assist him. What was the point of escaping at all if he wouldn't be at her side afterwards? Was it so absurd to believe they might escape together? She'd once thought it impossible to fall in love, and now it seemed impossible to go on living without it.

Boots thundered down the stairs, and they were joined by Long Thomas Gordon and a second guard. The guard made a beeline for Finn, but Gordon loped towards Jory, striding quickly but gingerly across the Hall.

She transferred the torch to her left hand, drawing the sgian dubh with her right, but she felt completely exposed and unprepared.

"Still here?" Long Thomas sneered. "It's time I showed you what happens to people who cross me. A clue: they seldom live to try it twice."

"Perhaps it's you who should be wary of crossing me."

"You? You're nothing. A broodmare who doesn't know when she's beat. No, my girl, the only solution for you is to be broken. And I will relish breaking you."

Jory focused on Gordon, even as she followed the sounds of Finn's skirmish, his huffs of breath and the clangor of swords as he worked to fend off the two guards single-handedly.

Gordon wore a sword but hadn't yet drawn it. She needed to keep him focused on her lest he join the fray, further lopsiding the odds.

"How disappointing it must have been for you, to find me unbroken," she said.

Furiously, Gordon lunged at her, and she waved the torch in his face to keep the monster at bay.

Finn had, as usual, been correct. Armed with a sword, if Gordon got close enough for her to use her sgian dubh on him, she'd be dead.

He came at her a second time, and she jumped away, swinging the torch at him once more.

"Have a care, mistress," Finn shouted at her before a third guard came flying towards him, drawing his attention back to his own fight.

Next thing Jory knew, the tapestries were going up in smoky flame, melting into even more grotesque images as they burned and curled, and she dropped the torch in surprise. Long Thomas retreated towards the middle of the Hall. She froze, trying to think what on earth to do next.

"The door," Finn yelled, seizing the moment's distraction to run his blade through the back of the smaller guard's neck, snatching up the man's weapon as he fell. "Get to the door!"

But the flames were spreading, up and sideways, and more rapidly than Jory would have thought possible as black, oily smoke filled the room. Even if she made it to the door, she couldn't leave him here.

He pivoted to face her, still defending blows from the massive guard when yet another appeared.

"They're all gone, milord," the guard called to Long Thomas as he flew out of the shadows towards Finn.

"Gone?"

"All the rooms are empty," the guard replied, before landing a blow Finn absorbed with his own weapon as though it were nothing at all.

The girls had all escaped. Jory breathed a sigh of relief, but when she looked to the massive wooden doors, she found they'd been enveloped in flame.

"You set that fire on purpose, didn't ye?" Finn teased, stepping up beside her.

Jory blinked and he tossed her the two-handed sword he'd taken off his smallest assailant. It was heavier than she might have hoped given her exhaustion, but light enough to manage for now. She spun back in time to meet Gordon, whose eyes danced wickedly like the flames consuming his castle.

His blade clashed against hers, and she breathed in the jolt as it shot all the way to her jaw, rattling her teeth.

Back to back, she and Finn fought the three remaining Gordons the same way they had fought in the bailey yard at Castle Moy as children, giving each other the will to absorb and return each mighty blow, their feet moving to a rhythm only they could hear, like some kind of inside-out ceilidh.

The smoke choked her and burned her eyes. They might die in this room, but at least they'd be together. She drew strength from his strength and wielded the weapon more deftly than she would have imagined possible a week ago.

Finn dropped the newest guard, and they were down to the giant and Gordon, who danced around them gleefully waiting for his moment to strike.

"Keep your left elbow up, mistress. Ye've always had a habit of letting it dip and stick out like a chicken wi' a broken wing."

Jory tucked and lifted her arm immediately, and it gave her fresh power and resolve. This was what she was meant for, the woman she was born to be, fighting alongside Finn.

If they got out alive, she'd tell him the truth: they were one and the same—had been since they were children—and she loved him deeply. Perhaps she had since they were children, too, even before his mother gave him to her with the instruction to protect his left side.

His words looped through her mind again and again. *Ye've always had a habit,* he said, but she hadn't picked up a sword since she was nine years old. All this time she thought he'd forgotten, but could he possibly remember fighting alongside her that fateful day?

THE GIANT WAS BEGINNING TO TIRE, STRUGGLING FOR BREATH against the smoke. Finn thrust and parried, studying the big man's moves, until finally he could predict them, and with an apologetic prayer he thrust his sword into the unprotected fleshy gap below the ribs and heaved upward with every last ounce of his strength.

The guard fell back, nearly toppling Finn as he struggled to free his blade from the giant's ribcage.

There was no sign of Long Thomas now. Jory's head swiveled

frantically—she'd lost him in the smoke. The coward probably knew many escape routes out of his own lair.

The entire Hall was aflame, the very paint on the untapestried portions of wall beginning to shrivel and glow like hot coals, and their path to the other dungeon was cut off by a fallen beam. They would have to go up to find another way down.

Grabbing Jory's hand, Finn raced up the only staircase not yet aflame.

"Wait," she panted. "Wait."

"The air'll be better above," Finn coaxed, but still, he paused on the gallery of the second floor, rubbing her back as she coughed.

"You remember," she gasped at him. "All this time, you remembered."

She meant of course that he recalled the day when his sparring partners had turned on him and a little girl dressed up in breeks and cap had flown into the fray like a cat with claws, helping him to vanquish them all.

Despite personal danger, despite risking his ire, she had jumped in to protect his weak side. And though Finn had been childishly ashamed to be assisted by a lassie, he realized even then the wee Mackintosh could always be counted on. She'd been willing to cover his weak side for quite some time, and he didn't want her to ever stop.

"I remember every moment," he said, stroking a thumb across her cheek and kissing her quickly, chastely, before taking her hand once more. "Come, we must go."

"There's nowhere *to* go," she gasped. "There's no way out."

"There's always a way out."

They ran towards another set of stairs, the heat and smoke at last receding behind them. But then Gordon stepped out of the shadows, the devil who refused to die. Though she still held her sword, Finn pushed Jory behind him to confront the man alone.

234

"The girl is quite right. There's no way out, but give her to me, and you can try to save yourself."

Finn growled low in his throat. "You dinnae recognize me, do you, Thomas-Boy? Long Thomas Gordon to those who serve him, but Scarface among the rest of his kin."

Gordon shook his head. "You're no one. Merely a Shaw Wretch. An errand boy for the Chattan Confederation. A Jacobite drudge."

"So ye do recognize me? I'm flattered."

Then Finn leaped on Gordon, and they fought, sword to sword, groaning and stumbling and cursing blue oaths. Finally he landed a blow and Gordon yelped like a dog in pain, cradling his arm.

"If I were the best of men, I'd help ye escape along wi' us, though you're scum who deserves to burn in hell for your misdeeds."

"There's no escape," Gordon gasped once more.

"If I were a bad man, I'd kill ye now, and not even be damned for it, because it would spare you the torment you surely deserve."

Finn stepped up a stair above Gordon and kicked him in the chest so he fell down and slid across the stone to the middle of the floor.

"But I'm only a man, and this one mercy I will grant—the chance to find your own way out of this inferno if ye can."

Then he grabbed Jory around the waist hauling her up the stairs, and they continued their feverish ascent.

Stumbling more than running, Finn half-dragged Jory along behind him, until the stairs finally came to an end. Then he pulled her through to the battlements and they ran along the top of the castle, gulping in fresh air as the salty wind whipped their faces.

"This is your plan?" she asked. "To what, wait until the fire burns itself out?"

Finn shook his head. "In some places the stone may well grow stronger, but in others it'll be weak, brittle, almost hollow. Far too treacherous. Nae, we go now."

He slowed his gait, searching over the parapet for the perfect spot.

And then the lass understood his plan and hung back. "You can't be serious."

"Aye. You jump, I jump, mistress. That was our agreement."

"Into a placid loch, not off a cliff into the raging sea, that's madness."

"I willnae let you drown. Come."

He held out his hand, unsure what he would do—what *could* he do if she refused him?—but she met his hand with hers and allowed him to draw her close.

"You're right about one thing. It'd be madness to do it fully clothed."

Working quickly and deftly, she untied her skirts while he loosened her stays, and then he helped her step out of them so she stood before him shivering in only her shift, the very picture from his vision in the dungeon.

He took the sack of money, and she reached out to stop him. "It's too heavy," she said. "It'll weigh you down."

She was probably right, but he couldn't leave it, so he reached over the wall to drop it in. If the tides were with them, maybe they'd wash up on the same shore.

"Wait!"

Finn brought the purse back to her, and Jory reached inside, removing his brooch and a ruby ring. Then she nodded her consent, and he tied it closed and flung the bag into the sea.

She leaned out to watch it fall, and Finn held her back, breathing in her smoky scent before he took her hand and helped her up onto the embrasure. "I must ask ye one thing first," he said, though the wind carried away most of his words like a whisper.

"Yes?"

"I cherish the sun because it shines upon your face, and the earth, though it's a pale imitation of your eyes. I love that your fingernails are always dirty from digging in the soil and that you never give me so much as an inch if we argue. My soul has been joined to yours for... I don't even know how many years. My heart —my body. You are exceptional, Marsali Mackintosh, and you have all of me. Will you have my hand and my name as well? Go to war wi' me, against the world?"

He looked down at her, saw a battle play out on her face, a storm of colliding sentiments as she smiled and frowned and licked her lips and blinked back tears, an eternity of emotion.

She shook her head and nodded at the same time. "Yes," she said, laughing and crying, and he bent to kiss her as she clung to him. Then he took the ring from her palm and slid it onto her thumb as a promise. He pinned his clan brooch onto her shift, and together they clasped hands and jumped.

Epilogue

TWO MONTHS LATER...

F inn stood on the fringe of the Great Hall, absently chewing a sprig of mint, watching and listening as the Chattan Confederation discussed issues of land deeds and rents. He was grateful to have been restored as his brother's heir and right hand, though such tedious palavers sometimes made him half-wonder if it was worth it. He was beginning to daydream about diving into the loch, when his ears pricked at the mention of Clan Gordon.

"They've sent coin," the Borlum said, "which is unexpected."

"But not unwelcome. It's the least they should do," Angus added.

"The question is, can they be trusted?" the elder Farquharson asked, waving a chicken leg in the air as he spoke. "For my money, they cannae. Not for all the gold in Scotland."

"Och, there's trust and then there's *trust*. Gold goes a long way towards the one if not the other," MacPherson chimed in.

"Aye, 'tis so," Borlum agreed.

"Can we take the money and to hell with the trust?"

Farquharson laughed, deep and guttural, taking a bite of his chicken.

"What say you, Tordarroch? You're uncharacteristically quiet."

Angus nodded. "I should hear Finn's opinion on the matter."

"You seek counsel from your second?" Borlum asked, his tone surprised but not unkind.

"He's a great deal of experience in the matter of Clan Gordon —as well as personal interest after the very ordeal for which they attempt to atone."

Angus waved Finn over to the head of the table, and, trying not to look too eager about it, he pushed himself off the wall he'd been leaning against and swallowed the mint. Four heads watched him amble over, none disputing his right as Angus's heir to be present and to be heard.

"What say you then, young Shaw?" Borlum asked. "On the matter of the Gordon reparations?"

Finn rubbed one sweaty palm along his kilt. He still wasn't accustomed to being heard.

"Gordons aren't to be trusted. And ye shouldnae read this as a promise they'll have any sway over the Watch. But, though some were certainly privy to the deeds of Long Thomas, I dinnae believe the laird could have known, for he'd have at least demanded his cut. And as we found when we raided Bearradh Dearg, it was mostly his own clanswomen who were taken."

"Aye, 'tis true, 'tis true," Angus agreed.

"He dealt... swiftly and brutally with the priest and Baen Grant for their involvement."

The assembly shuddered, for word of the men's tortured imprisonment had filtered back to the Highlands by way of Leask.

"But lack of trust doesnae preclude a peaceful alliance. One party must make the first move, and by accepting their offer of friendship—wi' our eyes full open and our heads on a swivel—we might take steps towards trust and lasting confederation. 'Tis as you say." Finn nodded at MacPherson. "There is trust, and then there's *trust*."

The others nodded soberly, all except his brother who looked Finn up and down as though seeing a man for the first time instead of a boy. Angus inclined his head and turned back to face them.

"We're in agreement then," Borlum said, handing off the Gordon gold to his steward. "Next we have a complaint about grazing rights along the river."

Through the open door, Finn spied Jory as she entered the kitchen, heading for the stairs. He made a quick bow to Angus and the others. "If you'll excuse me," he said before striding across the Hall and taking the stairs two at a time.

On the landing Jory paused to stretch her stiff and aching neck. She was accustomed to walking in the boots Finn had ordered to be modified for her, but stairs still tired her out, especially after such a long night hunched over assisting with a difficult birth. Then she made a trip to an elderly patient, and a small boy with a chronic cough. She was exhausted, but the good kind of exhaustion that came with the satisfaction of doing necessary work.

"And where've you been all this time, mistress?" a voice asked from the stair below her.

Jory smiled. The gravelly timbre of Finn's words never failed to give her a little thrill of expectation, from her throat right down to her knees. And though she'd been quite busy, she'd missed his steady presence at her side.

She turned in time for him to take the last step, filling up all the space in the corridor with his broad shoulders and those arms, pressing her back against the wall gently.

"You know me," she said, a little breathless at his nearness. "Out riding around, curing the ills of the world."

"Mmphm," he said, burying his nose in her tangled hair, his breath tickling her neck. "I've been thinking it's time we found ye a proper horse. Younger, wi' a bit more spirit."

"And abandon dear old Nell? Never!"

"Ye'll need it—if we're to ride all the way to Auld Reekie and buy you a place in that medical school."

A terrifying thrill ran through Jory. "I'll have to pretend to be a man."

He laughed and tilted her chin up for a better look. "As ye wish. You always did look verra fine in breeks. Ye seem tired."

She beamed back at him. "I delivered twins today. Two healthy baby girls. And I finally convinced Mrs. MacGillivray to let me treat young Jamie's cough with mullein."

He kissed her cheek and took a step back, holding her hand. "So ye'll be wanting to rest."

"I'll be wanting a bath. Why? Did you have something else in mind?" she teased, though she had felt exactly what he had in mind when he leaned in close. One night apart, and he was hard with need.

He shook his head shyly, though his lips quirked up in a little grin. "Wanted to show you something in our chamber is all. D'ye need assistance with yer bath, Mistress Shaw?"

"You know, I am quite worn out. I think perhaps I will."

His smile widened, and he scooped her up in his arms, carrying her down the corridor shushing her as she giggled with delight.

Author's Note

Maybe it's the revolutionary in my American-born soul, but I find Scottish history—particularly those Highlanders who stayed, as well as the ones who became early settlers of Appalachia—endlessly fascinating. Most readers will be familiar with the 1745 Jacobite Rising made all the more infamous by the Outlander series. But three generations of Scots fought and died for the Stewart restoration. First, from 1689 to 1692. It was in the aftermath of one of these battles that Jory's mother and father met.

1715, sometimes called "the First Jacobite Rebellion," actually marked the next short-lived attempt. William Mackintosh of Borlum was, in fact, the forth laird of the Borlum sect, although he has been completely fictionalized in my novel. Borlum, like so may others, was captured in the 1715 Battle of Preston, but he escaped from Newgate Prison before his trial.

Angus Shaw, who I claim as an ancestor though we can't yet trace our Shaws further than Virginia, was the 14th Chief of the Clan Shaw of Tordarroch, fighting alongside Mackintosh at Preston. He and his brother Robert were also imprisoned, but they didn't fair so well as the Borlum. Robert died at Newgate, and Angus was transported to the Virginia colony. Unlike his fictionalized counterpart, however, the real Angus was eventually returned to Scotland only after giving an oath of loyalty to the King of England, and he refrained from any future Jacobite activity, though there are some who say he was sorely tempted to join the '45.

The Black Watch, a regiment of Highland soldiers loyal to the British crown, was officially established in 1725 as a response to the 1715 Rising, in the hopes of keeping the Jacobites under control. Their name represents a contrast between the dark tartans they wore and the infamous bright red coats regular British soldiers wore. They still represent an infantry division in the British Army today. There's no evidence they ever helped kidnap girls in Aberdeenshire.

The Chattan Confederation represented an alliance of traditional clans within a larger clan. The full history is a bit spotty, but over the years a dozen different clans closely aligned with Mackintosh joined together for mutual protection and benefit, each retaining their own clan status and leadership, but each answerable to one central chief, as well. They often had similar mottos and battle cries, variations of "Touch not the cat without a glove," and were collectively represented by whortleberry, the plant depicted on my series broach.

Acknowledgments

In addition to reading all the things, writing this book is really what kept me sane during the pandemic. For that, I have to first thank Sarah Blair for the push. It was during an inspiration drought in early 2020 that Sarah begged me to drop everything I was attempting to do and write a Highland romance. Six months later I finally did, and it was the most fun I've had writing in years. Sarah, I owe you big.

My deepest thanks also to Emma Tennier-Stuart, who faithfully read that very first draft, and to Hanna M. Long, whose expertise informed the fight scenes. And Krista Walsh—I hear your voice in my head every step of the way, as I'm writing and editing, challenging me to go deeper, inspiring me to be brave. Your craft, your wisdom, your experience, and generosity—I learn from reading your work, your feedback, and every moment in between.

To the rest of my word herd, I owe you all so much: Jennifer Iacopelli, for encouraging me to lean in to my cinnamon rolls; Angi Griffee-Black, for inspiring me to stretch and grow, and for unabashedly loving every word; Megan Paasch, for reading the whole darn thing on the plane; Mark Benson, for all of it, always. Christian Berkey, Jennie Ritz, Tabitha Martin, Trisha Leigh, Sarah Henning, for every moment of advice, encouragement, and support.

So much work goes into these books, and I'm especially grateful to the crew that are always eager to share my excitement, to let me blather on about the latest episode in this rollercoaster of a publishing journey: Amy Copeland, Brenda Dyck, DeAnn

Hays, Jessie Parker, Rhonda Foxworth, and Vandita Singhvi. And to the village who helped make this book possible: Brigid Bello, for your thoughtful guidance; Susan Semadeni, for your amazing attention to detail; my extraordinary cover designer, Poshie, who brought Finn and Jory to life before my eyes so I could fall in love with them all over again; and my incredible designer Chris Reddie, who not only created the amazing Eridani Press logo, but also the fantastic Brides of Chattan brooch for this series. Your talent and craft are next level—I'm continually amazed by what you can do.

To my parents, who are tasked with warning the rest of the family that this one is steamier than the last. And most of all, my thanks to DJ, my love, who helps me believe in the impossible and dare mighty things. Thanks for making sure the wheels don't fall off.

And to you, gentle readers, who give it all meaning at the end of the day. My deepest and most humble thanks.

About the Author

Rose Prendeville was first diagnosed with scoliosis at the age of twelve, and after wearing a brace, underwent spinal fusion surgery in her late teens. Now a librarian, she lives in Middle Tennessee with her husband and a garden full of bees, writing stories about found families and flawed people doing their best. The 2022 Bronze IPPY winner for her debut *Last Blue Christmas*, she is passionate about books with happy endings and their ability to brighten a sometimes dismal world.

If you enjoyed this book, please consider leaving a review at your favorite marketplace.

To stay up-to-date on the Brides of Chattan series and other news, scan the QR code to sign up for my newsletter.

roseprendeville.com

Also by Rose Prendeville

Last Blue Christmas